INDIANA HORROR 2013 REVIEW

Edited by James Ward Kirk

Copyright James Ward Kirk Publishing 2013
Internet: jwkfiction.com
Twitter: @jameswardkirk
Facebook: James-Ward-Kirk-Fiction

Cover art and design copyright John D. Stanton 2013
Photography by Mike Jansen copyright 2013
Alternate art Jerry Langdon 2013
Copy Editor Krista Clark Grabowski

ISBN-13: 978-0615922836 (James Ward Kirk Publishing)

ISBN-10: 061592283X

Contents

POETRY

MONSTER
John D. Stanton

Robin Wyatt Dunn
Falstaff in Indiana

*Wise Old Falstaff, the man who came to Will in Dreams,
became a lich late in life and put a gemstone where his eye had
been and wove holly into his hair, the crown of the hill, a Celtic
witch in an Indian land, Falstaff made his home.*

What lands are these, traveler?

"My Name is FallStaff and I have a Son, his Name is Abraham,
and My Son, He is the Richest in America, Spiritually I Mean, for
From his Eyes Flow Chemical Bravery, he Changes Water into
Beer, with his hands, his name is Abraham, he moves over the
land, bringing the beer, from the chaff into the wheat, from my
heart.

This land is your land, this land is my land, from California, to
my crotch. I get all the dead hoes here, all the cups of canary
baby, from the Islands, to my mouth, I watch you grow old.
Gonna eat you when you dead.

My Name is FallStaff! I am a Staff and I am a Falling and When I
Touch Down like the Nuclear Sunrise Submarine at Your Gate
Elektrika, I will bring a sound in the collapse, I will sound out
your charm and your agony, I will relive your own life, to take it
from you, I am a Lich, that means I do mean things; I am
undead; I wear holly on my head (the Crown of Celtic Thorns)
the knowledge that is mine is mine to lose, and I would like to
give it away to you--would you like it? Just hold my hand as we
go down into the land of Indiana, land of the Indians, land where
Columbus dreamed, land where my canaries came to Roost.

Harry is dead. The Harries always die. A war or another.
Fallstaff plans ahead. For Lo though my staff falls it falls slow,
and my eye is on your own: you're growing sleepy, hand me over
your wallet, not too much in there, let me see your wife, not
much to look at, bare your soul before God or at least put it on
the table; it's tarnished but alive, I accept the bet.

My bet, all the oceans of my mind. The hurtling world. The hurt
beneath the hurt. The gem I keep where my eye was that I took

out of my head, here I'll put that on the table, along with my daughter, her name is

(James Windward)

Her name is

(Jack Kerouac)

Her name is

(Ruth Simpleton)

She won't let me say it, she's clever like that, well anyway she's my daughter, and I put her on the table too. So let's see, that's the oceans of the world, the hurt beneath the hurt, the gem of my eye, and my daughter, hedged against your tarnished soul:

Just look behind you there will the crow fly at dawn or do you think—

Ha! Well, you're soulless now. Welcome to my kingdom.

I greet you for you are mine.

Let me show you around.

This here is the Crown Cemetery, I rule, and it's nice to know you, brother, hand me your hand, I'll chew on it, thank you, now this, this gravestone is interesting. You see the carving here, it says:

I Will Shakespeare, Obviating the Need for an Explanation, Do Hereby Condemn this Hexed Backwater to—

Well, he did go on, Old Will did. Wrote on our graves and such. I do it too. Like this one, I wrote here, see?

"Let me out of here."

Ha, I like that one. You must undress now. Lie down. Look up at the sky. You're going to be here a long time. I'm glad you came to visit.

Shall we sing a song?

My name is a word. My word is the ocean. Can you hear it rustling its words? Like a canary to the shore? I need a cup, do you have one? Only a dram?

I want more blood.

Legend has it that long ago the Indian lived here. I am older than they; William Burroughs saw my face; he knew the evil was here, waiting, before the Bering Land Bridge, Before Pangaea, Indiana was Cursed, I know the reason, would you hear it:

A canary is at fault. It is why I drink. The fucking bird. Chirps, chirps, chirps, always making noise.

It went into its nest one night. The little fucker really got around on Pangaea, making lots of little babies and such, fucking this little yellow bitch and that little yellow bitch, thinking he's God's yellow gift to little yellow birds, well he wasn't, this is what happened:

He ate one of his own children. And so the curse began!

Ha! I lie, because I know your brain is rotting already. I don't know why Indiana is cursed, it may be because of me. I am not sure. Certainly I've been cursed enough. By women and men, children even. My face is ugly. My soul too. At least I have one, not like you. I chose this life after life, you, what did you choose?

A passage on a ship? A name for your child?

I chose a destiny. I chose this landscape itself, and drew it, did you know that?

I put this color blood on your temple. Rise, Adjutant.

Rise and dig me a new outhouse. And bless it with the names of all of your countrymen. We will make such music.

Mathias Jansson
The Next Chapter

In the cellar of The Next Chapter antiquarian
I found a room filled with horror
From floor to celling

In an old box on the floor
Lay a copy of Indiana Horror Review
To my surprise I found my name
In the table of contents
I started to read the poem
And felt fear crawling over my skin

"I stood in a room filled with horror
Reading a poem
When the door slammed behind me
The light went out
Alone I stood in darkness
When all the horror and fear
All twisted fantasies and perverted thoughts
Came climbing out from the books..."

Suddenly I heard the door
Slamming behind my back
And the light went out
I wished by God
That they haven't got more
Of my horrifying poems
Or the collected writings
Of my perverted soul
In that damn store

Bric Barker
Driving My Plow through the Bones of the Dead

The day peels away like sunburned skin
     leaving a blushing sky.
I pull my lids up again,
     propping them with routine and caffeine.
I harness the horse and we
     contemplate the turning of soil.
The worms and half worms forgive
     because it's honest sweat on my brow.
As seasons change, the work remains.
     I clutch slick clods in callused hands
searching for signs the womb is ripe.
     I find a bone I've plowed in two.
I've lived off the flesh this bone once held,
     through rains and stalks and animal dung
flung for encouragement.
     I never knew my plow divided life.
I never knew it makes no difference
     which side of the sod I'm on.

David S. Pointer
Fang Geriatrics

The old vampire
lugging his coffin
catheter-tamponade
around that told
more of the story
than he ever would
shopping for an
artificial airway or
implanted suction
device increasing
flow pressure from
kiss to bubbling red
stomach contents

David S. Pointer
Pistolero West

Night walking
fatalities on both
sides bludgeoned
two bartenders, and
commenced to
stockpiling those
half-eaten carcasses
inside the Logan
cabin for winter
meat, as the
Comanche gun
went through
six Mexican
bandits faster
than a grizzly
eating gold-
seekers before
turning back
for the dead

David S. Pointer
Indy Wagon Wheel Rodeo

The inspectors found lungworm droppings
at the host-parasite-popsicle stands then
handed off proper awards accordingly
amongst circlets of fruit fly buzz as the
cowboy and Indian extravaganza started
up by scalping the new robots with can
opener bionic grip taking off the tops and
wheelbarrow clownoids taking off the rest

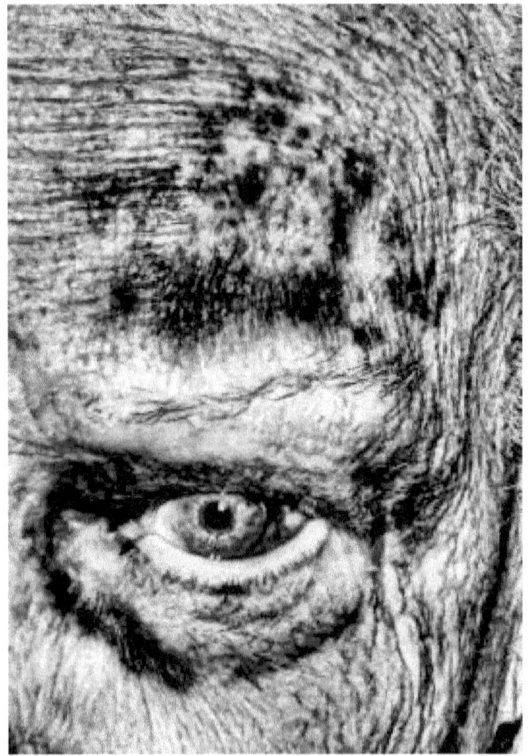

Roger Cowin
Charlie

The moon is shiny bright this sunny day
But Charlie's too dead to come out and play.
He doesn't really mind,
Being dead is better than being half alive,
He only wishes the flies
Would stop laying maggots in his eyes.

Charlie was only twelve years old when he died,
The victim of a most gruesome homicide.
His killer, bless his murdering hide
Became a civil servant in Hell
And Charlie went to stay with his late Auntie Nell.

Charlie has his odd little quirks,
Sometimes he's afraid of floors
And ceilings must always be shirked.
Other days he simply refuses
   to pass an open door

He finds school a dreadful bore,
Though he is quite adored
By the other boys and ghouls.
He is highly regarded by his teachers
Who consider him a most charming creature
Despite his being the class fool.

They laugh about the golem he made
Out of sticks and strings and straw
 "Golems are supposed to be made from clay,
Yours will never come alive at all."
But come Halloween day,
His was the one that danced and played.

Despite the fact that he is dead
And if not careful, his head can pop off his neck
Charlie remains a most normal boy,
Who loves his friends, his home and his toys
But most of all, though he would never tell,
He loves his dear, sweet dead Auntie Nell.

Roger Cowin
The Coming of the Old Ones

I.

Under primordial skies,
Ancient aeons ago, the Deep Ones
Raised their twisted, batrachian limbs
In subjugation to their mad,
Malevolent gods.

II.

In darkness they watch,
Corrupt gods from the dead past,
Dreaming while awake,
They await their summons
From the Hunger beast who never sleeps.

III.

The naked eye cannot perceive
Those strange dimensions
Where weird beings wait and watch
For their opportunity to wrench
This world from humanity's grasp.

IV.

The Laughing Magician opens
The forbidden tome locked for millennia,
He recites from the Passages of the Damned,
His sanity broken
As Hell pours into his sanctuary.

V.

The Abomination of Desolation,
The dweller between the stars,
Out of time, out of space,
Comes with his screaming hordes
To rape the world.

VI.

Deep beneath the earth, generals plot
Defensive scenarios to wrest
Victory from the mouth of defeat.
They die writhing in agony
At the teeth and jaws of Hell's hounds

VII.

Our gilded cities fall like so much
Chaff before the rising storm.
Our fearful weapons of mass slaughter
Are like unto pebbles tossed in the ocean.
The earth is consumed in its own fire.

VIII.

Those who resist perish,
They are the lucky ones.
All others are forced into servitude,
Slaves to the Old Gods,
They pray in vain for death.

IX.

The mongrel races of man
Undulate in sensuous celebrations.
The foul *Tcho-Tcho* offer up
Obscene sacrifices to Lloigor and Zhar,
Feasting on the flesh of their fellow men.

X.

In his house at R'lyeh,
Dread Cthulhu opens his eyes,
Rises from his ocean tomb.
The very planet itself shudders.
An Old Evil is reborn.

Roger Cowin
Friday Night Monsters

It began with the slow, ominous thunder
of funeral bells, the creeping groan
of a creaking door, then the hushed,
whispering voice of a woman intoning,
   "In the dead of night,
   When the moon is high
   And the ill winds blow
   And the banshees cry
   And the moonlight casts
   An unearthly glow,
   Arise my love with tales of woe."
The camera would cut to a coffin,
its lid rising slowly to reveal
an ashen faced ghoul with dark, shrunken cheeks
dressed in black clothes, gloves and brown hooded cape
who introduced himself as Sammy Terry
with a deep, diabolical laugh
and would bid us welcome
to Nightmare Theater
just as at the end of the night he would
wish us "Pleasant nightmares," before
sending us off to bed with the same
sinister laughter.

It was the Friday Night Monster Movie Bash
and no youngster growing up in central Indiana
during the sixties or seventies could fail
to recollect WTTV's resident horror host
and his sidekick, George the rubber spider who spoke
in a high pitched chitter that only Sammy could understand.
So camp and obviously fake
yet it never failed to frighten us.
The movies were of secondary interest;
bad 1950's B-films of bikini clad babes
being pursued by atom age monsters from the sea,
giant insects, robots from outer space
and bug eyed behemoths from the deeps
sprinkled with an authentic classic

like "Dracula" or "Frankenstein" or one of those
lush gothics from Hammer Studios.
Instead, we watched for Sammy's dry
gallows humor and comically
convoluted commentary
or that night's cinematic snack.

We always had to beg our parents to stay up late,
promising extra chores and dismissing their concerns
that such ghastly images would give us nightmares
or that we would grow up to be psychopathic killers
or even worse, Democrats,
wearing them down with a child's insistent persistence.
We'd pan pop our popcorn, slather it in real butter
and salt then leave half of it uneaten
when the movie's frights became too much
for our eight year old brains,
spend most of the night peering at the screen
through spread fingers and giggling
as we tried to out-scare our siblings.

Later, in our bed, all assurances to parents aside,
those horror flick beasts, no matter how cheesy or faked,
would follow us into our dreams to chase us
through the nightmare labyrinth of sleep
but it was Sammy who came to us most often,
rising from some dark grave to pull us
screaming into his dungeon where even George,
that rubber, dime-store Halloween prop
was transformed into a hideous, fanged giant
from the blackest reaches of Hell.

Roger Cowin
The Killing House

Near the old killing house,
a restless agitation
stirs the air.

Windowless and gutted,
it watches over
the malnourished field
like some ancient,
primal totem.

On humid days,
sweat seeps
from its gray cinderblock walls.
The spray of graffiti disguises
the deeper,
permanent stains.

The solid, death
thump
of the hammer is silent,
the killing tools
sold at auction.

But if you listen,
below the hard
quiet,
you can still hear
the distant,
startled lowing.

Short Stories

Allen Griffin
A Symbiotic Fix

Days moved in a grey dream, addiction riding like a god, speaking through me words of feral hunger. Dealers come and go, but old junkies never die. I have been around long enough to suckle from a million suppliers. Most quit the game, some go to jail, but despite what Hollywood would lead you to believe, very few are murdered. I've known a couple to go down into the black abyss at the barrel of a gun, but none went out like Skinny Mike.

Skinny Mike had been my hook up for the past year or so. He proved fair and reliable, not overly ambitious. The arrangement was low drama. So, imagine how I felt when he was murdered. They found him in so many pieces identification only became possible when the junkies started to line up at his door, like some twisted vigil.

We were in a pinch, no doubt. Everyone dug deep to find their next fix. I felt used up. My body shook upon hearing the news, not so much for Skinny Mike, god rest his soul, but my body already anticipated withdrawal. If you use for long enough, you know one of those withdrawals will be the end of you. I was getting to that point.

I resolved to do something I swore off long ago. This gnawing desperation led me back to Victor. He dealt out of a bodega not far from where I slept. In fact, he was closer and cheaper than Skinny Mike but the dude was drenched in bad mojo, enough to put in the extra effort to go to anyone else, but when you're hurting, you do what you gotta do. Last time I got hard up, Victor made me poke myself with a syringe and spray my blood on the crumpled money I used to pay for my fix. 'Never again,' I told myself.

So there I was, standing beneath the jaundiced lights of the bodega, figuring shit couldn't be as bad as last time. Aqua walls and flickering ceiling lights bathed empty shelves in a vespertine glow. The clerk radiated a sense of lurking menace. I bet the thug couldn't work the cash register if his life depended on it. They don't get those kind of customers around here, so the bastard really didn't have much to worry about.

I headed straight to the back of the store, straight to Victor's office, anxious to get the whole thing over with. I noticed the drink coolers had been replaced with aquariums. Tentacled, squid-like creatures floated dormant in murky green water. I wondered if they were alive, until I saw one thrash momentarily and then settle back into its stupor. I got the chills, and they had nothing to do with getting a fix.

I knocked on the office door and then stepped inside. Victor sat behind an old and filthy desk. A small hatchet lay on the surface exerting a silent menace. Something rust-colored coated the blade and handle, dripped onto the desk top and dried into a crust they seem to meld the two objects together, as if the desk slowly absorbed the smaller axe. I learned long ago not to ask too many questions.

"Glad you finally made it."

"Excuse me?"

"Nothing . . . forget it, kid." I don't know why he acted like he expected me. And why did he call me kid? I was easily ten years his senior. 'In and out, don't ask . . .' I reminded myself.

Victor swept a hand across his face, brushing away wet ropes of dirty blond hair that hung over his eyes. He leaned back in his chair and opened one of the desk drawers, pulling out a small vial and placing it next to the hatchet on the desktop.

"Here you go, kid." He turned his hand palm up and wiggled his fingers, indicating it was time to pay up.

"I wanted a dime bag." I said, my voice shaking. My need for a fix fought with my fear of Victor.

"This'll cure what ails you, kid." He turned a bloodshot glare directly into my eyes and I immediately wanted to cower in the corner, shoot up whatever he gave me and be done with it. I couldn't decide if he looked like a serial killer or drowning victim.

I pulled out a wad of bills and tried to place them in his hand, but the pile fell apart and scattered across the desk. He nodded at the vial as he started to gather up the money. I snatched the concoction up and thrust it into my coat pocket. I turned and darted for the front door.

"We'll see you real soon, kid." Victor called after me. The thug at the register kept quiet, and still looked like he wasn't worried about a thing.

I held the syringe between my fingers, the needle pointed up toward the paint-peeled ceiling. I tapped the side with a cracked fingernail and exhaled the tension of a hunger soon satiated. Ignoring the sick yellow of the narcotic solution, I pierced the skin between my toes and pressed down on the plunger.

I told myself I'd seen worse looking junk before, but within seconds, I admitted that Victor sold me something other than what I sought. Everything dimmed and started slipping away, a visual disintegration. I stared at the cigarette smoke stained walls and became lost in the patterns of cobwebs. The room drained away like a motion picture caught in a broken projector, and I became lost in the opiate void.

My heart pounded a Morse code, the arteries a drum skin stretched across the idiot face of the cosmos. I gibbered strange words, strained to hear them reverberate throughout the room. The surface of my mirror rippled, the television vomited strange colors, bathing every surface in crepuscular light.

I was unsure of my own consciousness. The high took me outside of the familiar parts of my mental map, yet I found myself bursting from the apartment and into the street, guided by an alien rapture through a maze of alleys and back streets. The moon tracked my delirium and the stars flickered above me. Finally, I reached a wretched house on the edge of an industrial park.

Walking without hesitation through the front door, I found several people standing in the candlelit interior. The smell of body odor and the ocean overwhelmed me. The shadows cast by the candles seemed fractal and unrelated to the shapes in the room.

The people resembled a congregation in a church where an insane deity reigned. They wore tattered rags over their faces, chanting strange psalms. One could imagine the contortions of their mouths and throats; painful efforts to form those strange syllables. My mind and body stood paralyzed before them.

The ceremony burrowed deep into the flesh of the night. I felt my spirit rise within me, clawing up my spine, threatening to burst forth from my vein cage. I fell to my knees as an invisible force exploded from my forehead. I threw my head back, eyes cast toward the ceiling.

One of the ritual participants stepped forward and stood over me. She was one of Skinny Mike's regulars, but the recognition flickered and escaped, the rapture reasserting control. The junky fed a length of plastic hose down my throat.

The chant of the congregants rose in intensity. My stomach heaved and a fountain of black viscous liquid geysered from the top of the tube. I fell hard to the floor and the others worked to gather my expulsion.

I was nudged awake, the comfort of blackout denied. I rose to my feet and the black substance was placed in my cradled arms. It felt somewhat solid yet seemed as if it would return back to liquid at any moment.

I was led upstairs to a rear room. I saw only darkness. The moon slipped through a few holes in the walls but the feeble light proved insufficient to illuminate anything of substance. At first indistinguishable from the other shadows, an amorphous shape rose before me. Sound slurped and gagged, and I felt horrible appendages flick at my skin. I felt suckers grip and release my flesh. Somehow, through some alien agency, I understood what needed to be done.

I pulled loose pieces of the tumorous mass cradled in my arms and offered them to the horrible creature. I felt the chunks of slime snapped up from my hands, and they were consumed with great vigor. My own intoxication mirrored the bestial feast, rising to a new intensity. I never knew a high like it before.

This, this was the promise my addiction never fulfilled, nurturing a strange sensation of life in the moment, creation and subsistence rather than willful destruction. I wanted to cradle the creature as I fed it. This was the ultimate fix, a symbiotic high.

The days turned from grey to a luminous black. Old addictions shed themselves like cold dead skin. We lived as Victor's progeny. He shepherded us, acting both as mother and father. In return, we eliminated the other dealers one by one. Death spread like a plague, each neighborhood yearned for a fix of Thanatos, and we supplied the whole metropolis.

Numerous creatures lay nestled in the womb of the city, the Nephilim in utero. We fed, placing their wellbeing over our own. Every tunnel and decrepit structure became a place of worship, sacred houses overflowing with the chants of opiate rapture. These were the churches in which we prayed, placed our hope in the future, that all may come to know the rapture of symbiosis.

A. Henry Keene
Lazy Acres

In the black sky, innumerable stars sparkle with faint, pastel colors, and the full moon glows steadily within its ghostly halo. Their pale light shines on the tall, undulating grasses and weeds of the field, which flows from a hilltop hovel down to the edge of a deep forest.

The house, barely visible amongst the tangled growth, is little more than a few rooms enclosed by a plywood exterior and topped with a simple, tarpaper roof, which pitches to one side away from a stone chimney.

Next to the ramshackle shack, Delores stands. She wears a white, satin nightgown, which shimmers and glistens in the moonlight, casting about her a surreal glow, which gives her the appearance of a nocturnal apparition. Her nightgown catches the breeze and collapses between her long, pale legs and twists around her body. The satin caresses her firm stomach, full breasts, and round bottom, and she closes her eyes to savor the sensations.

Barefoot, she strolls along a well-trodden path through the field toward the dark forest. Stretching out her arms, she sweeps them through the thick vegetation. Seed-laden grass flows through her hands and across her forearms. She hears seeds fall to the ground and giggles and coos, spins and prances; white satin flows and flutters around her knees.

Delores reaches the woods and stops. She stares past the trees, past the moist leaves, into the mysterious heart of the forest. She raises a hand to her heart and holds it there to feel her heart beat within her chest.

Her eyes fall closed, and her head leans to the side, as she feels the blood flow through her arms, neck, and face. She reaches up to the white ribbon, which binds her long, red hair, and pulls at the bow in the ribbon. Her hair falls in graceful, glistening spirals toward the moist earth. She runs her hands through her hair and feels the silky strands flow between her fingers.

Shrugging, Delores pushes the neck of the nightgown over her shoulders. It falls down her arms and past her narrow waist. The nightgown hangs for a moment on her round hips and falls in a loose pile on the path. Delores steps out of the nightgown, turns away from the woods, and faces the moon. She raises her arms into the air to embrace the pale disk.

Her body glowing like lamp-lit alabaster on black velvet, Delores slides a hand across her stomach. Up and down, she strokes the smooth, glowing skin of her midriff with the tips of her fingers. The hand wanders up to her breast, which she cups and massages gently. Her tongue slips through her lips to taste the night air, and she draws a long, slow breath, as the fingertips of her other hand reach her vulva.

Delores massages the fleshy mound with gentle pressure, until her juices flow. She parts the labia and slowly, gently, strokes her swollen clitoris with the rhythm of her breath. Tingling radiates through her body. Her knees press together and she bends at the hips. Reaching her free hand toward the ground, Delores lowers herself to her knees.

Leaves rustle in the woods nearby.

Delores gasps, bites her lower lip, and elevates her bottom. Goosebumps rise up on her arms, as a breeze blows across her toward the woods.

A tree limb snaps.

A startled owl hoots and flies away, crossing the nearby gravel road as a dirty, dilapidated SUV crunches along the gravel road. Inside, two couples ride beneath the illuminated dome light.

Al, an excessively thin man in his thirties with longish unkempt dark hair, struggles with a paper road map of Southern Indiana. He turns it this way and that, and pokes a finger into the paper. The red stone of his University of Louisville ring sparkles on the map.

"We were here. We know that." He slides the finger to the left, "Then we turned—here?"

He lowers the map to reveal Candy, his wife. She is younger than Al by about ten years and looks as though she has just walked from a salon. Her freshly-bleached hair, pulled back in a tight ponytail, shines in the dim light. Her pale make-up gives her symmetrical features a flawless finish. The neck of her snug black tee shirt is cut and stands open to reveal full breasts and deep cleavage. She looks at Al and raises her precisely-plucked eyebrows. Al frowns and turns back to the map.

"Hey, Chucky. I can't find us on this map." Al's voice cracks.

"I don't think we're on that map."

"That's swell." Al drops the map. "What the fuck are we gonna do?"

Candy pokes Al with a sharp elbow and shoots him a stern, wide-eyed look.

"We're gonna keep on keepin' on."

"Well, I hope we have enough gas."

Chucky licks his lips and casts his eyes to the side.

"We're all good," Chucky says with conviction. His thick fingers grip the steering wheel tightly, and muscles work beneath the skin of his forearms. He runs a hand across his balding head.

Kendal pats his leg. "Let's do it, Chucky." Her chubby cheeks plump up and she tilts her head to look into Chucky's eyes.

"Lazy Acres or bust." Kendal smiles.

"Bust is right." Al rubs his forehead. "Ya break down out here, and these fucked-up-country-bastards will bust their nuts in all our asses."

"I get it." Chucky locks eyes with Al in the rearview. "Campin's not your thing."

"No. Squeelin' like a pig aint my thing."

"Hush, Al." Candy sighs. "Where's your sense of adventure?"

Al huffs, tosses the map aside, and sinks into his seat behind Chucky.

The group rides quietly along the bumpy road, listening to the static-marred reception of Blondie's "One Way or Another." A ring tone rises above the droning vocals on the radio. Al reaches into his pocket and pulls out his cell phone.

"You still have reception?" Chucky glances at Al in the rearview.

"One bar."

Al swipes a finger across the screen. Up pops a picture of Candy posing cheek to cheek with another man. Al's heart pounds violently in his chest, and the muscles of his arms contract stiffly. His teeth clinch, as he looks at her, smiling sweetly from his screen. The man beside her stares defiantly to proffer his challenge.

Sweat beads up on Al's forehead. His teeth clamp, and his brows knit. His fists clinch and shake. His face tenses, his eyes twitch, and tears pool up on his eyelids. He is drowning in a flood of jealousy and he glares at Candy as though she were pushing him beneath the rushing flow of dark emotions. She looks at Al blankly and looks away.

He wants to strangle her right there in the car. He wants to gouge out her smiling eyes, shove his fist down her throat, and watch her squirm as she dies.

Chucky's phone vibrates three times. Al's head snaps around. He catches Chucky's eyes in the rearview, and the two share a brief look. Seeing Al on the verge of tears, Kendal reaches up to turn off the dome light.

Kendal's phone goes off. Chucky and Kendal sneak a peek at one another. Al feels his face flush with blood. He closes his eyes and breathes deliberately. Dizziness overcomes him, and his stomach churns. He swallows hard and wipes sweat from his forehead with the back of his forearm.

"Sure are a lot of deserted houses around here." Chucky turns his head to study a crumpled structure, as they pass.

"Seems like this whole area is deserted." Kendal's voice is light and sweet.

"I wonder why." Chucky muses. "Maybe the fluoride in the water made everyone go crazy and kill each other with pitchforks."

Chucky and Kendal laugh.

"No. I mean it. Why are all these houses empty? Where did the people go?" Chucky continues. "And why did they leave?"

"I heard about a witch that lives in these parts."

"A witch?" Chucky chokes back a laugh.

"Yeah. It seems that a mother was fed up with the cheating and hurtful ways of men and wanted to spare her young daughter the agony of being desired. So she held the girl's face to a fire just long enough to sear the flesh. Then she pulled her out and took her to a witch, who nursed the girl back to health.

"During her recovery, the girl became close with the witch and learned about medicinal herbs and such. As time went on, she learned more and more of the witch's craft. She also became increasingly lonely as she matured and longed for a man.

"But no man would come near her, until she returned home and caught her step-father's eye. He would study her legs and rub her shoulders and brush up against her when he could. And then it happened. The step-father took her down to the stream below her mother's house and laid her out on a blanket. Well, she learned what it is to be a woman. And every chance they got, they would make love.

"Then one evening, the mother returned home from picking strawberries and found them together. The woman stabbed her husband in the back with a butcher's knife, and, after some thrashing about, the wretched man died a bloody death.

"The livid daughter took the woman by the neck and said, 'Look what you did to me. You made me hideous. You killed my true love. Now you will pay.' She strangled her mother to death and stuffed her body in the hollow of a tree.

"She wept over her lover's corpse for three days, then dug a deep pit and lowered him into it. Then she set out, using her knowledge of the dark arts, to bring him back to life.

"She killed her mother's dog and threw it into the hole, then, over the next several days, she sacrificed chickens, puppies, cats, caterpillars, and any living thing she could find. She killed them all and dropped their bodies into the hole.

"When the full moon came, she concocted, from ingredients found in the forest, an elixir, which she added to the bloody mess. She chanted the incantation, and the grave became a bubbling, seething, smoking pit of organic ooze.

"Slowly, over several days, there formed a hideous chimera with the overall form of a human, but covered with fur, and having a dog head, and --"

Chucky stomps on the brakes. The truck slides to a stop. A cloud of grey, moonlit gravel dust billows into the air to obscure their vision.

"What is it, Honey?"

Kneading the steering wheel, Chucky peers into the opaque haze.

"Wait a minute, Kendal."

Everyone looks through the windshield, as the dust cloud settles to reveal that the road ahead seems to disappear. The car's headlights illuminate the grey gravel to a point and then— nothing. No road. No trees. Nothing.

Chucky eases the clutch out, and the SUV crawls toward the apparent precipice. Gravel snaps and pops beneath the slowly-rolling tires. Chucky rolls down his window and sticks his head through the opening.

"I can't see a thing."

He puts the SUV in neutral, sets the parking brake, and opens the door.

"Be right back."

He walks into the light of the headlamps, which cast a large shadow down the road and over its edge. Al peers through the windshield and watches Chucky walk slowly toward the end of the road. Al feels like he is at the movies watching a horror show. He knows that this point, when someone is isolated and vulnerable, is when the monster strikes. Al squeezes the back of the driver's seat in his hands.

Chucky reaches the end of the road and steps over it. He descends quickly as though free falling.

A small cloud of gravel dust rises from beyond the precipice into the moonlight.

Al feels his nerves crawl beneath his skin. His toes curl inside his shoes. His stomach tightens. Breath only reaches as low as his throat. He fumbles for the window button, and finally hears the electric motor lowering the window. The rush of cool air chills him, as it flows across his dewy skin.

He stares through the windshield and wonders if this is the end for his brother. What would he do? Would he go out to search for him? What if he found his brother badly injured? How would he get him home? What if he found his brother dead? Al's head vibrates on his tense neck, and his eyelids twitch.

He forces himself to take a long, quivering breath and releases it slowly through barely-parted lips. The breath hisses, and Al focuses on the sound.

Chucky climbs back over the edge at the end of the road.

Everyone smiles, and Chucky walks back to the car.

"I think we can make it." Chucky gets in and closes the door.

"The road drops off steeply, as it curves to the left and descends into a ravine." Chucky releases the parking brake and puts the truck in gear. "We'll take it slow."

The truck creeps forward toward the drop off. Chucky slips the clutch and gently pulses the accelerator. The front wheels crest the pinnacle. The SUV thumps down onto the frame and skids, grinding toward the vehicle's tipping point. The floorboards scrape along the gravel peak. Chucky gooses the gas and the truck tips forward onto its front tires and slides over the crest. Chucky steps on the brake pedal and the SUV slides slowly down the hill toward the edge of the road. The passenger side tires slip off the gravel, and Chucky, cutting the wheels to the left, lets off the brakes. The SUV rolls back onto the one-lane road, and Chucky attentively works steering wheel and brakes to guide the truck slowly along the edge of the ravine.

Into the cool river bottom, they descend. The sound of running water echoes through the valley and grows louder, as the truck descends. Al's mind wavers between fear of going over the edge and the certainty that his wife is having an affair.

He thinks about Candy and the other man together; he holds her hand, strokes her arm, and gazes into her eyes. Her eyes hover in Al's imagination and wait for him to break. He refuses. He endures.

He endures the nude portrait of her that the other man has sent to him. He endures the cheek to cheek, lap-sitting, love-in-full-bloom images that come to his phone. He endures her it's-all-over lies, and the other man's attempt to shame him by spreading the word that they are a couple.

He endures all of this because he knows her fragility, her weakness, and her need for attention, which he fails to meet. He knows that the love they had faded because he turned away from it, failed to nurture it, and under-valued it.

Now he holds on stubbornly as the other man contaminates his mind with images and poisons his soul with humiliation and rage. He holds on because it is best for her. She is weak and drawn to any light that shines on her, and Al knows that the other man's light focuses on her so that he can objectify her, possess her, and beat off.

At the bottom of the hill, the road levels and curves sharply to the right then angles up to an old bridge that crosses a stream. Chucky stops the truck to study the bridge. It is a dilapidated, one-lane structure with a crumbling wooden deck and metal guardrails.

"I don't trust it." Chucky looks from side to side, but sees no place to turn around.

"Can we back up the way we came?" Kendal knows Chucky will not turn back, but she asks anyway.

"Not in the dark."

The truck rocks back and forth as Chucky anxiously pumps the clutch.

He rubs his eyes, takes a long breath, and blows it out in a sudden huff. He looks at Kendal, who shrugs.

Chucky revs the engine.

Candy and Al stare at the fragile bridge.

Chucky gooses the accelerator. The engine howls.

Kendal swallows hard.

"Do it, Sweetie."

Chucky floors the gas pedal and dumps the clutch. The rear tires spin and throw gravel. The truck accelerates toward the old bridge. Gravel dust spews into the air behind the truck. Chucky slams the transmission into second gear, and the SUV jolts forward. Faster and faster they go. Chucky hits third gear and floors the accelerator. Their backs press against the seats, as they reach eighty miles an hour. Fists clinch. Teeth grind. The vehicle travels the approach ramp and launches ten feet into the air.

The passengers scream, as the SUV soars.

The vehicle lands with a thud, breaking planks and beams on the bridge. Everyone jolts forward. Seatbelts lock. The passenger side of the truck grinds on the guardrail. Sparks fly down the side of the speeding SUV, which rebounds into the air and lands against the other guardrail. It grinds to the end of the bridge. Chucky stomps on the brakes, and the vehicle slides off the side of the road and dies.

Chucky and Kendal roar with laughter.

"Man, we must have flown fifty feet!" Chucky pumps his fist in the air. "Take that Duke boys!"

"Yeah! Dese nuts!" Kendal laughs.

Al throws open the door and falls out of the truck onto the slightly-sloping ground. His body quakes, and cold sweat envelops him, as he struggles to support himself on hands and knees.

Chucky turns the key, and the starter whirls, but the engine doesn't start. Again, he turns the key and pumps the accelerator. Nothing but noise.

"The truck's overexcited. We'll let it rest a bit."

Al lay on his stomach and focuses on the rise and sudden fall of his chest, as he breathes heavily. He feels the cold, moist ground beneath him and lets his tension flow from his body into it. Warmth returns to his face, and his breathing slows. He feels himself sink deeper into the vast indifference of the Earth, and he recalls the early days with Candy.

She smiles. Her eyes beam with joy and laughter and something quite the contrary; her expression reveals a wistful longing for something unknown and unfathomable to him. Al breathes deeply through his nose to take in her scent. A cascade of hormones responds to her presence. Her scent ties him in twisted knots of longing, binds him to her through the cruel tyranny of chemistry.

Her succulent scent impels him beyond reason. He longs for and pursues her without regard for her marital status or his. Both have lawful partners. Both risk their marriages and reputations for the sake of chemical bonding.

They meet at the river. It is a cool evening in early fall. The trees cling tightly to their drying leaves. He looks at her, gazes at her small features, her flowing, dark brown hair. He touches her constantly as they walk together. He rubs her shoulder and her hip and feels his body rouse itself from a deep slumber. He is thrilled to feel the forgotten longing, the deep yearning for another. He submits to the allure of her scent and he buries his face in her silky hair.

On a subsequent walk along the river, Al takes Candy off the trail and leads her into the woods toward the river. He lays out the plaid blanket on a level, secluded spot and sets her down upon it. Small and delicate, Candy looks up at Al, who wants nothing more than to be with her; damn the consequences.

Al gets down on his knees next to Candy and looks into her eyes. She meets his gaze. He breathes her in deeply. He smells her sweet aroma and feels blood flow through his body. He sniffs the air again and smells faintly her tangy richness through her panties.

His erection presses against his jeans. He looks again into her eyes, which consent, and they, kiss gently.

Chucky turns the key. The engine turns over until it starts.

"Wake up, Al." Chucky looks through the lowered window. "We're getting' outta here."

Chucky puts the transmission in gear and lets out the clutch. The SUV spins its wheels, as it tries to climb the bank toward the road. Chucky depresses the clutch. The truck rolls back a little. Again he revs the engine and pops the clutch. The engine roars, and tires spin.

"We're stuck. How 'bout a push?"

Al walks to the back of the truck and puts his hands and shoulder against it. Chucky revs the engine. Tires spin. Al pushes, straining and groaning, as the spinning tires splatter him with chunks of grass and moist dirt. The SUV climbs half way up the slope. Al gives out, and the truck stops. Chucky applies the break. Al bends over, breathing hard.

Leaves rustle in the nearby woods.

Al looks over his shoulder. He sees only trees. He stands up straight, takes a long breath, and lets it out slowly.

Chucky revs the engine and pops the clutch. Again the tires spin.

A loud bellow rumbles through the darkness.

Al looks over his shoulder and sees a tree shaking at the edge of the woods. His eyes grow large, and his heart beats wildly. He gasps a great gulp of air, and a surge of energy jolts through his body. He pushes against the truck with all his might; every muscle firing at once. The SUV slowly climbs the hill until it reaches the gravel road.

Al rushes into the back seat. He slams the door shut, locks it, and collapses.

"There's, something out there." Al pants

"What are you talking about?" Chucky turns to him.

"In the woods."

"Like Sasquatch?"

"It howled at me."

"Okay."

Al turns to Candy. She looks him in the eyes and sees his fear. She takes his hand and feels it trembling.

"It's alright, Honey."

"Lazy Acres or bust." Chucky chuckles.

"Do it, Honey."

Inside her candlelit home, Delores picks dry, yellow leaves from one of many bundles. She places the leaves in a mortar and grinds them up with a pestle. She adds some lard to a small copper bowl and places the bowl over a candle flame. As the lard begins to flow, she stirs in the herb powder, which tints the concoction a sickly yellow. She adds a bit of clear alcohol, and stirs the pot until it catches fire.

Blue flames flit and flow from the copper bowl. The flames reflect in Delores' blue eyes and illuminate the rippled and pock-marked, red and beige flesh of her disfigured face. She sprinkles another powder into the burning pot. The powder sparkles and sparks as it falls. The flames extinguish.

She opens the front of her nightgown to reveal her breasts. Thick scar tissue and fresh wounds surround her nipples. She reaches a hand into the pot to gather up some of the hot ointment, which she smears on and massages into her breasts. As she massages, she squeezes the nipples, which exude a small amount of fluid.

Something scurries in the next room. Long nails scuttle across the bare wood floor, and a cat's meow lingers in the still air of the candlelit shack.

"Come, Baby."

Delores makes kissing sounds and looks to the doorway near the floor.

A small hand grabs the door frame.

"Come on, Honey." She squeezes more milk from her nipples. "Dinner time."

Through the doorway bounds something black and shiny, trailing a long tail behind. It leaps onto her lap. Immediately, it goes for a nipple. The thing purrs, as it licks with its rough tongue and chews with its sharp teeth.

When it is satisfied, the creature stretches its wings and curls up on Delores' lap.

Bright lights illuminate a large, dilapidated, wooden sign: Black letters on a faded white background spell out Lazy Acres.

"This is it." Kendal turns to Al, smiling.

"Grand."

Headlights, shifting to the right, light up the forest and come to rest on a chain link gate.

"That's just great." Al huffs. "Place is closed."

Chucky looks at Kendal, then across his shoulder to Candy.

"Y'all stay here. I'll check it out."

Chucky opens the door. The cabin light comes on overhead to reveal Kendal and Candy, staring at Al. He looks at them for a moment, then opens his door and steps out.

"Wait up."

The girls watch the brothers walk into the light of the headlamps toward the gate. Al is tall and lean. He walks with military stiffness. Chucky is big and thick and has a more lumbering gate.

"Sasquatch almost got me." Candy mocks.

"Eeeeeeee! Eeeeeeee!" Kendal joins in, and the two laugh, as Chucky and Al reach the gate. The girls watch the brothers inspect the gate. Chucky points to something. Al throws his hands up in a huff. Chucky lifts a chain over a post, swings open the gate, and walks back toward the car. Al rubs his face, dumbfounded, and hurries to catch up.

The two get back in the truck.

"No problem."

"Do it, sweetie."

Al groans.

The SUV rolls through the gate and down the road, past a dilapidated guard shack. They bounce through pot holes, until they arrive at a cabin. It is a small, faded white, wood clapboard structure with dangling window shutters and an asphalt shingle roof in need of repair. One of the posts that once supported the roof of the front stoop has given way, and the porch roof leans dangerously close to full collapse.

"I say we skip the tents and try this cabin." Chucky points.

"Might as well add breaking and entering to trespassing and reckless Evil Knievalism."

"Yeah." Chucky grins.

Again Chucky and Al walk into the headlights.

"So how long have y'all been married?" Kendal turns to Candy.

"About four years."

"Yeah. So, how is it?"

"What?"

"You know."

"What? Sex?"

"Yeah. How is it?"

The boys disappear around the corner of the house.

"Nothing special."

The girls laugh. The sound of shattering glass nearby silences them.

Chucky and Al stand beneath a broken window.

Running a stick along the lower edge of the window, Chucky clears away the remaining shards of glass.

"Alright. I'll give you a boost."

"Me?"

"Yeah. Unless you can boost me through."

Skinny Al snorts.

They look at one another silently. Chucky smiles.

"Come on." He laces his fingers together and holds out the makeshift stirrup. "Upsidaisy."

A wave of heat sweeps through Al's body, which shivers with tense energy. His stomach quivers, and his eyelids twitch, as he reaches up to inspect the window frame for remaining glass. Finding none, Al grips the window frame firmly. He takes a deep breath and, letting it hiss between his teeth, looks down at Chucky's cupped hands.

"Attaboy."

Al steps up onto Chucky's hands and extends his leg to raise his eyes level with the window. Al peers into the dark interior of the cabin and sees that boards lean at different angles against the walls, plaster rubble lines the floors, and, just beneath the window, broken glass awaits his head-first arrival.

Al's pulls up with his arms. Chucky follows Al's movement with a strong boost, and, like an infant entering the world, Al glides steadily through the opening into the unknown. His torso passes through, and he reaches his hands blindly toward the floor until they come to rest in a pile of broken glass. Chucky gives another boost, and all of Al's weight transfers to his hands, which press heavily onto the broken glass. As Al scrambles to pull his knees and feet through the opening, a shard of glass penetrates the palm of his right hand.

He gets his feet beneath his torso and straightens up to the sound of crunching glass. He looks down at his hand to see a gleaming shard protruding from his palm. He grips the wrist. His arms shake. His heart thumps heavily. Pain pulses from his hand up his arm. Deep red blood pools in his cupped palm and trickles over the round edge to fall onto the filthy floor.

Al looks up and sees a doorway with light from the truck beyond. The doorway sways. Al loses his balance and, staggering to the side, falls against a wall.

"You okay?"

Al stares at his hand, as the blood flows in long, dark streams down his forearm.

"Al?"

The image from his cell phone rises in his mind. Candy smiles at the camera, at the viewer, at him. Her cheek nestles lovingly against the other man's. Flesh presses flesh. The warmth of her body soaks into him. His energy flows into her. Al's heartbeat turns jazzy. His stomach churns down deep, and his mouth fills with saliva. Sweat runs down his cheeks and mixes with tears from his eyes.

Al's mouth stretches open. His strained voice wretches. His stomach convulses, and Al vomits.

"Al!"

His head hangs loosely. Drool flows slowly from his hanging lips.

"You okay in there?"

Al raises his head slowly.

"Yeah." He wipes his mouth with the back of his left forearm. "I'll be alright."

"Good. Find the front door."

"Alright."

Al, pushing his elbow against the wall, regains his upright posture and takes a clumsy step toward the backlit doorway.

Inside the car, the girls wait.

Chucky comes around the corner and walks into the light from the headlamps. He walks under the leaning porch roof up to the door.

Al opens the door from the inside.

Chucky turns and beckons the girls.

"Our rooms are ready." Kendal smiles.

"I can't wait."

The glass dagger shines brightly in the flashlight's beam. Al stares at it. He looks at the exact spot where it enters his flesh; the intersection of inside and outside. He imagines the tip of it; slicing his muscles, nerves, and blood vessels. *How strange this world is. This world of stuff, where no two objects can occupy the same space.*

Candy stands behind Al and strokes his thinning hair, as Chucky grips the glass dagger between his finger and thumb. He slowly, ever so slowly, pulls the bloody shard from Al's palm. Candy's eyes grow large, and the corners of her mouth pull back, as she watches the glass slide from Al's palm. She feels empathy pain in her own hand. Her fingers tingle, and tears well up in her eyes.

"Poor Al."

Kendal wraps Al's bloody hand with a torn tee shirt and ties the fabric with a tight knot, as blood soaks through.

"Alright. Let's eat." Chucky pats Al on his shoulder and rises to his feet. "I'll get the food."

"Get the booze, too."

"Coming right up."

Bourbon flows from the Dixie cup. Caramel color. Smooth on the tongue. Rich like butter. Bourbon flows from the Dixie cup.

Kendal and Candy make sandwiches by the light of a red lantern, while Chucky piles wood from a stack into the fireplace. In the background Al sits in a side room with a bottle. Chucky douses the wood with a heavy stream of charcoal lighting fluid. He strikes a match on the side of the box and drops the match into the fireplace. Whoosh! A red and orange fireball rolls from the fireplace. Smoke rises up into the rafters of the collapsed ceiling, as the fireball dies down to a steady burn in the firebox.

"That should do it." Chucky looks over his shoulder to see Al drink from the bottle. Leaving Candy and Kendal to make the sandwiches, Chucky walks into the side room to talk with Al.

He walks into the room and notices that it is in much worse condition than the main room. Wallpaper lay in twisted strips on the floor from where someone ripped it from the walls. The ceiling bows down in the middle, a gaping hole reveals the inner structure of the wall, and the one window in the small room has been painted black. Chucky feels uncomfortably constrained in the tight confines of the wrecked room and wants to turn around and leave, but he needs to talk to Al.

"How's the hand?"

"It hurts."

"Guess so."

Al's text alert goes off. He ignores it.

"You gonna check that?"

"I don't know." Al drinks from the bottle.

"I've been getting' them for a while." Chucky looks at Al intently. "Kendal too."

"Pictures?"

"Yeah." Chucky raises his eyebrows and nods his head. "Who's the guy?"

A shudder travels through Al.

"I don't know. Some old boyfriend that found her online. Guess they got together a bit."

Chucky takes the bottle from Al's hand. He takes a long swig and hands it back.

"She said it was nothing." Al drinks. "Looks like something to me."

"Yeah."

"She said he's obsessed. She broke it off. Now he's trying to ruin our relationship, whatever that is. He sends texts, 'Where's your wife?' Shit like that. And the pictures; they're all over his page."

"Yeah."

"She denies the pictures. Say's they're hoaxes. I know better."

"Yeah. So what are you gonna do?"

"I'm holding on. We're bound for life." Al drinks. "A lot of it is my fault. I don't give her the attention she needs."

Chucky nods.

"Boys, y'all ready to eat?"

"Be right there." Chucky pats Al on the shoulder, turns, and walks into the front room. Al takes another swig.

Candy, Kendal, and Chucky gather around the fireplace. Kendal rubs her hands together by the fire.

"Nice fire, Sweetie."

"Thanks, Kendal. It wasn't too hard to make. The wood is dry. There's no tellin' how long it's been in here."

"Yeah. It looks like the place has been empty for quite a while. Could be a nice cabin if somebody fixed it up."

Chucky nods and bites into his sandwich. "Good sandwich. Is that Swiss cheese?"

"Yep. I like Swiss. How 'bout you, Candy? You like Swiss?"

Candy nods her head.

In the background, Al pulls out his phone, looks at it for a moment, and runs a finger across the screen. He stares for a second. His eyes fall closed. His head falls back.

A loud bellow rises above the crackling fire.

Chucky and Kendal look to one another with wide eyes.

"What was that?" Candy's face fades to white.

Al falls over, unconscious.

A guttural grunt.

"Something is out there!"

Kendal looks into Chucky's eyes.

Chucky goes to the window and, cupping his hands to the sides of his face, looks into the darkness.

He sees the truck and gently swaying trees, glistening in the moonlight.

"What do you see, Honey?"

"Nothing."

"Well, something is out there. A dog or something"

"I know, Kendal. I'm gonna check it out."

Chucky picks up a two by four from the floor. He shakes it to get a feel for its mass and turns toward the door.

"Be careful."

"Okay. Lock the door behind me."

Chucky opens the door and steps out beneath the leaning porch roof.

Kendal rushes to lock the door.

"He'll run it off."

"Good idea."

The girls peer through the window and watch as Chucky, walking away, fades into the darkness.

Four eyes shift left and right. Large pupils search the night. The girls huddle close. Their hearts beat in unison at a rapid pace, as the girls join sweaty hands and wait.

"Something's wrong." Kendal whispers. "I can feel it. Something happened to him." Her chin quivers. Candy holds Kendal close and strokes her cheek.

"He's okay. He's just looking around."

"No! Something happened to him." Nervous energy jangles in her limbs, and she squeezes her eyes shut, causing tears to flow. "I can't take it." She reaches for the deadbolt.

"Stop, Kendal." Candy pulls Kendal's hand away from the lock.

"I've got to find him!" Kendal looks desperately through the narrow glass in the door and sees something. She can't make it out at first, can't comprehend what she sees beneath the full moon.

Kendal stares out the small window and breathes slowly, a bit of saliva drips form her lower lip.

"What is it, Kendal?" Candy places her right palm on Kendal's shoulder and feels the energy flow through Kendal's body.

"What do you see?"

Kendal does not respond.

Candy squeezes up to the glass and watches something stride along at the edge of the forest. The thing walks on four legs. It is black and fury with an enormous head shaped like a dog's.

Transfixed, the girls watch breathlessly, as the creature sniffs at the rear, passenger-side, door of the truck. The thing huffs deeply and grunts. It raises up on its hind legs to reveal a strikingly human form. It strikes the window with a smashing blow. The window shatters. The thing sticks his head into the truck and sniffs deeply. Hair bristles on its back, and it grunts.

The girls stare, fighting back screams, as tears flow. A muffled sob escapes Kendal. The beast turns quickly toward the cabin. Bright yellow eyes glow in the moonlight.

The thing approaches.

Candy runs into the side room. Kendal slides down the door and presses her back against it with all her might. She breathes heavily, as tears stream down her cheeks. Bloodshot eyes search the cabin for a safer place.

Beyond the door, huffs and growls grow louder and more frenzied. Kendal, holding a shaking hand over her mouth, stifles her sobs, until a forceful blow jolts the door. She screams and presses her back against the door.

Frenzied growls fill Kendal with terror, and a mighty thump rattles the door. Kendal screams. Another thud on the door. Kendal and Candy share a desperate look, and the chimera crushes the door on top of Kendal.

Pinned beneath the door and panic stricken, Kendal wriggles and screams. The beast throws the door aside to reveal Kendal, mad with terror. The beast reaches down with a human hand and grabs her by the hair. The dog-faced thing, flashing long, yellow teeth, pulls Kendal from beneath the wrecked door onto the porch.

Kendal kicks and screams, as the thing tugs at her hair. Kendal grabs the thing's fury wrists and digs red fingernails in deep. The creature, grunting and snarling, jerks her across the porch. Kendal slides around and kicks the post that supports the leaning roof. The roof shakes. The creature stares down its long muzzle at her and bares it sharp teeth; drool flows in long streams from his mouth.

Kendal kicks the post again. The post slides a few inches to the side, and the roof heaves above the creature's head. The thing barks fiercely, and Kendal kicks again.

The roof collapses with an enormous rumble onto the creature and knocks it, yelping, to the porch.

Kendal struggles to get free, as the thing bellows and growls.

She slides from beneath the collapsed roof and stumbles toward the woods.

"Chucky!"

Through the dark woods, Kendal stumbles. Looking left and right, straining her eyes to see, she frantically searches for and calls out to Chucky.

Sweat stings her tear-filled eyes, and she runs blindly into a quagmire of hanging vines and low brush. She falls face first into a blackberry bramble, which binds her arms, legs, and hair. Gasping and grunting, she struggles against the young tendrils, and the bramble binds her tightly.

Ensnared by the bramble, Kendal sinks deeper into the vegetative trap and wallows upon the thicker, prickly limbs, which rip and gouge her flesh. Blood flows across her freckled, moon-lit skin, and, mixing with sweat, smears into a translucent red stain, which stings as it flows across her lacerated skin.

Stinging pain and face-down bondage exasperate the torment of her certain knowledge that the creature is not far behind her. Her muscles twitch and strain against the bramble, which gives but doesn't release.

She hears herself panting for air and feels her heart beating hard. Desperate energy flows through her desperate body, and tears flow down her blood-smeared nose and drip off. She hears the chimera scurry nearby.

"Oh, God!" Kendal pushes hard against the flimsy mass but finds nothing solid to press against. So she tries to roll over onto her back. Prickles, digging into her arms, hold her tight. She knows she will suffer the pain of the prickles or the pain of the thing's yellow teeth and she chooses to turn herself no matter how much flesh she leaves behind.

She rocks. Prickles rip.

Kendal, groaning the hero's groan and exerting herself beyond the limits of pain, tears her body from the bramble.

She reaches shredded hands up to a low-hanging vine. She pulls her hair free and stands, as the thing comes into view.

Kendal looks into the chimera's eyes. Its pupils stand wide open, leaving only a thin ring of yellow to glow in the dim moonlight against its massive, black haunches.

She stumbles into the open forest and picks her way between the trees. Her pace slows as exhaustion overcomes her body. The thing closes in on her. She looks over her shoulder and watches the chimera approach. Head hangs low. Hairs stand on its back. Tail twitches.

The thing snarls viciously. Kendal picks up a stick.

"Back!" "

The creature stalks. Kendal turns to run and falls into a web of guts, strewn about the low limbs from tree to tree. She, becoming ensnared, struggles frantically against the web of innards until, from its perch on a broken limb, Chucky's head falls, thumping into her lap.

Kendal breaks. The will to live flies from her, and she accepts her imminent death, as the monster descends on her exhausted body.

"Wake up, Al." Candy shakes Al. "Wake up!"

Al grumbles.

"Wake up!" Candy, weeping, smacks his face.

"What?" Al wipes his eyes.

"We've gotta get outta here."

"Why?"

"Something's out there. It got Chucky and Kendal."

Al struggles to his feet.

"What?"

"Just come on. We gotta go!"

Candy leads Al by the hand through the doorway into the front room. Looking at the entrance, Al freezes. His face goes pale, and his heart pounds in his chest.

Candy turns toward the entrance just as the creature lunges, knocking her to the floor.

The thing stands up to its full seven foot height and stalks up to Al, who shivers in place. The beast swings a mighty backhand and knocks Al through the air into the wall.

The beast turns to Candy, sliding backward across the floor. It seizes her by the foot and thrusts its long muzzle up her short skirt. Sniffing and snorting, the thing presses its moist black nose heavily into her crotch. The thing's shining red penis slides from the furry sheath, and the beast rips the black, satin panties from her body.

Candy gasps.

Al, frozen in place, watches.

The abomination descends between Candy's legs.

Al stands breathless and frozen. Tears flow from his transfixed eyes, as he watches the horrible beast arch its back and thrust into Candy. Its bushy tail swirls in the air.

Al's body goes cold. His arms shake. His head shakes. His legs shake. The thing moans, and Al's face draws back into a mask of terror. His stomach convulses, and air hisses between his chattering teeth. He holds the breath until it escapes him and he pants.

Al forces himself to draw a long breath and lets it slip slowly through barely parted lips. He draws another breath and focuses on the sound. Warmth flows back into his limbs and his neck regains some flexibility. Al takes another breath and feels the heat rise to his face, as the horrendous scene plays out before him.

Al wiggles his fingers and looks to his left, where he sees the can of charcoal lighting fluid. Al looks at the beast, still pumping. He tentatively stretches his arm toward the can. Slowly, he reaches for the flammable fluid.

With the can in hand, Al grabs the box of matches with the other. He takes another deliberate breath and rises, shaking, to his feet. He takes an uncertain step toward the hairy beast. Again, he breathes a long, quivering breath. He takes another step toward the gyrating chimera. Al looks at the thing fiercely and raises the can above it. He squeezes the can, and a steady stream of flammable liquid flows through the air onto the thing's furry back.

The beast growls and turns toward Al, who drops the can. The thing stares deeply into Al's eyes. It snarls, licks Candy's face, and thrusts deeply into her.

Al pulls a match slowly from the box with trembling hands. He fumbles with the match, which refuses to light on the first attempt. Again the thing stares into Al's eyes. It licks its lips with its long tongue and moans. Al strikes the match again. The flame comes to life in his hand. He holds it for a moment and stares into the thing's terrible eyes.

Al flicks the flame toward the abomination. The flaming match flutters through the air and lands on the creature's accelerant-soaked back. A huge fireball erupts. The beast howls as it leaps to its hind legs and twirls in excruciating pain.

The thing whirls about, growling and roaring, as the smoky blaze consumes its flesh. The cabin fills with the stench of rotten eggs and burning feces.

The hideous monster falls onto a pile of wood.

Al looks at Candy, who murmurs.

The hairy interloper sizzles and smokes.

The fire spreads.

Al helps Candy from the floor, takes the keys from the hearth, and the two run through the doorway, as the cabin goes up in a great inferno.

Dale Hollin
The Last Eulogy

"I want another kiss," he said.

He began to feel warm as her face moved slowly forward. The last touch of her lips upon his seemed an eternity ago. A cool, plush softness brushed his mouth like an autumn breeze and he craved the pale contours of her throat.

"Michael, I'm not leaving you. I never really have."

The long, dark hair seemed to lift and cascade across her shoulders in the still room. He reached to grasp it with his fist, but couldn't quite take hold of her. It felt to him like finely spun black glass dissipating into vapor. Her eyes moved to the open window across the room. The first tendrils of dawn wisped dark shades of violet in intervals along the Eastern horizon. Her face became slack and withdrawn.

"I have to go for now. The other will be near soon. He mustn't know I've come here."

Michael inhaled deeply as she moved slowly from atop him, her eyes never deviating from the window. He wondered vaguely about this "other." She had spoken of him before, but he had rarely asked her for any details about his meaning or status to her. He only knew that she still came to him in the nights, and that was all that mattered for now; that she came to him at all.

"I will wait for you again," he said.

She looked at him, her face still slack, but somehow paler than before.

"I will be here tonight, when he releases me."

He watched as she drifted sullenly to the window. She placed her head and upper body outside of its frame and fell forward into the early dawn. *She's gone again.* He never questioned why she wouldn't use the door. It had been months since she had walked through the rest of the home. She seemed content to remain confined to his bedroom at night. The clock on the wall above the mantle read 5:09am. She always left at exactly this time. It seemed ritual to him, for some reason; as if the numbers themselves were a painted portrait, speaking volumes in a language not conveyed through simple words.

He rolled over and pulled the pillow over his head to close completely the dim light of the rising dawn. He thought how blissful the walls of sleep would be in this hour, but knew these walls were illusions. If ever he did sleep now, it was an experience he carried no memory of. Not since . . . the parting. Not since "the other" swept his love away like so much magic dust under an old and frayed rug.

He smiled lightly beneath the enclosure of the pillow. It was as if his face were wrapped in a soft tomb. He blinked his eyes and stared into the darkness. *Danielle.* Her once smiling face, from a time past, materialized within this created tomb. *She was once happy here.*

"Time to crawl out of here," he whispered to himself.

He threw the cushion to the floor beside his bed and sat up. His mind felt awash in vertigo and he covered his face with his hands, peeking through his fingers until the room leveled. He uncovered one eye and glanced at the half empty bottle of Chianti still set on the bedside table. *Ahhhh...breakfast is served.* He poured the draught into the stained glass set beside the bottle. The wine looked to him like liquefied garnets, swirling a toxic sheen through the fine crystal stem. He lifted it to his mouth as if holding and inhaling a delicate red rose. *Danielle.* He drained the glass and stood.

He heard a door open and shut somewhere in the house. There always seemed to be a door opening somewhere when he was alone. What did it matter? He used to wander the rooms and corridors, searching for strangers or possibly her. No sign of a soul could he find. Just doors and the myriad of photos hanging on the walls. He grabbed the stem and Chianti and walked to his desk in the front room.

He sat in his chair and glanced over at the TV in the corner of the room. It was cold and dark. It hadn't been turned on since the parting. He had a gun and often thought of shooting it just to hear the glass break. It would seem such a more decorative piece, he thought, without the constant and dusty reflections held in that glass. He could gut the box after he shot it and place something pleasant to look at within. Like a picture of her. Perhaps the one of her dancing to the beautiful, droning sound of the cicadas when they once camped by the river. He had always loved to watch her dance. Within the gutted box, she could dance eternally for him.

The wine flowed again and he smiled at the thought of it. He turned his attention from the TV and stared at his monitor centered atop his desk, gently running his fingers across the keyboard. He had grown tired of writing these eulogies for people and families he had never known. It was what he seemed to do best, though. Prominent mortuaries across the tri-state area paid him well for this service. Since the parting, he had taken to infusing certain blasphemies into the sermons for his own personal amusement. His last eulogy was written for a locally famous Jewish woman who had died of emphysema. He had purposely inserted a line which was a direct quote from Mein Kampf toward the end of it. Hitler's words intertwined and fit beautifully within the rest of the memorial. No one seemed to notice. No one cared.

His newest corpse to memorialize was a partner with a major law firm in the city. He died of heart failure. So many attorneys did die of heart problems, it seemed. Probably because they had so little heart to sustain anyway. He scanned through his personal life details quickly. Father of four. Divorced twice. Involved in various civic and community organizations. Fairly generous in his monetary charitable donations. All useful to him in regard to the eulogy, but meaningless otherwise. He stared for a moment at the man's photos. One an obvious high school senior photo, one a wedding photo with his second bride, the last one a more recent photo taken recently before his death. All of them shared in common the same set and plastic grin most people wear as a kind of mask when posing for pictures. He wondered how the people at his service would react if the mortician would sew his lips in place to mimic this same grin in the casket and almost laughed at the thought of it.

He pushed the photos aside. He couldn't think of this man now, or his petty life accomplishments. He could only think of this "other." This man who had stolen his wife, as if she were some golden trinket he could possess when the sun had risen. Could she only come to him while he slept? There had to be a reason she only saw him on such a precise schedule. He would find out. He would find this man and release her from his bondage. He knew he would have to kill him. He raised his head and glared at the ceiling. *Danielle. I will save you from him.*

The screen of his monitor drew him forward. A eulogy. Yes. He would prepare for the death of this other by writing his eulogy even before his demise. The man should be grateful. Generally only the very wealthy and elite were privileged enough to have him write their final memorial. A problem was he really knew nothing of the man's life. Knew nothing of his accomplishments, besides of course, having the exceptional talent of taking what was his. Yes. A thief. A very skilled thief he was, and he would receive a thief's memorial.

He opened a new file and stared at the screen. He had to pay this other homage, no matter how much he hated him. He had accomplished what no other could. He had purloined his beloved's heart. The man was probably a fairly handsome chap. His wife was an extraordinarily beautiful woman and would surely not accept another not fair in appearance and charming in the extreme. He closed his eyes and tried to visualize him. He couldn't do it. He decided to place a mask on the other much resembling his own features, but with lighter hair. Maybe a better physical build. Better dressed. He opened his eyes and began to type.

Today, we gather as friends, acquaintances, and loved ones of the other. Not in mourning. For no man's life should be truly mourned; but in celebration of having held the privilege of knowing and experiencing his intervening presence. He came to us not through an extended invitation, but from his own bold and perceptive heart having heeded a call from each one of us. Each one of us who has held the longing and necessity within our own hearts to lose everything so that we may find strength within ourselves.

We may compare this man to the Sainted Patrick of Ireland who had the divine grace to lead the serpents from the plush and green land of his people, so they would know the serpents amongst them no longer. For these serpents were within their hearts then and ours now; and today, we celebrate this other who has freed us from them, so they may strike at our heels and poison our souls no more.

Although I have only known this other for a short length of time, his grace and wisdom have gathered the snakes which had coiled around my feet and soul and led them into the far away Netherworld where such creatures dwell. With my serpents followed my transgressions, and with my transgressions followed . .
.

Michael glanced above the monitor as the slim figure of a shadow passed across the wall. He turned quickly around in his chair. No one. Always no one. He slowly turned to the dark screen of the television. Danielle's reflection stood still and staring back at him. Her image sometimes materialized in the black glass, but she was never there. She was with him. Always with him until the sun closed its dimmed scarlet eye and the night fell upon his bedroom window like an old and tired companion. He closed his eyes and wished her reflection gone. He hated the television. Hated the dark glass which tormented him when he looked within it. He opened his eyes and she was gone. All that stood there now was his image staring back.

He opened the drawer of his desk and pulled the blued thirty-eight caliber revolver from it. He pointed it at the screen and fired. The sound was deafening. It angered him that he wasn't able to have the pleasure of hearing the glass shatter. He ran over to the television and began kicking the rest of the glass in with his bare foot. Again and again his foot went through the screen until his own blood began staining the carpet and plastic frame of the set.

"Michael!!! What are you doing!!!?"

He felt hands and arms pulling him to the ground. He sat there stunned for a moment and looked up to where the scream had come from. It was her. *Danielle.* He glanced over to the window, scratching down the side of his face. He glared at her.

"What are you doing here, Danielle? You don't come till night. You're not supposed to be here till night. You're supposed to be with him. Your "other." Where is he? Is he here? Maybe I have a little something special for him, too. Maybe I'll shatter him the same way. WHERE IS HE????"

She covered her eyes and began sobbing.

"Michael, there is no other man. I have always been here Michael, but you don't see me. I bring your food and your wine, but you don't see me. Sometimes I stand behind you while you write these god-forsaken eulogies, but you don't see me. There is no other man, except you. You are the other, Michael . . . AND YOU DON'T SEE ME!!!!!!!"

He scratched into the side of his face deeper and stood up, moving toward her.

"Bullshit, bitch. Every morning at 5:09am you leave out my window. Every morning. You leave me here alone to be with your other. You said so. You said you return when he releases you. Your words. He releases you at night. Your words. Now where is the bastard?"

She wiped the tears from her face and looked at him, sullen.

"No, Michael. 5:09am is when you leave me. I am in this house all day long and you don't see me because YOU ARE THE OTHER!!!"

He snorted laughter and shook his head. He wanted to kiss her, but he knew better. She was his now. This other's. He pictured the soul of a woman and saw an image of a desert filled with beautiful reptiles, writhing and mating in a wasteland of refined white sugar and jewels.

"Leave, Danielle. Go to your other. Go see him. When night falls, you come to my window. You are my beloved. Always. Just go."

She turned and fled, weeping. He went to the television and carefully cleared the remainder of the glass from its gutted frame. He looked above the set to where their wedding picture was hung on the wall. He stood and removed it, placing it carefully within the empty space he had created within it. He smiled at the photo in the television. The faces in the photo smiled back at him.

He sat back in his chair and stared at the eulogy. He had to finish it. He would finish it for her. She loved this other as she loved him. He knew this now.

. . . my beloved. I will heed the wisdom of the other. For he has shown me the way. He has shown me that it is my duty. My honor. My love to release her from his bondage. *Danielle.* **And release her I now must do.**

He slowly picked up the gun and placed it to his temple. He smiled.

"My beloved Danielle. Your other is no more."

A. Henry Keene
Delores

Blue and orange flames consume the young girl's face and lick the interior of her gaping mouth. Tongue and lips swell and split to expose more delicate flesh to the flame's frying fury. Teeth crack. Cheeks sizzle and smoke, and the floral print blindfold catches fire. Flames travel delicate, red curls, and the small room fills with the smoky stench of burning flesh, the girl's screams, and her mother's insistent words, "This is best for you, Delores."

Pulling back a fistful of singed hair, Mother removes the girl's head from the fireplace. She thrusts the girl's face into a grey metal tub filled with water, which sizzles, bubbles, and steams. Delores pushes against the bare wood floor with her small might. Her arms shake, as the girl struggles against her mother's strong hand. Relenting, Mother pulls the girl from the water. She gasps, and black skin slides down her face and falls from her chin onto the floor.

Light from the waxing moon flows through the window onto Delores, writhing small on the mattress; bare feet constantly rub each other, and fingers twitch, as she moans. Her head rests on a white pillow, over which red hair, singed at the ends, spreads.

A fly crawls from her hairless eyelid across the blisters that surround the puss-covered, raw flesh of her cheek. The fly crawls across the gooey, yellow layer onto her swollen, scabby lip and feeds.

Mother stands over Delores with a small glass of water. "Pray with me, Girl." She looks sternly upon her daughter's ruined face. "Pray for forgiveness." Mother takes the girl's small hand in her own. "Dear Lord." Mother pauses for a long moment and closes her eyes. "We are weak beings. We think not in advance of what we do." Mother presses her lips together tightly, as her chin quivers. "My child has led another astray." Mother raises her free hand into the air to beseech God. "We pray for your mercy." A tear runs down mother's smooth cheek. "Forgive the child, oh, Lord. She knows not what she does." Mother quakes. "Amen."

The day after a rainy spring day, Delores, cloistered in the small hovel, sinks into the filthy mattress. Puss oozes from her wounds into her red hair, which grows stiff and matted. A thin stream of tears flows from the corners of her eyes, down the sides of her face, and into her ears.

Motionless, she waits for an end to her suffering. Motionless, she watches a dark figure creep in through the window.

The sweet and pungent aromas of herbs and drying sassafras, ginseng, and mandrake roots fill Delores' mind, and she, feeling unusually rested, stirs from sleep. The young girl opens her blue eyes to see an old crone smiling a gaping, one-toothed smile. Delores gasps.

"Oh, no, no, no, Child." The crone strokes the girl's red hair. "You mustn't be afraid."

"Who?" Delores speaks her first word in weeks. "Who are you?"

The old crone runs her tongue across her tooth and studies the child.

"Me? Well, I'm just an old woman. I live here in this cottage in the woods." The crone sits at the girl's side and takes a porcelain jar from a table, holding many such jars. "Perhaps you've seen my house when you played?"

"Oh, no. I'm not allowed in the woods."

"Well, you're in the woods now."

Delores glances through the slightly-parted curtains and sees nothing but trees. Her heartbeat flutters and she desperately studies the old woman's face: White hair pulled back into a bun. Long nose. Sagging, wrinkled cheeks and eyelids. Soft, caring eyes, shining bluebird bright.

"Are you . . .?" Delores feels her heart beating fast and she pants. "Grandmother?"

"Yes, child. I'm your Grandmother."

"But you—"

"Yes, child." The crone smiles gently. "I died."

The child's mind reels, and she looks around the small cottage. A rough stone hearth and fireplace with a cauldron, hanging from an iron arm, occupy the center of the back wall. Above the fire, a wooden mantel holds a menagerie of wood and stone trinkets, some of which resemble people; others favor animals in their shapes.

To the side of the fireplace stands a cabinet. The door hangs slightly open. Delores peeks inside to see jars filled with fruits, vegetables, and animal parts. One jar contains eyeballs, floating in a clear liquid; another preserves a small brain. Delores wonders what her grandmother does with these things.

The old woman notices Delores looking into her cabinet and gently closes the door.

"We will have time for these things. But not now."

Grandmother dips her fingers into the porcelain jar to scoop up a thick, translucent green ointment. She leans over Delores and looks into her eyes. In the tenderness of Grandmother's gaze, Delores feels the warmth of love and lets her eyes fall shut.

Grandmother gently smears the viscous, green goo onto the girl's face, which is deep red, pitted, and rippled like molten lava. Her fingers flow over the rugged undulations and leave behind a shining layer, which shimmers red and orange, reflecting light from the fire. A tear trickles down the crone's wrinkled cheek.

Bright sunlight winnows through the thick forest canopy. Amidst blue and yellow wildflowers, Delores frolics in the full, sweltering heat of summer. Grandmother watches, as the child wanders over to a low plant with broad, bubbly leaves. The old crone smiles and walks outside to join Delores, who now kneels over the plant. The young girl runs her fingertips over the dark green leaves and presses her nose into the rich blue flowers.

"You have an eye for the Alraun." Grandmother smiles; "Time to see what you will."

Grandmother kneels down next to the child and gathers up the leaves in her fist.

"Cover your ears, Child"

Slowly and with great power, the old crone pulls the plant. As the root breaks free of the earth, Delores hears a strange shriek, and her eyes stand wide with awe.

The old woman smiles. She looks down at the bifurcated root, which resembles, with its knobby growths and curvy form, a fully-developed woman.

"Yes, child, you have chosen well."

Grandmother clips the flowers from their stems, binds them with a bit of twine, and hangs the bundle from the mantle.

"We'll let these dry for now." The old woman smiles. "Now for the poppet."

"The what?"

"The root, Child. Who does it resemble?"

Delores holds the root before her eyes and, turning it about, recognizes the figure. She squeezes her eyes shut.

"Who is it?"

"I don't know."

"Yes you do. Who is it?" The crone stares.

Tears flow down the girl's ruined face; she shudders.

"Who is it?"

"Mother! It's my Mother!" Delores drops the root and collapses onto the floor in a fit of weeping.

"Yes, Child. It is your mother. Do as you will."

The visitor is welcome. A man, wearing dirty jeans, work boots, and a white tee shirt, stands at the door of Grandmother's cottage. The two chat before the man enters. Delores skitters behind her cot in the front room and watches.

Grandmother crosses the room, reaches into her cabinet, and retrieves a small bottle filled with a blue liquid. She carries the bottle to the waiting man and hands it to him.

"Guaranteed to win her heart."

The man gives grandmother a heavily-loaded paper sac in exchange for the vial and, glancing over his shoulder at Delores, walks through the door.

The old woman carries the sac to the cot.

"Now, let's see what we have."

She rummages through the sac and pulls out an assortment of glass canning jars, some string, a few candles, and a photograph, which she stares at for a long moment before placing it on the mantel.

After grandmother turns in for the night, Delores gets up, lights a candle, and walks to the mantel. She steps up on a small stool and sees, among the effigies, the photograph; it holds the grey images of two women, standing in fine clothes and embracing. The younger woman glows with the radiance of beauty, and Delores knows immediately, from the woman's resemblance to her mother, that this is her grandmother. But the older woman?

Once the flowers have dried, grandmother grinds them in a mortar and places the resulting powder in a small copper pot. She adds a small amount of clear alcohol to the powder and sets it over a candle's flame. After a few minutes, grandmother pours the tincture into Delores' cup.

"Drink this, Child."

"What is it?"

"Tea. It will bind your will to the poppet."

Uncertain of the meaning of grandmother's response, Delores, trusting the old woman, raises the cup to her lips and drinks. She winces at the bitter taste of the tea but manages to finish the cup.

"Now, think of your mother, as you hold the poppet."

Grandmother hands her the Alraun root.

As the tea takes effect, Delores feels her body expand, rather her awareness of her body becomes greater, and her mind becomes clear and bright. A smile crosses her face.

"Think of your mother," Grandmother commands.

The image of mother's face comes into focus in Delores' mind. Behind it, red and yellow flames burn brightly. The girl's heart thumps in her chest and waves of heat engulf her body. Delores squeezes and twists the poppet in her hands. She hears her mother groan in agony. Delores laughs. Her peals of laughter grow in intensity, as she realizes the power she has.

"Slow, child," Grandmother advises. "Slow vengeance is the best."

Delores eases her grip on the poppet, until she, smiling a crooked smile, steadily bends the root against its resistance.

Delores listens as her mother whines and, at length, the girl falls into a deep sleep to the gentle sounds of her mother's suffering.

As the months and years pass, grandmother teaches Delores about the plants in the forest and their medicinal uses. She also alludes to more obscure knowledge, which she promises to impart. Delores, enjoying the use of her poppet, anxiously awaits instruction.

Two mysteries remain with Delores, as she develops into a young lady. First, who is the woman in the picture with her grandmother? Second, and most profound, how did her grandmother return from the dead?

On a night of a nearly full moon, Delores dreams of her father. She feels his touch on her skin and smells his breath rich with bourbon. He lays her down in a field of grass and caresses her cheek.

As Delores sleeps, she rubs her budding breasts and licks her rough lips. She presses a hand against her crotch and writhes and moans with pleasure on her cot.

Grandmother, standing over her, realizes it is time for her take a lover. But who would have her?

In the morning, grandmother sits down with Delores for a discussion. She holds in her hand the photograph from the mantel.

"I have seen you study this picture." The old woman looks at Delores. "Is there something you would like to know about it?"

"Who is the older woman?"

"I thought that might interest you." Grandmother smiles. "She was my lover and mentor. She was my reason for living and the reason I live."

"You died, right?"

"Yes. When John found out about me and Gwyneth, that was her name, he lost his temper and killed me with an axe." Grandmother opens her blouse to reveal a long, gnarled scar on her chest. "Then he dumped my body in the woods. Gwyneth, who lived in this very cottage, found me there and brought me back to life."

"How did she do that?"

"I will teach you."

Over the next years, Grandmother instructs Delores in the higher arts of extraction, lunar cycles, and incantations. The girl learns everything she could ever want to know and gains great power. As she reaches the fullness of womanhood, she completes her training in the dark arts and sets in motion a diabolical plan.

Beneath the full moon, Delores stokes a fire. Light from the flickering flames flashes on the surrounding trees, illuminating their moist, green leaves, which shine translucently.

Settling down before the fire, Delores feels the thick scar tissue of her face drawing tighter. She takes a bundle of herbs and tosses it into the fire. The dry plants ignite, sending a violet plume of smoke drifting into the cool night air.

Delores breathes deeply, inhaling the pungent aroma of the herbs. Her heartbeat slows and her neck loosens. Deeply she breathes; deeply she relaxes. Having reached a state of near-total relaxation and heightened concentration, she begins the work.

"Night messenger, winged friend, witness my desire."

In her imagination, Delores conjures the image of herself and her father joined together, limbs mingling, flesh sliding on flesh. She feels her ovaries pulsing.

"Take this to my father as he sleeps."

With a flurry of sound, an owl bursts, flying through the silent forest, from the bough of a nearby tree.

In his drink-induced sleep, Delores' father feels her touch: a gentle glide of fingertips across his cheek. His mouth waters, as she stands naked before him. He studies her luscious curves, undulating like the body of a fiddle, and watches her rub her perky breasts. His penis grows erect, as Delores guides his hand to her vulva. He runs his fingers through the curly hairs. Delores slips a finger into his mouth. It tastes like smoke. The odd sensation heightens his desire, and he calls out to her.

"Delores. I want you, Child."

Mother stirs in bed next to him.

"Delores. I want to cum in you, give you a baby."

Mother gets out of bed and goes to the next room.

The next evening, Delores, naked with the exception of a black cloak, takes a candle from the cabinet. She stands before the mantel, lights the candle, and stretches out a yard long piece of twine. She snips the length of twine from the roll and takes the poppet down from the mantel.

She holds the poppet, studded with pins and needles, and looks at it intently. She smiles a crooked smile and begins to bind the poppet with twine. Round and round, she wraps the twine. Tighter and tighter, she binds her mother. She ties off the loose end and, leaning the candle above the tightly-wound ball of twine, seals the deal with wax.

Delores laughs and draws the hood of her cloak over her head. Slowly her form dissolves into smoke.

Through the open window, the smoke flows into the hovel. At the foot of the bed, the column of blue-grey smoke condenses into the form of Delores, wearing only her black cloak.

She glances into the bed to see her father, bloody and dead; an axe protrudes from his chest.

Delores screams. The high-pitched wail rattles the windows of the old shack.

"You, Bitch!" She looks about. "Where are you?"

She bursts into the next room and finds her mother stretched out, rigid, on the floor.

 Mother, moaning and motionless, stares through wide eyes, as her maimed daughter approaches.

"Now you will pay for what you have done to me."

Delores stands over her mother. She raises her hands. Mother, stiff as a board, floats straight up into the air. With subtle gestures, Delores causes her mother's body to rotate slowly around its vertical axis like the blades of a helicopter. Delores' fierce eyes stare. Her hands shake. Mother's body whirls faster; her floral print nightgown trails behind. Faster and faster she rotates until she is a blur of motion.

The room fills with wind and the swooshing sound of solid matter ripping through air. Another slight gesture sends mother veering away from Delores. Mother grazes a wall. In an instant, blood sprays a wide, red stripe around the room and douses Delores' bare chest.

Delores laughs and, with a strong thrust of her hands, sends mother crashing through the wall in a bloody explosion.

In the morning, Delores removes her father's heart and puts it into a jar. She drags his stiff body out to the trash pit and throws him into it. She calls her mother's dog, an old Stephens Cur. When the dog comes, Delores strangles him with a wire and tosses the corpse into the pit with her father.

Over the next weeks, she kills every animal she finds and adds it to the festering mess. Caterpillars and birds and cats and snakes; all join the putrefaction party. Flies and bees buzz about the corpses, and maggots wriggle in the eye sockets.

As the corpses liquefy and stew, the stench of rot fills the air, and the full moon approaches. Delores returns to Grandmother's cottage in the woods.

"Child." The crone glares. "What have you done?"

"Only what was right and proper."

"Slaughter is neither right nor proper."

"You taught me vengeance."

"Slow suffering is vengeance. What you have done goes beyond our craft."

"I have mastered our craft and taken it a step further."

"No, child. We are healers."

"And what of me? Who will heal me? Who will be my lover? The father of my child?"

"There is time, child."

"Enough talk, old woman."

"But..."

"I've come for the potion."

"You may not have it."

"I will." Delores slaps the old woman to the floor.

"So you can create your abomination?"

"So I can know what it is to be a woman."

Delores extends a hand. Grandmother raises feet first into the air.

Delores looks deep into the old crone's heart, searches through the secret recesses of her mind in flashes of images. A rush of emotions flows through Delores. For a moment her hard heart softens, as she feels Grandmother's love for her. But her ovaries call out to her, demanding satisfaction.

Delores slings her Grandmother aside and goes to the cabinet. She riffles through the jars of organs and parts. She casts each to the floor in her search for the potion.

She pulls out a jar of luminous violet liquid.

"This is it."

She turns and looks at her grandmother.

"Now I will go."

"Never return." Tears flow from the old crone's eyes. "You are dead to me."

Beneath the full moon, Delores builds a small fire next to the stinking pit. Wearing her black cloak, she chants an incantation. Dark smoke gathers around the pit. Holding her father's heart to her chest, she closes her eyes and prays to the dark forces. The smoke dances around the pit and flows into it.

Delores, crying, pours the potion onto the pile of bones and pool of organic goo. The mess begins to sizzle and glow, illuminating her and the surrounding trees a ghastly green.

She takes a burning stick from the fire and drops it into the pit, which instantly erupts in a short-lived fireball.

Delores collapses to the moist earth.

Inside the pit, connections are made, tissues form, and the heart begins to beat.

Justin Hunter
The Maternal One

June watched her husband die. His body lay still on the blood spattered concrete floor of the fighting pit. The people called it the killing floor. It was 'double-death' week and the bent rebar railings surrounding the pit were full of screaming on-lookers. People of all ages crammed the event to capacity and over capacity. There were always two or three people crushed or trampled to death each night by the crowd. Some of the crowd cheered, drained large glasses of foul liquor and grabbed their betting wins. Others cursed their losses. Rocks, spit, and fouler debris rained down on those in the pit. A small stone hit June on the left temple. It opened a small gash. Blood dripped in a small stream down her jaw-line. She hugged her child closer.

Even though her husband was dead the ritual of the kill still had to take place. The man who killed her husband wept as he picked up a long knife from the many crude weapons that were scattered around the pit floor. He had heavily muscled arms and a ponderous stomach. It made his movements slow and ungainly. The men didn't so much fight, but struggle in a torrent of tearing fingernails and desperate gnawing bites. The larger man overpowered the lithe figure of her husband and that made the difference. Her husband was dead. The big man was not.

The man picked up her husband's head by the hair and chopped hard with the rusted blade. The head came away with five hard whacks of the knife. The man threw the head into the crowd and sat on the hard floor. His heavy frame shook with pitiful sobs. June didn't watch her husband's decapitation. The body on the floor wasn't the man she had fallen in love with. Nothing was the same since everything fell apart. First the jobs went away. The country that couldn't support its poor during times of prosperity was completely worthless during recession. Then other countries called in their debts. The superpower that was America defaulted. The dollar became worthless. The riots started. Police were helpless to stop it. Government collapsed.

The fat man rose to his feet. He wiped tears and blood from his face. His own wife and child were huddled at the other end of the concrete circle of the killing floor. He turned away from June and her child and walked over to his family. He hugged his wife and kissed his boy. A rope ladder was lowered into the pit. The large man boosted his wife and child to the dangling rungs. He watched them climb to the relative safety of the mass of people above. The ladder was raised before the man could climb it. It was double-death night. One more person had to die.

June met Steve at his high school youth group at the local Methodist church. She had gone with the intention of meeting boys. Steve liked the sight of her. A sign-up sheet was being passed around for a local clean-up project and Steve took her phone number off it. He informed rather than asked June he was taking it. She shrugged. Three weeks later Steve was at his friend's parent's house and found the phone number in his wallet. He called June and she invited them to come over and watch a movie with her and her friends. When he and his friend arrived at her house, she didn't remember which one Steve was at first. (She still enjoyed teasing him about whether or not she made the right choice.) They left her house to go rent a movie. Steve and June got in the back seat of his friends' car. The back seat wasn't very big and Steve had to lean way over to get inside. June grabbed him as he entered the car and hugged him. It was a whim that felt right to her in the moment. She didn't let go the whole way to the video rental place. That's when Steve fell in love with her. She didn't fall in love with him until later, but that was okay.

Six years later Steve bought an engagement ring for June. They had been dating for a long time. Everyone who knew them couldn't imagine one of them without the other. It had been assumed for some time that they would get married. Steve didn't assume anything. He was terrified. He was going to propose to the June that upcoming weekend and he was making arrangements for the perfect opportunity. He was sitting in his bedroom of the lower half of the college area house that he and two of his friends rented for an exorbitant amount of money. Students of the area were fleeced by landlords who assumed their parents paid the bills for their hard-up children. Steve wasn't going to school. He was working. He had saved long and hard for the ring. It was a paltry diamond with even smaller diamonds spread out amid waves of silver. He'd paid for it in ten dollar bills; every last cent of his savings. He knew it was in the style that June liked. (He wished he could have afforded something nicer, and still does to this day, but he doesn't think June would trade it now, even though they have the money.) He set the ring on the bedspread and wrote out plans for the weekend. He orchestrated the perfect time and place to ask her. She lived a couple miles away, so he didn't have the slightest idea that she was about to barge into the room looking for postage stamps - which she did.

"Do you have any stamps?" She said.

He just looked at her. She saw the ring. The perfect plan went out the window. He got down on one knee.

"Will you marry me?" Steve said. He was never more painfully aware of how little he had to offer her than at that moment. He had nothing but himself.

She looked shocked. She stammered.

"I have to go," June said. "I have to think about it."

She left. Steve sat back on his bed. He didn't know what to think. He sat there for over an hour. The phone rang. It was June. She asked him to come over. She said to bring the ring. Steve did. Her apartment was empty of roommates. Candles were lit all over. She led him over to the couch. He went meekly. He never felt so small and powerless in his whole life.

"Ask me again," June said.

"Really?" Steve said.

"I just got off the phone with my mom," June said. "She asked me how long I was going to make you wait. She said you weren't going to wait around forever."

There was a pause. She was patient.

"Ask me again," June said.

"Will you marry me?" He said.

"Yes," she said.

The man shifted his heavy bulk and picked up a wooden baseball bat from the killing pit floor. The bat was stained red, cracked and ugly from heavy use. The man walked toward June and her child. He stepped around the headless body of her Steve. He didn't even give the gory form a glance as he moved toward his target. June shoved her child behind her, blocking him with her body. The crowd roared in approval. The din was so tumultuous it threatened to rupture June's eardrums.

She looked so small compared to the hulking male that stalked toward her. She was barely five and a half feet tall. Her simple white dress was stained yellow from sweat and dirt. It hung in tatters around her emaciated frame. Her curly hair hung in unruly clumps. Most of it was tied in a knot on the back of her head, giving her a vague ponytail. The man stopped a few feet from her. His body reeked of old sweat and death. He held the bat in his right hand. His muscles tensed on the wooden shaft of the bludgeon. June wondered if he would bring the bat down on her or if he would just try for the child. The man opened his mouth, revealing several broken teeth from other fights on the killing floor. He spoke to her. His voice sounded deep and weary.

"Give me the child," he said. At his words the crowd surrounding the pit quieted a bit. They strained forward to hear. Many shoved each other, cursing for quiet.

"You can't have him," June said. "Kill me." The man waited a moment to answer. His words came slowly. It was almost a plea.

"The child has to die," he said. "That's the rules. It's either him or both of you."

"You'll have to kill me, too," June said. The crowd grew tired of the parley and screamed for June's blood. They came for death and were impatient when it was withheld. Their blood lust threatened to take the whole pit down with them. The man raised the bat and swung hard for June's head.

June shoved her child to the side and lunged toward the man. She bit hard into his neck. The man screamed low and steady as she ripped a parcel of flesh from his throat. The man tore the flailing woman off his body. He flung her against the wall. She hit the concrete hard. Darkness clouded her vision. She nearly passed out. She tried to rise but her legs wouldn't work from the shock of her blow against the wall. The man shook his head. He turned toward her child. The boy, nearly four years old now, his shadowy brown hair plastered to his face, stood stock still in fear. He wouldn't move when the death blow came. The man raised the bat to kill the boy.

June panicked. She picked up a rusted spike off the pit floor and rose on unsteady legs. The bat came down at her child. June hurled herself at the man, driving the metal spike deep into his back. The bat's course altered slightly from the pain of the wound, glancing off the side of her child's head. June ripped the spike out of the man's back and stabbed him again. The man swung his arm back and knocked June sprawling. He tried to pull the spike free from his back but couldn't reach it. June picked up a hatchet off the killing pit floor. She rose to her feet again.

"You can't have him," June said. The crowd roared its approval.

Steve's cell phone rang. He groaned and rolled over in bed, covering his face with a pillow. June prodded him in the ribs. Steve sat up and rubbed his face.

"Answer your phone or I'll never sleep with you again," June said.

"It's not fair to use sex as leverage," Steve said.

"Nothing is fair this early in the morning," June said. "Answer it or die."

"I don't know why you're so cranky at a quarter to three in the morning," Steve said. He leaned over the bed and fished out the pair of jeans he had worn the previous evening from a small pile of dirty laundry on the floor. He found the cell phone and answered the call. Fifteen minutes later June and Steve were in their car, driving to the Department of Child Welfare social services building.

June loved children, always did. She just didn't want to go through pregnancy in order to have one. She had to endure a lot of misunderstanding from friends and family over this. Her mother tried to coax her by telling her that she would make beautiful children. June told her that even beautiful people could have ugly babies. One of her friends told her that maybe she just wasn't 'the maternal type.' Needless to say, she wasn't friends with that person anymore. June and Steve longed for a child and decided on going the adoption route. Steve was on board with the plan. He believed that he could love an adopted child just as deeply as a biological one.

The problem they faced was that adoptable children were treated like a commodity. Their family, being solidly blue collar and desperately hanging on to middle-class status, couldn't afford the ten to fifteen grand it would cost to adopt a child overseas. They decided to become foster parents after speaking with a few families that worked for the system.

"Those parents never pull their act together," a foster parent told them. "They hang on for a few months but don't do what they have to in order to get their children back. They prefer drugs to their kids. You foster a child and they eventually become free to adopt. It doesn't cost you anything. The kid is already in your home and under your care. The State won't want to move the kid to another family. You'll be first choice as an adoptive placement." Steve and June didn't think they had any other option of getting a child. They enrolled in foster classes and became a licensed home.

Weeks had gone by and no children had been placed with them. They had gotten a couple calls about some teenagers that needed placement, but they didn't accept. They wanted a baby. The call finally came. A child had been removed from a home in a trailer park near the north side of the city. June found herself saying 'yes' to the social worker before she had even finished telling her about the boy. She roused Steve and they went to pick him up.

The night emergency social worker, a heavy set blonde with large bags under her eyes, led them to a waiting room. She walked hurriedly, speaking at the same fast clip of her step.

"He's been taken for severe neglect," the social worker said. "The police went to the home on a domestic disturbance call and found the child in the parent's bedroom."

"Is he hurt?" Steve said.

"If he was he would be in a hospital now," the social worker said. "What he needs is some food. We can send some with you. The kid looks like he's spent most of his time strapped into a little bouncer seat, back of his head is kind of flat. You're going to need to get him to a doctor as soon as you can. He's got some skin issues from lack of proper custodial care by the parents. I doubt his immunizations are up to date. I don't know what else to tell you now. I won't know much until I get the police report."

"Thank you for calling us," June said.

"Thank you for helping the child," The social worker said. "I can give you one of the agencies car seats too. You need to bring it back by tomorrow. It's the only one we have. The one he came here in is filthy. I can't send it with you in good conscience."

"We have one already," Steve said. "It's in the car."

"Good," the social worker said. She stopped by the door of the waiting room and turned to June and Steve. She saw the look of concern on their faces and put a warm hand on June's shoulder.

"First time?" The social worker said.

"Yes," June said.

"Honey, it will be okay. The kid is looking pretty rough but he only needs a few things; good food, love and a bath." She opened the door to the waiting room and they saw their baby boy for the first time.

"He's beautiful," June said.

June couldn't move her left arm. She had taken a shot from the bat at the elbow. She thought her arm was probably broken. She no longer held the hatchet in her hand. It was buried in the big man's chest. He was dead. It all happened so fast. The man had swung the bat sideways at the same time June struck with the axe. She hacked with desperate hopelessness. The bat crushed her arm. Her hatchet struck deep, hitting the vitals and killing the man. The crowd was louder than ever. Fighting pit was filled with debris as people threw everything but themselves over the rebar railing onto June and her child. It was double death night. Two people were dead. June and her boy would be leaving the killing floor alive.

She felt her son lean tentatively against her. She hugged him with her right arm and waited for the ladder to drop. It seemed to be taking longer than usual. The result of the fight was unusual. June thought that maybe they were deciding whether to kill her anyway, but she heard the crowd and noticed that the cheers were drowning out the curses. They loved her. Their blood-lust was placated. The pit bosses had nothing to lose in letting her and her boy go.

The rope ladder was thrown over the side. Her boy climbed up first. June had to be hoisted up by the rough hands of the crowd. She felt startling pain from her arm as they dragged her up over the side of the railing. Her boy was almost swallowed up in the jostling throng of people, but she clutched his shirt with her good arm and held him close. She walked away from the pit and was stopped by a diminutive man by the door. He wore a stained powder-blue suit, no shirt underneath the vest. His skin was covered in some untreated disease. He was shoeless. June halted several feet away from the man. He was the reason that she was here.

"You can consider our contract paid in full," he said.

Elijah was growing quickly under the care of June and Steve. He was a voracious eater, demanding feedings every three hours. He squealed his demands with an ear splitting screech. Steve had taken to wearing earplugs everywhere he went.

"I can still hear him," Steve said. "It just takes some of the edge off." Even though the child was the loud, June was still calling him "little silent one." The baby didn't make a single sound for the whole first week he was a part of their family. It wasn't that he didn't know how to cry. Crying was apparently one of his greatest talents. It was that he used to think that nobody cared when he did. One of the first things a baby finds out about this world is if anyone loves him. He learns if anyone will come to his call. Nobody used to answer his cries and Elijah, like many children in his circumstances, gave up and stopped crying. One night around midnight his stomach hurt from hunger and he let out a small peep. June heard him and entered his bedroom. She picked him up and fed him a warm bottle of formula. Elijah stared into her eyes as she cradled him. He studied her face and the sound of her soothing voice. He felt a warmth in his little body that he never felt before. He was too little to understand what it was, but it was love - Plain and simple, yet fiercer than any emotion, love. Someone cared about him when he cried. From that night forward, Elijah found his voice.

Elijah grew quickly. His head rounded out all on its own. Steve was secretly pleased. He was worried the kid would have to wear some sort of head shaping helmet, and he would have been a little embarrassed at the attention it would receive. The malnourished child they picked up from the social services building two years ago was now a stout little man. He toddled at a sharp pace on chunky legs. He thrust his stomach out forward as he moved. June was worried that he was eating too much, but her mother told her he was a healthy boy. She said all that extra girth was just baby fat and would disappear within a couple years.

It was around that time that Elijah's biological father was released from jail. Termination of parental rights was never finalized by their state court system. As soon as Elijah's biological father was out of jail, he was contacting the system to find out what happened to his child. He demanded visits and was granted a couple hours supervised a week. June and Steve didn't worry about Elijah's biological mother demanding her child. She had died of a heroin overdose that same year.

Steve and June drove Elijah to the social services building. It would be the first time Elijah had seen his father in over two years. They were concerned with dropping Elijah off because government control and regulation was tenuous. It had been several months since they received Elijah's foster maintenance stipend. Their last check from the state bounced. Steve had driven over to speak with the foster case worker about it and found the building overrun with people demanding food stamps, disability payments, clothing stipends and every other type of government welfare support. Steve didn't even bother trying to get into the building. The throng at the doors was too thick. The people had a look of desperation about them that spoke of danger. Steve left before things got out of hand. June and Steve watched the live news feed at home of the riot police descending on the crowd. Families were tear-gassed, beaten and arrested. Three police officers were wounded in the struggle. He needn't have bothered to worry. Elijah's biological father never showed for the visit and they never heard from him again.

A week later they received a note from the state about the default on the payment.

Dear Foster Placement Providers,

Due to unsustainable demand of funds the state will no longer provide the contracted amount previously stipulated for maintenance of foster children. Clothing, food stamps, education and daycare support is also terminated immediately. Medical care through the Medicaid program will also be ending at the end of this month. Please get the children in your care into their doctors and get their medicines refilled before then. Families are encouraged to put the foster children under their own personal insurance plans. If this is not possible, please utilize your local emergency rooms for any medical care the children need.

We understand that these changes may make affording appropriate care of the children in your home difficult to manage. If you cannot afford to care for your foster children, a state run home is being arranged. Foster children will be able to be dropped off at the home for permanent transition beginning at the first of the month. If you have any questions, please contact your immediate foster case manager. I'm sure we all understand that these are not best practices in ensuring appropriate care of children who are wards of the state. We have no other feasible options at this time. State and federal resources have been exhausted. We are doing all we can to ensure we are meeting the immediate needs of our children.

Thank you,
Nancy Kraftwood
Senior Management Coordinator
Child Welfare Social Services Division
St. Louis, Mo 63104

"That state run home is nothing but an orphanage," June said. "Those kids are just going to sit there and starve."

"There's not much anyone can do about that," Steve said. "We all know what's been going on in this country. No money finally means no money."

"What about all those other kids?"

"There's bound to be other families like us," Steve said. "We wouldn't think of putting Elijah in one of those homes. I doubt many other families will do the same."

"Can we afford it without the subsidy?"

"We'll have to."

"We are free to go?" June said.

"Indeed," the man said. "You put a hell of a show on for us tonight. You could stay. We could make a whole lot of money together. I didn't know you had that killing streak in you."

"We're going," June said.

"Have it your way," The man said. "I doubt you'll make it five blocks down the road. It's a jungle out there. I dare say you'd be safer down in that bloody pit."

June knew he was right. Death was certain, but outside it was on her terms. She pulled her boy close to her, her Elijah, and walked past the man, out the building and into the night.

Two years had gone by since the State had eliminated the foster care subsidy program. Steve, June and Elijah had survived, though not very well. There were many days where none of them got enough food. The state-run home for children was open and willing to take care of Elijah but Steve and June had heard hellacious rumors about the place and couldn't bring themselves to leave Elijah there. If they knew the boy would have enough to eat and a safe place to sleep that may have swayed them, but from what they heard the home was a place where children went to die. Many foster parents that they knew weren't allowed to see the children they left there after the state-run home opened.

June was standing with Steve and Elijah in a long line outside the building with other foster families. Once a month the families had to check in with the social services building. This eliminated any home visits, meetings or court dates. All that the official needed to see was that the child was alive, then they would sign a piece of paper affirming that fact, then they would be free until the next month. June left Steve and Elijah in line to go speak with an older man that was crying a little away from the building. His body racked with sobs. She put a hand on his shoulder and he didn't startle. He just looked at her.

"Are you okay?" June said.

"They won't let me see my grandson," the old man said. "I bet they just killed him. I never trusted this place and I hate my daughter for leaving him here. I would have taken him. I would have cared for him. This place is death to kids. It's like an abattoir for children or something."

"Do you really think they actually kill children?"

"Nothing surprises me anymore," the old man said. "I've heard that any parent that wants to drop their children off there, they can, no questions asked. I know someone who did this. She said that her kid was starving and she didn't have a choice. She said the home promised to take care of their child. More than that, I've heard that they sometimes actually *pay* parents to leave their children at the home. Why do you think they do that?"

"I don't know," June said.

"I bet none of us really wants to find out."

June gave the man a reassuring squeeze on his arm and turned to see Steve walking toward her. She was surprised to see him since they were still very far away from the front of the line. Elijah wasn't with him.

"Where's Elijah?" June said. "Is something wrong?" Steve tried to meet her gaze but couldn't. June began to panic. "Where's Elijah?" She said. June could feel her stomach churn with acid and she almost retched. It had been weeks since she'd had a decent amount of food to eat. Her body had become bony and slightly bent from malnourishment. Steve had fared worse than her. She knew he was giving as much food as he could to Elijah so that the boy would live. Steve had spent the last several nights sobbing against her shoulder about not being able to provide for him or her.

"Elijah is gone," Steve said. He pulled a thick wad of dollars of out his pocket and showed her. "He told me that Elijah would be safe." June looked at the money. There was so much, but nowadays it would be barely enough for a single day of food. The paper currency meant almost nothing.

"You sold him to somebody!" June said. She slapped Steve in the face over and over. He grabbed her hands and held them to his chest.

"He would die staying with us," Steve said. "We can't care for him."

"Better with us than whoever you sold him to." She shoved Steve away from her. He fell backward to the ground. He had been so weak lately. There wasn't much left of stature or power to the man she married, her high school sweetheart. June scanned the throng of people. She caught a glimpse of Elijah being herded with other children into the back of a cargo van. She screamed, but nobody paid attention to her. A small man closed the back doors of the van and slapped a palm on the glass window. The van drove off. June ran up to the man. She was screaming a waving her hands. Steve trailed behind her. She finally caught up to the small man and pulled him to her.

"Where are you taking my son?"

"He's mine now," The man said. June raised a hand to strike him. "Hit me and I'll feed him to the dogs in one of the preliminary bouts to warm up the crowd." June stayed her hand.

"The killing floor?"

"At your service," The man said.

"I want my son,"

"He's mine now, bought and paid for," the man said. "Maybe we can come to some sort of deal."

The man looked at June and felt her strong hands gripping his shirt. He felt her depthless anger in her love for her child. He saw ferocity in her eyes. He looked over at her husband. The man looked like most of the others did now. He still lived and breathed, but there was no fire in him. He might as well have been dead already. The man looked back at the woman and felt hate in her glare.

"Maybe we can come to some sort of deal," The man said. "Have you heard about my business?"

Dona Fox
Lost in the Wind

I spun in frantic circles but I couldn't see my dad anywhere. Just nasty dead bats and flies. Some of the bats had been dead a long time and were jerky dry, others were fresh meat. I was lost.

The blades of the wind turbines rotated in huge arcs above me, casting overlapping shadows on the ground. Fun to run through, but then they made me woozy. That must be what happened to the bats. They lost their way just like I did.

My dad works for the State of Indiana. The State sent him out to this wind farm to figure out why the bats' radar wasn't working, why they fly into the blades and get killed. My dad can figure it out. He's really smart. I hope he can find me. Maybe if I go up to that ridge over there . . .

Something huge and white smashed into the blades right above my head. I ducked and covered as it crashed onto the ground next to me.

I peeked and saw only a pile of greyish cloth. I walked over to it. Just a pile of cloth. I kicked it. There was something solid inside. I backed up.

It moved.

I backed up a little farther.

It groaned.

I was ready to run. Large hands with long narrow fingers pushed the cloth aside to reveal a bloodied face. The face was grimacing until it saw me; then it smiled. "Hello, Timothy."

My mouth dropped open. Did I know this . . . person? I knew to be careful. I took another step back. "I'll go get my dad."

"You don't know where he is, do you?"

"No." I shouldn't have said that.

It sat up. "I don't think you want to bring your dad into this."

It had wings. Huge dirty grey wings. Feathers. Really. Feathers. Not in very good shape right now. The wind turbine had taken a big chunk out of one of them.

It stood up. Bad ankle, too. It sat down again, right away.

"Darn. I'm going to heal, but not in time. I had two missions to complete."

Tears ran down its face. "Darn. Darn. Darn." It held its head. I think it was dizzy. It lay back on the ground and shut its eyes.

"Can I help?"

It opened its sky-blue eyes and evaluated me. "No." It shut its eyes again. Then the eyes popped open. "Sure. Yes. Yes, you can. Give me your hand."

I bit my lip and, in a moment of pure stupid trust I held out my hand. The angel took my hand and squeezed and I saw the two tasks that were now mine. "Thank you, Timothy."

"Sure, I can do it."

"Now, quick, your dad is coming up over that ridge. Get up there before he sees me. Oh, and just in case I don't heal quick enough and I don't get back in time to warn Aziel about the wind farm, there is one other big problem coming up." The angel whispered in my ear one more time, one more task that might be my responsibility if the angel Aziel didn't arrive in time.

I ran up the ridge on rubbery legs and my dad hugged me.

"Thought I lost you, Son. Don't go off like that, there's a lot of acreage here. You're shaking. Hey, there, it's okay." He put his arm across my shoulder and I looked back and watched the angel until we went down the other side of the ridge and it was out of sight.

I cut English the next morning so I could be sure to be at the hospital before 11:11am. I was standing next to Bobby's bed at exactly 11:07. No one else was in the room. His lips were scaly and dry. He was having trouble breathing. He opened his eyes, surprised to see me.

"Timothy." He smiled. "I'm glad you came."

"I had to come, Bobby." I took his hand.

"Did you know?" He coughed a phlegmy cough. I handed him a basin to spit in.

"Know what?"

"I'm dying. It won't be long. I might as well tell you. I love you, Timothy."

I processed Bobby's words with no expression on my face. "I love you, too, Bobby." I knew what was coming. This gave me time to get ready, to decide how I was going to react.

"No, Timothy, I mean I am in love with you. I always have been."

I smiled at him and prepared to lie.

"No, Timothy, you don't have to lie." He smiled. "But would you kiss me?"

And I did, full on the lips, and that, I meant.

It was 11:11 when Bobby died.

As I looked up, there in the hallway hung a spectral Frank, mouth agape, the school bully and my next task.

That afternoon I heard screams and chanting by the lockers. This must be it, I thought as I ran to the source of the noise. Sure enough there was Frank, a circle of students around him. He had Tudy Baker's backpack and he was holding it over her head as he pulled item after item out of it.

"Whoa! A romance novel! Got a lot of romance in your life, Tudy? Listen to this" – in his passion he ripped her bodice and pulled her to him – "whoa Tudy, did that happen to you last night? Did you have a hot night, baby? No?" He tore that page out of the book. "Well, how about this" – she looked up into his eyes."

Tudy weighed at least three times more than any other girl in our class. And she had a lot of other problems that were immediately apparent. Both Tudy and Frank were foster kids. Neither one deserved to be bullied, not even the bully, Frank.

As I walked up, Frank focused on me. "Ah, here's the perv, who you pervin' on now, Tim-O-thy?"

I went straight up to Frank and whispered in his ear so that only he could hear: "This ends right now or I kiss you on the lips, right here, right now."

Frank laughed. "Hey, I don't have time for this. I'm cutting last class. Anybody with me?"

I helped Tudy pick up her things, and then I went to my last class. I was getting nervous. I hadn't seen Aziel yet and the final task was supposed to come down tomorrow morning just before lunch.

The next day in English class, the last class before lunch, my nerves felt like a drop of water on a hot griddle. I was sitting by the window so I could watch for Aziel. Tudy kept smiling at me. I think she thought I was sitting there to be next to her. It looked like she had more books in her backpack than ever.

There were only about fifteen minutes left in class when I saw a man in a long dark trench coat running up the sidewalk toward the entrance to the school. It was Aziel. The tip-off was the white feathers falling from under his trench coat onto the sidewalk. There was no way they would ever let him into the school. This was all on me.

I looked around the classroom one last time. That's when I saw it. Sticking out of Tudy's backpack, like an empty eye, was the end of a shotgun barrel. She hadn't quite got it zipped inside. A girl? Who would have thought of a girl? Who would have thought of Tudy? I looked around. She had to be acting alone. She had no friends.

I wrote a short note and casually walked up to Ms. Perkins. I handed her the note and stood there while she read it.

"Okay, Timothy, we've had about enough of this kind of crap. We're not putting up with it any longer. Andy, you're in charge of the class. Timothy, come with me."

Ms. Perkins took me to the principal's office where I got a lecture on bullying. I tried to explain about the angel in the windmills and Aziel coming to the school and Tudy really did have guns in her backpack, but they checked and she didn't. Aziel must have made it into the school after all. I just didn't have enough faith.

I don't go to school, anymore. I just sleep in this little room. And when I can manage to stay awake the angels keep me company.

Darn windmills.

Lee Forsythe
Up North

Dan Blackwell punched the Jeep's accelerator, spraying gravel off a row of parked cars, as he and his three South Bend legal partners spun out of the Sportsman's Lounge lot onto the Canadian highway. Seconds later they were back up to speed, night air whistling past the two canoes on the roof rack.

The sound of the ricocheting stones had portly Franklin Lahr giggling in the front passenger seat.

"You believe those bohunks?" Tim Henley asked from the back. "The Mackenzie brothers' night out, eh?"

Sitting next to him, balding Alan Peterson laughed. "Definitely not the white wine and brie set." He sniffed in mock disapproval.

"They've got more of a taste for moose burgers up here," Dan said.

Off on their annual Ontario fishing trip, the anticipation of a week without corporate or family responsibilities, coupled with a bout of power drinking, had loosened them up considerably.

It was raining by the time they put the small town behind them and began climbing into the hills. As they approached a blind curve, a rusted-out Toyota rumbled up from behind them.

"You're not passing me in that piece of shit," Dan announced, speeding up.

The driver of the car pushed ahead anyway and drew even with them just as oncoming headlights swept around the corner directly in its path. The lawyers stared openmouthed and braced for an impact.

The third vehicle veered onto the narrow berm before plunging off the road into a ravine. The Toyota continued around the bend, careened back over the center line, and disappeared in the distance.

"Oh God, they're not stopping," Dan shouted, blasting the horn in protest.

"Pull over," Franklin said. "We've got to see if they're okay."

Dan reluctantly pulled onto the shoulder, turned off the engine, and flipped on the emergency flashers.

For a long moment they watched the arrows on the dash blink and felt adrenaline surge into their systems.

Dan got a flashlight out of the glove box. "Frank and I'll check this out," he said, his previous bravado replaced with apprehension. "You guys wait here in case anybody stops."

From the road's edge Dan and Franklin could see an old pickup resting flush against a dirt embankment at the bottom of the gully. A thin line of light from an obscured but still functioning headlight defined the lip of the crumpled hood in the darkness.

"Maybe we should just get going," Dan said. "Drunk driving isn't exactly the crime of choice anymore. We could call someone down the road."

Franklin gently took the flashlight from him. "Come on," he said. Leaning backward they worked their way down the bank, occasionally slipping and catching themselves with their hands. The tall, wet weeds soaked their shoes and pants.

Alan produced a battery-powered hook sharpener and set to work on his lures. "This really puts an edge on these trebles," he said. The device made a low-pitched grinding sound each time a point was inserted in its tip. "More hook-ups and fewer lost fish."

By the time the others returned he was finished and his tackle stowed in the back.

"They okay?" Tim asked when they were under way again.

"Yeah, but their truck was totaled," Dan answered. "The driver's pissed. He got a wrecker on his cell and we gave them a description of the other car."

"Tough break," Alan said. "Glad it wasn't us." Franklin looked over at Dan, but said nothing.

Of all the locations Dan had picked off a map and dragged them to over the years, the Waukeecha River seemed the most remote and pristine. They had somehow moved beyond even sporadic cellphone coverage. After hours on the water they had not heard nor seen a trace of another human, not even the tiniest scrap of litter. Franklin and Dan hurried downstream to throw the first casts into each pool, while Alan and Tim fished slowly, enjoying the scenery and the sweet smell of pine.

No wider than fifty feet in most places, the river twisted and turned between thickly wooded shores through boulder-strewn pools and rapids. At first the white water worried Alan and Tim a little, but after negotiating several surging straights, their previously rusty canoeing skills returned and they grew comfortable with the wild surroundings.

It was as if they were lost in time on the river. They steamed around a bend and surprised three white-tailed deer that bounded off helter-skelter into the woods. On another stretch an eagle kept flying ahead of them and landing high up in the treetops. As their canoe approached the bird would head off again downstream.

"Quite an escort," Alan beamed, pausing to adjust his sunglasses and pork pie hat.

Later with the sun low in the sky, Tim and Alan rounded another bend and spied Dan and Franklin sharing a bottle of whiskey in a clearing set back from the shoreline. Smoke twisted up from a campfire between them. Their tent stood at a distance, pitched at the base of a hemispherical grassy hill.

"A bad sign," Alan said. "Must have limited out to be celebrating already."

"Don't show our stringer first," Tim cautioned. "First liar doesn't stand a chance."

When they'd drifted within hailing distance, Tim yelled, "Any luck?"

"All bad," Dan yelled back. "Not a bite. You guys do any good?"

Alan held up a northern pike and six smallmouth bass, flopping against one another on two stringers.

"Good job. At least we're going to eat," Franklin shouted.

On the shore Tim found the end of another stringer and pulled a mesh bag full of ice-cold beer out of the water. "Ready for a cold one, eh?" he yelled and, without waiting for an answer, removed four cans. He tossed one to Alan, popped the top on another, and toasted his fishing partner with a broad grin before taking a long drink.

Alan stretched his cramped back, put his beer down on a rock, and pulled their fish out of the water long enough to run the tip of his filet knife down the lateral lines on the sides of the northern and two smaller-than-legal bass that Tim, the quintessential meat-fisherman, had insisted on keeping.

"Yeow," Tim laughed. "What'd you do that for?"

"Just bleeding dinner a little. It's supposed to improve the flavor."

At the campfire Tim handed beers to the other two, already heavy-lidded from the whiskey and wood smoke. "We caught enough for you sad losers to fix our dinner and breakfast," he boasted, the exhilaration of the day settling into his bones. "If we'd left it up to you, we'd be breaking out the feves au lard."

After a meal of fish and fried potatoes with onions, they lay sprawled out around the campfire. At the edge of the fire's glow a curtain of inky blackness had fallen. They could hear the waters rush but could no longer see the river or much else except their tent and the outline of the soaring mound behind it.

The perfectly hemispherical mound, a surprisingly common woodland feature wherever Native Americans buried their dead, consisted of earth, rock, grass, and something more. Something ancient and powerful and just beginning to stir from a long sleep.

They stared into the blaze, listening to the pop and snap of the wood against a background of night sounds. A small animal scampered through dry leaves nearby, sounding huge. A strong breeze rustled the trees and made the ancient trunks creak and groan.

"With all the noises out here," Alan said, "easy to see why primitive people were so superstitious."

Dan, his face transformed by the firelight into a pale mask, gave Alan a look of disgust. "It's easier to see you spend your nights in the suburbs watching reality TV, pup."

"It never gets this dark in the suburbs," Tim said. "In those trees over there I couldn't see my hand in front of my face."

"Maybe because we're so far from any city lights," Franklin suggested, yawning.

Something thrashed around in the water. "Those damned fish are still kicking," Dan said in amazement.

Tim chuckled. "You would too," he said, gesturing toward Alan, "if you saw what Charles Manson here did to their partners."

One by one they left the dying fire for the tent, its lightweight nylon rippling crazily in the breeze, to crawl into their sleeping bags and drift off.

The wind, water, and other sounds wove their way into Dan's dreams. He was kneeling before a sun-drenched rock slab on the bank, preparing to clean the rest of the fish. A dozen braves, clad only in loin cloths and moccasins, swarmed down out of the woods on the opposite shore. They flew down from the forest with supernatural grace and speed and waded into the river.

On his side of the stream, standing far back in the trees, someone pointed them toward him. Dan could see only an outstretched arm and the long strands of gray hair whipping wildly about the head. He somehow had been mistaken about the fish because instead before him on the rock lay the still body of a little girl, her long black hair sprinkled with diamonds glittering in the sun.

The raiding party, their eyes ablaze, had produced bows and were shooting arrow after arrow into him with loud, sickening thumps. He wondered how he could still be conscious with the thicket of shafts that had blossomed from his stomach, chest, and throat. An escalating scream ended his nightmare. He imagined it had come from him.

The next morning a sore and hung over Franklin stumbled out of the tent. He relieved himself against the hill and headed down to the river for a beer. As he sipped it, he pulled up the other stringer to find four mangled fish heads dangling at the end. Something, raccoons he guessed, had chewed their breakfast right off the line. The fish hadn't been splashing around on their own the previous night, he realized.

"Damn," he said, followed by a moan on behalf of his aching head. "What next?"

He glanced at the opposite shore and froze.

Hanging upside down against a broad tree trunk was Alan's naked, mutilated body, suspended from the branches by fibrous rope buried in his ankles. Blood from numerous incisions had tinted him bright red - his lifeless, staring blue eyes the only contrast - as a final few drops of it fell from his fingertips onto the trees gnarled roots.

Backpedaling in horror, Franklin tripped and fell down hard. He struggled to his feet and ran for the others as his beer gurgled out on the ground.

"Maybe he's still alive," Tim stammered, looking across the pool.

Dan glared at him. "And maybe you've lost your fucking mind, you stupid faggot!" he screamed, his face suddenly purple.

Tim stepped back, blinking rapidly. "But who could have done this?" he asked, unable to control his trembling voice. "We're not trespassing here; we're only fishing."

Franklin glanced at Dan, ashen-faced. Tim looked helplessly from one to the other. They decided against cutting the body down, afraid of what might be waiting on the other side of the stream.

Dan held his hand up for attention. "We've got to get away from whoever did this. I forgot the map, but the take-out landing can't be that far. We'll dock at the first sign of civilization and get help."

Without bothering to break camp, they tossed a few things in the canoes and headed downstream, glancing nervously at the shorelines. In the lead canoe Dan held his paddle lengthwise at different angles overhead to indicate his recommended line through the white water.

Around noon they saw their first sign that others had once been there. The weather-beaten remains of a kayak, split almost in two amidships, was lodged high and dry on the face of a large boulder in the middle of a particularly strong set of rapids. Sticks, leaves, and other debris, bleached white by the sun, overflowed the splintered cockpit onto its deck.

Exhausted, they hobbled ashore at nightfall. They had gone even farther into a wilderness that closed around them. Deep stands of pine lined the shores interspersed with thick undergrowth as far as the eye could see.

The Waukeecha had snaked in every direction: splitting, rejoining, and endlessly cutting back on itself. They'd had to retrace their path several times after paddling down dead ends that started deep and fast but dwindled into narrow pockets of stagnant water. Vines and branches intertwined overhead, blocking out the sun and harboring clouds of mosquitoes that descended to feast on them or fly en masse into their mouths, noses, and eyes. After shipping water in rapids that morning, Franklin and Tim had spent the day with their feet submerged in icy bilge.

All day in vain they had listened for an automobile, chain saw, or human voice; examined the wall of trees for any hint of a trail; and looked down river for a bridge or launching ramp whenever they came around a bend.

After camouflaging the canoes, they collapsed on the only moderately open ground they could find and, despite rank weeds and rock outcroppings, bedded down for the night.

They shared the rest of the food - two beef sticks and a can of beans - wolfing it down in the dark with warm beer. After discussing the pros and cons of seeking an overland route the next morning, they agreed to take shifts on guard, Dan, armed with a canoe paddle, insisting on the first turn.

Much later he awoke with a start, sensing something was wrong. He fumbled around on the ground for the flashlight, switched it on, and panned in the direction of the others.

In the circle of light Franklin's left hand spasmodically unclenched and clenched around a weed clump by his sleeping bag. Sweeping the beam up his arm, Dan let out a small yelp in a voice he scarcely recognized as his own and shrank back.

Perched atop Franklin with a knee firmly planted in the small of his back, Alan slid the curved blade of a filet knife along the top of his skull with one hand, gradually peeling back his scalp with the other.

The flashlight shook in Dan's hand at the sound of flesh being ripped from bone. His mind began to spin out of control. Alan continued in a trance, proudly displaying Franklin's blood-stained silvery scalp at arm's length when he was done.

Dan wanted to run, but couldn't look away from his friend's darkened face and body. Alan stared into the light with eyes wide and lips curled back in a maniacal grin, finally retreating into the forest with his trophy atop his own head.

As Dan moved the light around the perimeter of the campsite, the shadows of the trees shifted with the sweep of the beam, further unnerving him. He shook Tim awake. "They got Frank," he yelled, his eyes fixed on the woods.

Wrapped tightly in a blanket, Tim stood up, rubbing his eye with the back of his index finger. He looked down at the body.

A short, sharpened stick pierced Franklin's tongue and held it in place, protruding from his mouth. His sleeping bag was soaked with blood, mostly from his throat, slit ear to ear.

Tim sank onto the ground, hugging his shins and rocking to and fro. He shook his head slowly from side to side. "Did you see them?"

"No," Dan said, unable to admit what he had seen. He helped Tim up and they cautiously made their way to the river.

With Dan aft they cast off, every sound from the water and woods intensified in their heads by darkness and runaway panic. Although they didn't notice immediately, the river had changed. Instead of a twisting, boulder-filled obstacle course, a clear channel opened up before them in the night, bearing them effortlessly downstream.

"You never got the whole story about that accident," Dan volunteered as they eased along. "There were Indians in the other car -- an old man and his granddaughter. They both bought the farm."

"You mean nobody phoned for a wrecker?" Tim asked.

"They were pretty much dead by the time we got to them," Dan said. He proceeded to tell an altered version of the events of that evening, exonerating himself in the process. But as he spoke, the details of what really happened came stealing back to him with remarkable clarity.

Steaming coolant sprayed out of the ruptured radiator mingling with the aroma of freshly turned earth. Through the open window on the driver's side Franklin trained the beam on a gray-haired Iroquois slumped over the wheel, blood flowing from his forehead and throat.

"Help," he moaned; "My granddaughter."

Franklin moved the light to the windshield, a spider web of cracks punctuated by two holes: one where the old man's head had gone through until the steering wheel caught him and dragged him back and the other in front of where his passenger had been sitting.

Dan took the light back, climbed up on the embankment, and traced a probable line of trajectory beyond the accordioned front end. Thirty feet away he found the motionless body of a little girl curled up in the fetal position, her long black hair matted with blood and bits of glass.

He checked for a pulse then hurried back to the truck. "Let's get the fuck out of here, Frank," he whispered. "She's dead and Cochise here soon will be."

"They could charge you with leaving the scene," Franklin said. "It wouldn't look good..."

"I'm way over the legal limit and I'm not going to prison for this. Come on!"

"My granddaughter," the man repeated.

Dan flashed the light directly in the Iroquois' eyes. "She's gone to the happy hunting grounds, chief," he snapped, "And I'm afraid you are too."

The man set his square jaw in a look of transcendent fierceness. Dan turned and began climbing the hill.

Franklin spoke into the darkened wreck. "I hope you know, sir, we didn't do this. A Toyota ran you off the road. We saw the whole thing."

He quickly followed Dan up the bank. Halfway up, the old man screamed out an imprecation they couldn't understand, followed by a rhythmic chant. Something in the sounds made the hair on the back of Franklin's neck stand on end.

When they reached the road, the distance and a sudden, gusting wind rendered anything else inaudible. "What was that?" Franklin asked as they approached the truck.

"Non-Hebraic prayer for the dead." Dan wiped his forehead with the back of his hand. "The less these two know, the better, counselor," he added. "Let me handle them."

In his retelling Dan left out everything that implicated him, described the old man as if he had been as lifeless as his granddaughter, and even attributed the decisions to flee and keep their companions in the dark to Franklin.

"My God," Tim said. "But how's that connected to all this?"

"Others found out." Dan delivered the statement with somber finality.

Tim shook his head. "And want to kill me for something I didn't even know about?"

"They're Indians," Dan said bitterly. "I never believed that stuff about noble savages -- at least not the noble part."

"Have you seen Indians?"

"Not exactly."

"What then?"

Dan stared at the floor of the canoe. "I don't know," he said, his voice barely a whisper.

The pre-dawn light filtered in as the river narrowed into a long chute of boiling water scarcely wider than the canoe. Sheer rock walls rose up on both sides. They glided over the churning surface, staring down at the turbulence.

The canoe slid out of the passage into the bend of a broad expanse of black water blanketed by shifting patches of white fog.

"Help! We're over here," Tim heard someone cry over a muffled roar. Straining to see through the clouds of smoke, he followed the sound to a stand of birches on the far shore.

"It's them," Tim said. He paddled toward the voices. On the far bank he could see Alan and Franklin as good as new, waving their arms and laughing.

Dan neither heard nor saw them. He sat with his head cocked at an odd angle, trying to concentrate his frayed mind on the growing rumble.

When the vessel, sideways in the current, had reached the rivers midpoint, Tim, unable to hear the voices, looked toward the shore to correct their course.

The smiles were gone from their companions' faces, replaced by expressions of sorrow. Their hollow-eyed images stared sadly at him before vanishing in the gloom, leaving only the birches where they had been.

Too late Dan recognized the sound of falling water and felt the strong current pulling them toward it. The mist parted enough to reveal a line where the water seemed to end. Dan turned the craft perpendicular to the falls while Tim looked back a final time to the empty shoreline.

Their eyes widened when they saw what awaited them: halfway down, trapped in the rocks across the middle of the falls was the horizontal trunk of a huge tree. Twenty feet below that, dipping partly underneath the waterline, a tattered net suspended from log poles spanned the river.

As they were swept over the top, they instinctively leaned back as if to lift the bow over the hurdle. Instead the canoe fell straight down, its nose lodged squarely behind the tree, and they were catapulted out, head over heels, with their remaining gear.

Alan's unlatched tackle box flew down onto the net where it popped open, dumping lures across the weed-entangled mesh a split second before Tim landed on them. He shrieked as the razor-sharp treble hooks caught on the netting dug deep into his face and hands and snagged his clothing. A minnow imitation stuck in his ear lobe pivoted and a second set of its hooks were planted in his lower lip.

His weight sank that part of the net beneath the surface. Inhaling water, he battled to free himself. The harder he struggled, the more firmly the hooks were buried. Within minutes his dead body lay face down in the foaming ebb and flow of the falls as curtains of mist rolled over him.

Dan's spine had slammed into one of the long, wooden supports. The impact whipped the back of his head against the pole, filling his vision with tiny sparks of light, and he tumbled to the bottom of another section of the net.

He regained his senses cradled at the waterline, his face inches from the algae-coated skull of a skeletal fisherman trapped beside him in the folds of mesh. With each rise and fall of the pool, water poured in a stream from one of the eye sockets. Dan screamed.

After confirming Tim was beyond help, he returned his attention to his closer neighbor. The entire skeleton was covered with green slime, the ribs encircled by a fishing vest, and one bony hand still gripped a fishing rod with a broken tip.

Dan slipped into the water, swam ashore, and crawled onto the bank. The morning air chilled his skin, and tangled weeds snatched at his ankles. But he didn't notice.

This towering forest once stretched unbroken to the upper Hudson Bay, he thought as he ran, gasping for breath. He wondered if, somehow, it still did.

He listened as he fought his way through the trees and brush. It wasn't long before he heard them.

A legion of spirits, their task nearly completed, converged from along the water's edge. Without disturbing a twig or leaf, but with the sound of their swift and sure footsteps pounding louder and louder in his ears, they gained ground on him.

Kristin Roahrig
The Good Servant

No one ever told Aimee anything, no one noticed her enough to think of speaking with her. When Aimee first joined the household staff of the Marquis de la Rochebrune, she imagined her days to be spent waiting on fine noblemen and ladies. Her mother told her if she did as told, was discreet, and made herself a good servant, she would rise up.

She only learned by accident that the Marquis was to return home. Jean the footman and the maid Cecile were speaking of it one morning. Aimee stopped her work to better hear. The closest Aimee ever managed to so far be near the riches of the noblemen was when she washed the linen from beds or cleaned the fireplaces in the noble's rooms. She rose at four in the morning and her day didn't end until long after sun down; where she would go to bed with her back aching and her nails chipped badly from her work. Maybe with his arrival, he would bring guests and Aimee could finally wait on true lords and ladies. She had begun to worry maybe it wasn't the right decision her mother made in sending her to this house. Even if her grandmother had been a servant here before she left to be married. But Aimee would never have dared to say this out loud.

"The Marquis is to return home. I don't know if I like it or not," Cecile was saying.

"Because of more work you'll have to do?" Jean asked.

"No, because of the stories, haven't you heard them? His family sold themselves to a devil for riches and power. I don't want to be near a damned soul."

"Nonsense, don't you go listening to tales," Jean said.

"How do you know it's a tale and not truth?" Cecile challenged.

"It's only gossip, some story for people to tell at night when they've nothing else better to do. Isn't that right Aimee?" Jean asked.

Surprised that he asked her, Aimee only nodded, not being able to think quickly enough of an answer. The Marquis de la Rochebrune returned home unexpectedly as Jean and Cecile said he would. His arrival sent all the servants in a frenzied rush to prepare the rooms for him. It especially made Aimee flustered in her hurry to help. Even though she only been employed for two months and was the newest member of the household staff, she too was pushed out to stand in the long line to greet him when he arrived. Usually she was purposefully forgotten for special occasions because she was hired not for experience; but because the head housekeeper Gabrielle still remembered Aimee's grandmother. Aimee had nothing else to recommend her as a qualified servant. But for this occasion Gabrielle made sure all the household staff was ready to greet the Marquis. She only saw the Marquis for a few minutes and recognized a resemblance to the portraits she saw of his ancestors. He possessed their longish features that managed not to look horsey, but create a distinctive character. From the other servants she had learned he also inherited their perchance for Versailles, the unofficial capitol of France, with its favors that could be taken and opportunities to advance in one's powers while basking in the "Sun Kings" glow.

"This is strange," Jean said.

"How so?" Aimee asked. She whispered low to keep from being heard by any of the others.

"The master returned willingly to the family's home, and from what I hear it's not to collect taxes or escape a scandal at court," he said.

"How is that strange?" she asked.

"No one voluntarily leaves the court and he did."

With this unusualness was the woman he returned with. Aimee stood on her toes, trying to get a better look at the woman. She was unable to see anything for the woman wore a velvet black cloak that covered her completely. Even the large hood hid her face so all Aimee could see was a dark shadow. Despite this, Aimee knew immediately she was a Lady. Once the Marquis and the Lady had been settled in, it was time for the servant's dinner. After the servants finished their supper that night, all of them lingered, sitting around the large table.

"Why would he return here?" Gabrielle asked. She slouched with a slight resentment in her chair. With the Marquis return, work would have to be done on a tighter schedule rather than completed at the relaxed pace she'd grown accustomed to.

"Maybe he ran out of money," Jean suggested.

Most of the others shook their heads at his. Everyone knew that at Versailles there was power to be found along with the great pleasures that could be had in life if one held the money for such luxuries. And even if one didn't, money was always to be had by borrowing with no intent on repayment.

"No, that wouldn't be it, the family are unusually lucky in finding both money and power," Gabrielle said.

"Such luck is unnatural," one of the elder gardeners said.

Most of the others nodded, a few even crossing themselves. Aimee never said a word or nodded. Being both the newest and youngest member of the household, she tried to remain as insignificant as possible.

"Unnatural?" Jean said derisively. He had read a few books on the philosophy of Rousseau and Voltaire, thus considering himself a philosopher of the enlightenment. "The family is only shrewd with a good nose of where to gather money and find opportunities to advance themselves."

That night despite being tired from her heavy work that day, Aimee found it difficult to sleep. She turned over repeatedly in her bed, causing Cecile, who she shared the bed with, to complain. It was difficult for Aimee to turn as the bed was so narrow it could hardly hold both her small body and Cecile's. She thought on all she knew of this house and its family.

The ancestral home of the de la Rochebrune family laid miles from any nearby habitation. The closest village where Aimee was from was twenty miles to the south. No other great names of the nobility were nearby. The lands surrounding the single manor belonged only to the de la Rochebrune family. The land had passed from one generation to the next without mishap.

The de la Rochebrune's only ever returned for a brief visit in the country or when disgraced at court. The main residents were the servants who kept the place in good working order. Despite the well-kept grounds and family's little presence, there were tales half whispered in the dark that told nothing and explained everything. Strange sights were sometimes supposedly seen in the house. On Sundays after mass there would be whispers amongst the people at church that the house glowed red at night. Their priest often warned against such gossip, claiming they were tales caused by either drunkenness or too vivid an imagination. Aimee would have agreed with him except her own mother once saw this sight and she was neither given to drink or flights of fancy.

The following days she never saw the Marquis or Lady. Different women of the household staff were sent to the Lady to act as a personal ladies maid. The most experienced was sent first. Each woman would only serve for a short time before refusing to do it anymore. She'd quit and would be followed by another woman that could be found in turn until only Aimee was left who hadn't served the Lady.

Once when she was carrying a large bucket of boiling water to be used to wash linen, Aimee heard Cecile and another servant girl, Joan whispering.

"I wouldn't work for her, even if it meant I could then be the Queen's maid," Joan said.

"No reward is worth having to look after that woman," Cecile agreed.

They both stopped as soon as they noticed Aimee. The girl walked silently on by, careful not to spill any of the water on either of them. The Lady must be a difficult one indeed for them to even consider calling a Lady of such rank that woman. She probably had a fearful temper or maybe she kept them up all night with difficult duties. Whatever the case, Aimee thought the woman was a Lady, she was allowed to have a temper or be difficult.

As usual, Aimee never learned of anything further for none of the women of the staff would confide in her. Instead, Aimee only watched while one woman after another quit.

Gabrielle called Aimee to her office one afternoon. As Aimee made her way to there, she tried to think of anything she may have done wrong or forgotten to finish. She could think of nothing but that didn't mean anything. The closest thing she could think of was when she had to learn the placement of silverware on the Marquis' table. It was a lot to remember and Aimee took longer than the others to learn.

Before she was able to think any further she was standing in front of Gabrielle's desk. Gabrielle was rifling through a stack of letters and bills that were before her.

"You are to be the Lady's maid," Gabrielle said without looking up from her papers.

"Me? Are you sure?" Aimee asked.

"Yes."

"But I know nothing of being a Lady's maid," Aimee said.

"It's mostly doing what you're told, helping her dress, and keeping her clothes clean. You're duties begin tomorrow," Gabrielle said.

For the first time, Gabrielle glanced over her papers at Aimee.

"Speaking of cleanliness, be sure to get rid of the dirt from under your fingernails."

Aimee hid her hands behind her. Leaving, she forced herself to walk to her own room rather than dance. Excitement built within her at the prospect of her new position. She would now not have to do dirty work that was hard labor. She would for the first time be near a true Lady and feel fine fabrics with her hands. If she was lucky, the Lady may take a fancy to her and take Aimee into her service.

As soon as Aimee returned to her room, she scrubbed her hands with soap and water numerous times. Taking a small knife, she used the blade's edge to try getting the dirt out from under her nails. Once satisfied, she fell asleep, dreaming of velvets of many darkened hues.

Aimee began her new duties the next morning. When she came to the Lady's room, she found it empty. She waited, uncertain what to do. Finally the Lady appeared and Aimee saw her for the first time. The Lady was beautiful as Aimee expected, with her features finely sculptured. The only defect to distract these features of perfection was pensiveness in her brow. And the woman's eyes for looking into them were similar to staring into those of a stone statue; hard, with no sign of emotion or warmth.

Aimee lowered her own eyes from them, disconcerted. She tried staring at the woman's hands instead. Observing closer, she noticed the Lady's ring finger on her right hand was longer than all her other fingers. Aimee lowered her eyes even more at this, deciding it would be best just to keep her eyes on the floor.

"You must be my new Lady's maid," the woman said.

"Yes," Aimee said, keeping her eyes down. It occurred to her she should curtsy or do something of the sort. She did a slight curtsy, almost falling over.

The Lady had turned away by then, missing the attempted curtsy. Pointing towards a large armoire, she told Aimee to lay one of the gowns out. The Lady then sat at the vanity, idly picking up a small handheld looking glass even though she was sitting in front of a large mirror. She moved the glass along her arm and neck, minutely checking her skin.

When Aimee opened the armoire, she saw over a dozen gowns of a dark hue color, resembling the variety of wines that existed. Her eyes shifted across each gown, undecided which one to choose. The Lady had given her no instructions and Aimee didn't think to ask earlier. It hadn't occurred to her the armoire could be filled with gowns. Aimee owned only two, one for work and one for church.

"What is taking so long?' the Lady asked.

"Which gown do you want?" Aimee asked.

"Oh, surprise me," she said, sounding bored.

Aimee chose a dress that was a dark burgundy with gold trim. As she shuffled through the gowns, a smell seeped from the fabrics. The usual poultice to keep a pleasant odor was used and they were what Aimee smelled at first. However, the pleasant odors were soon overcome by a stench Aimee found hard to place. She guessed at first the smell reminded her of human waste. Then no, rotting flesh, then no, Aimee changed her mind again. The smell was acidic, one that left a taste in her mouth.

Aimee gulped and took a step back, almost stumbling over a small stool.

"Whatever is the matter?" the Lady asked.

"Nothing," Aimee lied. She wasn't going to lose this position and return to the drudgery of hard labor because of a bad smell.

The following days she learned how to dress and undress the Lady. She learned other things as well of how to be a Lady's maid. She would have enjoyed it had it not been for the smell. She thought the smell was in the Lady's clothes but then discovered it was on the woman as well. Aimee noticed this once when she stood right behind the woman, brushing her hair. The smell was on the Lady's skin. It penetrated all the artificial perfumes, passing through until it seeped into Aimee's fingers. Afterwards, Aimee washed her hands repeatedly, trying to get the scent out of them. Despite the number of times she washed them, Aimee still felt the Lady's skin on her hands.

Another day she found a strange wound on the Lady's skin. At first she thought it was only dry scaly skin. Then she realized it was a layer of skin, red scales that reminded her of a snake. Her fingers touched the skin as if by accident. They were truly scales, not dry skin. The Lady glanced down at her touch.

"Hand me my cream," she instructed.

Aimee never was certain what kind of cream it was but she grabbed the container, handing the jar to her.

The Lady spread the cream on her scales until the cream blended with the rest of her skin. It blended so well, Aimee began to wonder if the Lady's skin was what it appeared, if it wasn't in fact made of red scales.

Still, Aimee said nothing, trying to ignore what she seen. After all she was a Lady, who was Aimee to wonder at her strange skin condition. It was only dry skin and the woman had an odor that was difficult to be rid of, but people's stink was not uncommon. After this incident with the cream, the woman began having Aimee help her place the cream on spots when a small scale would appear.

Aimee rarely saw the Lady and Marquis together. She would be sent away anytime they were in the same room. The only guess Aimee could make of their relationship was that the two must have enchanted each other accidently into love. This must be the only reason for the two were devoted to each other, only wanting to spend their time unhindered by any other person.

One afternoon the Lady without warning announced she wanted to go for a stroll and instructed Aimee to follow, carrying her cloak in case it became cold. They walked around the gardens. Aimee followed at a discrete pace behind her. A large dog went past Aimee, barely noticing her. However, when he past the Lady he stopped. Sniffing the air, he snarled and the Lady barred her teeth at the dog as well. Aimee had to glance twice to be certain the woman was doing this. The two began to move in a tight circle, leaving Aimee to clutch the cloak tightly, trying to think what she should do.

The dog began barking wildly. He was barking so hard that Aimee could see the spit flying from his mouth from the distance she stood from them.

She was ready to call for help. The dog's coat was long and scraggly, clearly a wild dog. Opening her mouth to scream, she stopped short when the dog leapt towards the Lady. Her delicate hands grabbed the dogs head and ripped it off the animal. The Lady did the act so easily Aimee blinked her eyes a few times to be sure she saw right. But yes, there was the dog's body on the ground and the Lady holding the animal's head. The Lady sniffed the head before idly tossing it aside and turned to Aimee.

"And what do you have to say to all that just happened?" she asked.

Aimee's mouth went dry and she had to force herself to swallow a few times before she was able to speak.

"I say it's a lucky thing you were here my Lady; to protect us from the beast that is," Aimee said.

"Good girl," the Lady said.

She walked past Aimee, patting her cheek.

That night Aimee went straight to Gabrielle.

"I won't do it no more," Aimee said.

"Do what?" Gabrielle asked.

"Serve the Lady."

"You must, there is no one else after you to do it, all the other girls refused."

"But the Lady isn't human, I'm sure of it. She's a demon," Aimee said.

"Stuff and nonsense. You should be grateful for this opportunity, not many girls of your age and experience get such a one. If you're fortunate, the Lady may take a liking to you and take you into her service."

"But I've seen things that aren't human," Aimee tried protesting.

"Quit prattling on so," Gabrielle muttered. But Aimee noticed there was a slight hesitation before Gabrielle spoke.

Gabrielle held up her hand, signaling an end to the conversation. Knowing it to be useless, Aimee didn't press on.

She didn't try explaining about the stink, the red scales of the skin the Lady hid, and the dog's head being ripped off. She very much feared the Lady now and didn't want her to find out she was telling these stories about her.

Memories of the old stories, of the family's unnatural good fortune and the house glowing at night began to resurface in Aimee's mind. She slept in fits that night, trying to push away such thoughts. Cecile finally ordered Aimee out of bed, telling her to sleep on the floor. The rough boards made sleep impossible but at least in the morning's light Aimee was able to ignore the memories until night fell again.

That evening Aimee was closing the window in the Lady's room. The Lady sat on her seat before the vanity, gazing absently into the glass. It was a cool evening and the fire was lit. It blazed fully, throwing light to even the darkest corners of the room. Aimee was glad of the fire's bright light for she was now afraid of shadows. She was almost done when she heard the Marquis right outside the door.

"Hide behind the curtains, I don't want him to see you," the Lady instructed.

Aimee pulled the heavy curtains in front of her and stepped back as far as she was able, until she felt the cold glass of the window on the back of her neck.

The Marquis entered the room. Through a small slit Aimee saw the Lady lounge back on the velvet covered settee. Her dress' color matched the burgundy in the decanter. The Marquis poured himself a glass of this same burgundy.

"The day will come soon," he reminded her.

"What day is that?" she asked.

He turned, smiling ironically. "In a few days time we are to make our binding pledge to our own true Lord. One that I admit as most others I've paid no heed to anymore in this more enlightened time. An entity, who I never gave credence to until you invoked him." The Marquis gulped his brandy in one swallow before continuing. "Since then, I've believed in little else, except this one who can grant and take any desires."

The Lady shifted, suggesting the day should be held off. Indefinitely at best.

"Indefinitely," he said. "Why put off that which will bind us to the one and each other? I have anticipated this night for a great long while."

"You know as well as I do why," she answered. "It's such a risk."

Aimee wasn't certain, but she felt the Lady was not truthful in voicing her apprehensions. The Lady was playing a game of some sorts but what that game was she couldn't say.

"What care you for that?" he asked. "You who have always risked much without thought."

"This is different," she murmured in an undertone. "You'll only become as the others before you in your family. They always use what I offer to further themselves and become gluttons for my Lord to take in the end."

He gulped another burgundy down, not listening to her. "You have never exhibited such nerves before. Are you unwell? That must be it," he decided without waiting for a response.

Seeming to be comforted with the thought he relaxed once again.

"Why do you believe you love me?" she asked.

"Because you introduced me to the possibilities in worlds I never could have guessed existed. Which is why you can't doubt now," he said.

"Why?"

"Because if you begin doubting, I may doubt. I once already stopped believing in any faith or creed. But I've regained faith again, albeit of a different sort, and I can just as easily lose it. And that would undermine all that we've worked towards. Those nights of gatherings and searches would all be for nothing, only resulting in waste and oblivion," he said.

Despite her fear, Aimee was fascinated. She also thought the Marquis sounded not quite in his right mind. Despite the interest she felt, she hoped he would leave soon so she could as well.

Instead, he sat on the low settee and stroked the Lady's ankle she propped up. His finger tracing around its curve, he gently circled the small space within her ankles.

"I plan to live my life to the fullest," he unexpectedly said. "And when I die, I'll be willing to shed all my blood for the one."

Her thin eyebrows arched in mild surprise. Lifting her head slightly, she peered at him.

"Fine words to be spoken. Who taught you this?" she asked.

"You did."

"I never said such a thing."

"No, by your example I learned," he said.

The Lady removed her ankle from his grasp. Rising, she picked up a black velvet gown cover. Wrapping it around herself, she tied the cloth snuggly across her waist.

"Your family has always wanted prestige or wealth. Often both. That is what they asked me for; their wants and I must admit, it grew tiring to always be subject to their whims. Never offered simply to give as you have just done. Wanting nothing in return except to give," she said. The Lady strolled around the room, her eyes moving along the wall. Twice they passed over the curtain that hid Aimee.

"Tell me again," the Lady instructed him.

"Tell what?"

"The words you promised earlier."

He repeated what he had uttered, adding he released the Lady from his families hold on her. She was free from having to fulfill their desires. She tilted her head, partially listening to him. Aimee thought she looked like she was waiting for a signal from the shadows that circled along the floor. Aimee listened closer. No sounds came. The Lady moved nearer to him.

Holding out her hand, he took it, his fingers curling over hers. A question passed across his face. She placed her finger, the one that was longer than all other's on his lips. A slow realization came into his eyes.

The Lady turned and stared right to where Aimee hid. She smiled. The smile chilled Aimee and she pressed against the glass, leaning far away as possible. Fire filled the Lady's eyes when she turned back to the Marquis. The fire shot from her eyes out to him, devouring the Marquis in flames. Aimee wanted to scream but stifled the urge. The Marquis' body lurched in every direction in an attempt to run. The body finally collapsed on itself, bits of ash smoldering on the floor. Aimee nearly gagged on the smell and was surprised no one else in the household noticed the stench.

"You may come out," the Lady said once the Marquis was gone.

Aimee stepped out.

"What are you?" Aimee asked.

"You know what I am. I've been forced to serve his family for a long time. His willingness to give completely enables me to be free of the contract between his family and me."

"He expected to die?"

"No, I don't believe so," she said. "I will eventually need to return to my own home but until then I plan on staying in this country for a long while. I want to enjoy this world before I'm summoned home. I intend to leave this house tonight and will need a Lady's maid. Will you come?"

"I have little experience," Aimee tried saying but the Lady interrupted.

"You know my true nature. You never gossiped about my secrets to any of the other girls, you can witness the acts I do and not become a puddle. You didn't go running when you saw my skin as the other girls did and you have a respected fear of me. Those who aren't afraid end up like the Marquis. Say yes, after all, mine is an offer you can't refuse."

She laughed at this as if at a great joke.

"I, er, need to think about it," Aimee said.

"It's employment and I'll be no worse a mistress than many a human Lady. Besides, you've become complicit in the Marquis' death, you wouldn't want the law to learn that, of the part you played."

"I didn't kill him."

"No, you just watched me do it, doing nothing to stop his murder."

Aimee kept shaking her head, trying to recite a prayer of any sort in her mind. The Lady sighed and said, "It's not your soul I want, just a Lady's maid to help me retain my appearance. So no need to worry your pretty head about damnation, I won't make you perform a black mass."

The Lady held out her hand to Aimee, surprising her. Ladies of higher station didn't want to be touched by those of low birth. Despite knowing the woman's true nature of demon, she still couldn't stop thinking of her a grand Lady such as she heard were at Versailles. Unable to force herself to refuse, Aimee gingerly took the offered hand. At Aimee's touch, the Lady's fingers intertwined around the girl's own and she smiled sincerely while her eyes warmed for the first time in uncountable centuries.

"Come along then," she said, "For I have long been waiting for this night."

Matthew Wilson
A Private Indiana Home

"Mom, I heard a noise in the attic last night," Mark said at breakfast.

Helen found the milk, and closed the fridge with force. "No, you didn't." She said it matter of fact, like a minister.

I did, Mark thought, wounded. Mom was testy lately. Grandma was dead. Mom worked like a slave keeping Grandma comfortable, even changing sheets in her last days. Mom worked an eighteen hour day serving food, and never seemed rested at night when she locked herself in her room.

Private was a word Mark felt described Mom's life. No other Hoosier's bee's wax, thank you very much, she often said.

Though Helen gave him life, she'd little maternal instinct. She fed him, retained a roof over his head, but there were no hugs at night or stories in storms. When mom came home from work she immediately went to her room.

And sometimes, she went to the attic.

Mom didn't know he heard her steps upon the stairs at night. At first, he thought it burglars. Now his bridging the topic put a nasty edge in Mom's eyes.

"You aren't to go up there," Helen said, "There're Christmas presents I put up."

"It's November," Mark said, confused. Mom had made noise on her lack of money. Where'd this mention of presents come from?

Mark ducked as the milk she poured on his cereal missed the bowl, staining the red patch cloth. His principal at Indiana High complained he looked like he dressed in the dark; his shirt hanging out his trousers, and his tie askew drew attention.

Dust came down from the ceiling, spoiling his breakfast as the single sodium bulb swayed back and forth like a charmed serpent.

He dabbed the milk from his collar and dropped the spoon. "What's that?"

Earthquake, Mark thought. *No, ridiculous. The shaking was too slight.*

It was like someone upstairs wanted attention.

"Mom?" No mention of a man was necessary. Since dad walked out, she'd neglected makeup or any other effort toward looking nice. Helen liked to pretend she worked too hard for a social life.

Mark heard her hiss. She grabbed a rolling pin, leaving a small dent in the ugly flowered paper as she whacked the wall with it. "Damn pipes-- aren't you eating?"

Mark fished the plaster out of his bowl. "I'll get something later."

She handed him five bucks for the cafeteria and though he tried to kiss her cheek, she moved away, saying he would miss the bus.

"Bye, Mom. Love you."

"Yeah," she said, and waited till he closed the front door before she picked up the knife and headed upstairs. "Wait a minute, damn it," she said. "I only got one pair of hands."

The house was quiet when Mark came home, which was not unusual as mom was working. He wished he could remove the mausoleum quality with loud music, but then neighbors would make problems for him.

Mom liked her privacy, and didn't converse with people. The idea he'd bring them to her door would result in grounding, or a suspension of his pocket money or both.

He was in the kitchen when heard the banging.

"Pipes," he said, like a charm against a witch as the thumping grew in potency. He grabbed the wall and thought what the neighbors might say about this. To busy his hands, he decided on a sandwich and opened the drawer.

The heck's the bread knife?

He flinched as something drifted like a snowflake down on his head. A dead blue bottle fly had come loose from the lamp shade. "Man, nasty!"

The banging was growing worse, like a drumming tornado and Mark made a decision. Mom would be home soon and talk him out of it. With Dad gone, he was the man of the house and had to protect it.

"Hello?" He grabbed the banister to stop his hand from shaking.

Weapon, he thought. He should've bought a weapon. He hoped it was an animal that sought shelter, come in from the rain through a hole in the chimney and panicked.

He was attacked by a strange smell on the landing, like the reeking rot of a lake where dead leaves turned brown and gave off the scent of decay.

"Oh," he moaned as the carpet squelched and made his socks sticky. Mom didn't like shoes in the house. The carpet was wet. Maybe the pipes were acting up after all. Had one split and leaked?

Curiosity and fear tussled inside him like fierce wild dogs trapped in one cage. Fear didn't die, but did subside. If he was to live here, how would he sleep if he imagined some hideous monster lurking every time he closed his eyes?

He made fists of his toes to un-stick his socks and, as if walking in jelly, he pulled himself along the banister past Mom's bedroom, that, as always, remained shut, and headed up the second flight of stairs.

Toward the attic.

The base step creaked and Mark winced. Despite the noise, he was sure he'd been busted. He heard wood warp like a crushed can in a fist.

Breathing, he thought and touched his mouth to make sure it was closed. His breathing was hard, like running track at school.

"Hello?" Mark said, and stopped when he saw the knife near the door.

Where'd that come from?

Had someone been up here before?

"Mom? You home?"

What if she was doing something unpleasant, like killing a trapped animal? What if she had a man up here?

He was struck by the bizarre need to knock. Helen had brought him up a gentleman. Expecting the door to blow open with the built up pressure of explosive gas, Mark didn't take his eyes off it as he crouched and lifted the knife.

The brass knob was warm with body heat.

"Mom, are you alright?" He felt his tonsils burn like he'd swallowed sand. Grey liquid bubbled through the keyhole. Disgusted, he stepped back, afraid to touch it and be infected.

More of it oozed out from under the door and seemed to hold life. It came at him!

Mark shrieked like a cat with its tail caught in the door, and heard a clank.

You dropped the damn knife.

He didn't care. His legs had taken on a mind of their own. He turned and ran back down the way he'd come as quick as possible.

He jumped the final three steps and heard the door open behind him.

"Mark?" Something said, its mouth full of liquid as if drowning. Mark didn't stop. Tears felt like acid in his eyes and he yelled, nearly losing his footing, blind with sobbing.

He had to reach the phone!

He stopped when he saw Mom through the open kitchen door,

standing with her back to him at the counter. Fresh from work, Helen made coffee. Steam poured around her like fog. She wore headphones to blot out the banging.

She missed her sons shouting.

"Mom!" Mark wept. Thank God, he thought he'd lost her. He bruised his hip as he staggered into the door knob. Though she treated him as a guest rather than a son, at last, she'd have to give him some attention.

At last, she'd do what moms should and help her son against this terrible invader of *their* home.

"Mom! Mom! We got a problem--"

Helen jumped as he grabbed her arm and the kettle upended. Boiled water sizzled, eating into her forearm and knocking off the sound protection with her other hand. She darted back like the ground had opened up before her.

"Oh, God! What -- what the--" She stopped talking when she saw Mark. The boy was nothing but problems. "You stupid -- what are you doing home?"

Mark felt ill as the smell of burning flesh filled his nose. He thought of grabbing a towel and wrapping it round her affected area, but his feet would not carry him. He froze like a prisoner lined up against a wall to be shot. "I'm sorry, I'm so sorry."

Helen hissed and Mark saw her eyes darken like a shadow on a grave. The flesh on her arm completely peeled away like faded wallpaper. Mark saw there was another layer of membrane beneath. It was grey and sticky, like the liquid upstairs.

Mom craned her head upward when she registered the panic in his eyes and that familiar look of disappointment crossed her. "You did it, didn't you? I told you not to disturb your grandmother!"

The scalding seemed to have lost its effect on Mom, anger now making a home of her. She dropped her arm and Mark stared at the grey beneath her camouflage like a bull's-eye at some rifle range.

"What?" He felt his lips move but was unsure if he made words.

"Don't I have enough to do looking after that old cow, and keeping you out of trouble?" Mom said, heated, so Mark could believe the steam was coming out her ears. "You want to know why I don't let people visit," she asked. Mark yelped as she grabbed his hand but he registered no pain from the boiling water. *What am I?*

"I never get close to my kids because they always get curious." Mom sighed, quite unconcerned by the sticky texture of the carpet. She gained surprising strength and cut Mark's arm with her claws. He screamed when he saw what lay underneath his flesh.

"All my kids have gone against me." Mom muttered, like it was such a simple matter. "Why be maternal when you guys don't last long -- you wanna see what your grandma eats?"

Mark tried to dig his toes in, but his socks slid in the mossy grey slime that had the same quality as ice, and still Helen dragged him on.

Mark tried to say he would be good; he'd not go against her again for his curiosity was all used up. But though he worked at it, his mouth would not work.

It wouldn't open fully till mom pulled him round the landing corner, ignoring the advancing tentacles till one wound round Mark's feet, and carried him up toward the open attic door.

Glenn Rolfe
In the Basement of the Amazing Alex Cucumber

Growing up, you hear about the creeps and perverts who kidnap women, or children, and imprison them in dark, dank basements. You hear about the jars of hands, fetuses, brains, and on and on. In Bentleyville, two towns over from Fort Wayne, we had Alex Cucumber. Strange last name, stranger family. Alex was the only child of parents who were themselves quite outrageously talented in many dark and enigmatic ways. Kids whispered about his mother being a vampire, though no evidence of the charge ever made its way public. His father was assumed to be her creator. They both disappeared in 1998, the summer before Alex's senior year at Bentleyville High School.

Alex, who bore a striking resemblance to the late Doors singer, Jim Morrison, wandered the streets of Bentleyville night after night. Though not even eighteen at the time, he was seen with one beautiful lady after another, going in and out of Danny's All Night Diner, and the massive house he had to himself.

I was a senior myself three years later when I found an odd invitation—a black piece of construction paper with a red cut-out heart, and glitter-written message inside—upon my windowsill. The message read:

Nolan Lachance, your presence has been requested to join us at a party thrown by the Amazing Alex Cucumber. Come alone, or bring a friend. See you this Saturday.

9 pm sharp!

– Bev

I wasn't sure who Bev was, or when Alex Cucumber had established himself as "The Amazing," hell, I didn't think he was aware of my existence, but I couldn't deny that I was intrigued by the situation. The Cucumber house, on Haley Street, sat behind a line of massive pines that held its secrets along with those of young Master Alex. Rumors at school spread throughout the years that he could levitate, that he could read, or control minds, that he got whatever he wanted. No one said no to Alex Cucumber. And now, what of this invitation? It was childish in its make-up—construction paper and glitter. However odd, I could not resist the opportunity to be in the company of our town's strangest resident. I made up my mind the moment I finished reading its glittered lettering, I was going, and my buddy, Devin, was going with me.

I called Dev the next morning, informing him of the party.

"What if I don't wanna go?" Dev said, his newborn baby sister crying in the background.

"What if the rumors are true and his place is filled to the brim with chicks that look like Megan Fox?" I countered.

"What if the rumors are true and we end up strung up by our flesh, and sacrificed to the devil?" Dev had a little Money Mayweather in him—he could counter anything.

"Listen, just go with me. If you get bad vibes, and you want to get the hell out of there, we'll leave."

"I don't know, Nolan. Why can't you just take Billy?"

Billy Katz was our third wheel. His parents had money and Billy had every game, and console any teenager could ask for, but he was a bit of a nimrod, and pretty much useless in real world situations.

"Absolutely not," I said. "Billy would get me thrown out, or instantly cast as a lost cause the second I walked through the door with him."

"All right, I won't do that to you, but I want total stay-or-go power. If I get the creeps, we're out of there."

"Clash powers granted," I said, referencing Dev's favorite punk rock band. "We'll meet at seven? My house?"

"Deal, but one other thing—why does it say "the Amazing" Alex Cucumber?" Dev said.

I had wondered the same thing myself, but guessed it was a play on the rumors of his "abilities". "Maybe he's putting on a magic show," I said.

Saturday seemed to take a month to arrive (even though it was really only two days). I waited for Dev to show up as the night began to devour what remained of the day. Fall had come to northern Indian all too soon. Damn cold off from Lake Michigan—where rumor had it, Alex had washed his crimson hands after many nasty dates—wasn't doing us any favors. Leaves were changing colors, and the hard rains of the last week had forced them to the earth's floor. You would have thought it was Halloween already, not mid-September. Dev showed up on time, as always, dressed in a black Alkaline Trio hoodie and a pair of skinny jeans-- or girl's pants as I liked to refer to them. "Got enough gel in your hair tonight?" I said, staring at the wet-looking spikes of black hair covering his head.

"Fuck you, Nolan. I agreed to go. I didn't agree to fancy myself up like that," he said, gesturing at my clothes.

I had on the pair of black slacks, and the black button-up shirt my mom had bought me to attend my Grandpa Joe's funeral earlier this summer, and a fairly new pair of white Adidas. A white fedora Grandpa Joe had passed down to me finished off the "fancy" look Dev was shaking his over-gelled head at. "I didn't say you had to, but I look like someone who wants to get laid, you look like a slacker-hipster going to a Fall Out Boy reunion gig."

"Double fuck you," he said, flipping me off with both hands.

"Okay, okay, I'm sorry. You don't have to do this—"

"You're damn right I don't," he said.

"But I appreciate you coming with me."

I watched him fend off a smile, and then saw his eyes dart off somewhere behind me.

"What?" I said, turning to the patch of trees and unruly bushes that served as the end of my property, and the beginning of old man Peterson's. There was a brief rustling among a black pocket that looked as though it had been swallowed by the universe. I stood staring, my imagination attempting to get the best of me. *Alex, or one of his friends, is watching us to make sure we're on our way.* A few seconds later, Van Halen, my dad's fat gray cat jumped from the black hole, and plopped down on his rump to lick his paws.

I turned back to Dev, smiling from relief as much as from excitement. "Let's get going."

There were no cars near the Cucumber residence, Haley Street was devoid of any sense of life—even the crickets were holding their breath as we reached the driveway. I thought cars would be lined up down the road. Dev slowed down as we neared the line of pines that served as the home's fence.

"You sure you want to go in there?" he said.

I wasn't. "Yeah, of course," I said. I took the lead, taking us from the blacktop to the gravel driveway. The crunch beneath our feet gave way to the booming thump of music we should have been able to hear from a mile away. There had been nothing until we crossed onto the Cucumber property, and found ourselves standing before the impressive estate. I'd seen the home in the light of day (Gina Colby had dared me to go up to the porch earlier this summer. I did, and was rewarded with a make-out session and hand job later that night). Standing before it under a pitch black sky—the clouds casting out the moon as if it were uninvited by the Amazing One himself— goose bumps, like the zits that greeted me on my fourteenth birthday, broke out upon the canvas of my flesh. I passed off the fluttering in my guts as positive anxiousness.

"I'm following you, man. You ready?" Dev said.

I looked at my watch–it was not yet nine–then around once more, searching the scene for signs of *anybody* else: cars, voices, *lights*. Despite the music, the sprawling three-story house was in complete darkness. "Let's hang back a minute. We're a little early."

"And what, stare at the grass, or the tree-fence? Fuck it, dude, let's go," he said blowing past me, and heading straight for the porch. "Whoa," Devin stopped in his tracks. There was a shadowy figure standing on the steps. "Tell me you see that," Dev whispered from the side of his mouth.

I did, but couldn't make out whether it was a man or a woman.

"What should we do," Dev whispered again.

Run, run while we can. Get the hell away from this godforsaken place before we end up in the headlines as two missing teenagers.

Instead, I stepped forward. "Hello, we're here to see Alex–I mean, the Amazing Alex Cucumber."

"Invitation," the voice behind us said.

I nearly catapulted out of my skin, and noticed Dev do the same as I spun around. A tall woman, clothed in a long black dress that hugged every one of her curves, stood with her hands behind her back. I hadn't brought the invitation with me, and said so. "I didn't bring it. It didn't say to."

She took a minute to look us over, first Dev, and then me; her face– expressionless. Despite her awe-inspiring beauty– high cheek bones, full lips, and her dark, come-hither eyes– I found myself repulsed by her. The urge to flee swam over me again.

She gazed past us, and then back to me. "Come, the Amazing Alex Cucumber welcomes you." She moved between us, and led us to the porch. I searched for the shadowy figure, but found the dark space empty.

The large, wrap around, porch was shadowy and vacant–no chairs, no knick-knacks, no welcome mat. The lady in black pushed the door open. The foyer within, bathed in dim red light, was also empty of any possession. The walls were bare, or so I thought. A few steps in, a portrait hung near the bottom of the staircase across the room. As we got closer I saw it was a family portrait. Alex sat between his mother and father. His mom on his left smiling with her mouth closed; his father, on his right, wearing a thin moustache on a stoic face with handsome features.

"This way," the lady in black said.

The staircase, from what I could make out in the red light, looked like it was carpeted in dark velvet–either blue or red– and rose up to a second floor that seemed impossibly far away. The house looked humungous from the outside, but seemed oddly larger on the inside. *It's probably the lack of furnishings; mom says that really opens up the space.*

Dev trailed behind, he seemed much more comfortable than me–he kept poking me, and grinning at the lady in black's ass. Of course I noticed, but I was also aware of the heavy silence pressing down upon us when we should have been assailed with thumping music that had been audible from the driveway.

We reached the top of the stairs, where our hostess led us through a large white door. Once open, the music with the pounding bass blared out. Mixed in, were moans, whether of pleasure, pain, or both, I could not discern. Another red light was the only source of luminance in this room, as well. There were bodies moving everywhere. Men and women were swaying, and grinding all around us as we followed the tall woman in the curvy dress through the center of the room. I glanced back at Devin– his eyes looked black in the red light–and saw him grinning. He was under the spell; I felt sick.

We exited the red-light dance floor, and followed our mysterious hostess to a hallway lit by candlelight. The walls were bare here, too; the wooden floor squeaked at every step. I wondered if it would hold our combined weight. It did.

"Where are we going?" I said. She did not answer.

The hallway ended at an elevator. Strange, but true.

Bing

She stepped aside and motioned for us to enter. The voice in my head warned me.

"Aren't you coming?" Devin said, once we were both inside. Our hostess, standing in the hall of candles, smiled, but offered no verbal response. Her creep factor was at about a nine. The door closed, and the elevator began its descent.

"Why the hell did we go upstairs to get into an elevator to go back down?" I said.

"Beats me, but did you see the friggin' shit going on in that dance room?" Dev bit his knuckle. "Holy shit, if that's what's happening up here, I wonder what we're heading into."

I wished he hadn't asked.

"Hey man, are you all right? You asked me to come, and now you look like you wanna go home and suck your mother's tit. What's up?"

I didn't feel right. *This* didn't feel right. "I-I don't think we—"

Bing.

The door slid open. On the other side was a wooden door.

"Now what the fuck is this?" Dev said.

I didn't want to find out. I'd had enough. I no longer felt the spine-tingling sense of mystery and wonder the invite had given me. I looked for the elevator buttons, wanting to go back the way we came, and found none.

Dev stepped out into the small, torch-lit foyer. I followed, chewing at my thumbnail the way I always did when we were at Dev's house watching Halloween, or Friday the Thirteenth. I wished this was a movie. The door looked like something that belonged on a dungeon in some medieval black and white film. It looked older than the rest of the house. The wood was worn, splintered in some places. It looked like there had been a slat to peep through at some point but that had been covered, and bolted with a rusted piece of metal. The door handle was a thick brass ring, which ran through the mouth of a freaky-looking demon gargoyle thing. I was certain that if we passed through that door, we were either going to enter a wormhole, or head straight into Hades.

"Are we supposed to knock?" Dev said.

"Uh, I don't know. They must be expecting us, right? Your girlfriend wouldn't have sent us down here otherwise."

"I wish that was my girlfriend," he said. "I'm gonna knock." He stepped up and wrapped his knuckles against the wooden door three times. The sound died on impact. The smells of the room began to present themselves—mildew, rot, and something that reminded me of *raw hamburger*. Combined with our elongated shadows cast beside the demon door knob from the dancing flames behind us, the atmosphere was seeping into my blood stream like a narcotic. My affected brain conjuring up a parade of macabre images that would have fit in perfectly in the painting Mr. Adkins had shown us in Art class. Garden of Earthly Delights, I think. I can't remember the artist's name, but like it or not, my mind tunneled toward its darker corners

Dev moved forward, raising his hand to knock again—I grabbed his wrist, no longer wishing to be acknowledged by whoever was down here, but the door opened.

And I swear I shit my spine out right on the spot.

The room before us was lit by more candles and torches, and what their light cast upon was certainly more perverse than the sexually charged rave taking place above. There were people I didn't recognize, dressed in various leather studded outfits, chewing on severed arms and hands, or devouring what looked like intestines or organs. Devin screamed, and so did I. Clutching one another, we stumbled away from the door back toward the elevator. Not one of the cannibalistic heathens looked our way, they just kept on *feeding*. Two dark shadows flew at us. The next thing I knew Devin and I were snatched up by the unseen hands of shadow people, pulled apart, and taken into the heart of the ghoulish scene.

That's where we were introduced to our host, the Amazing Alex Cucumber.

He was mesmerizing. Clad in leather pants, an open white shirt–with his longish brown curls he looked like he could have stepped straight out of a Doors poster. Two devilish, nude girls writhed up and down his legs, groping at him all the while staring at me and Dev.

"Wine?" Alex said.

Two glasses, surrounded by black smoke, floated to our hands. I took mine, but held it, still trying to clear my head, and figure out what the hell was going on. I glanced over and caught Devin sniffing the glass; he shrugged at me and threw the dark liquid down the hatch.

"It's okay, Nolan, despite all that you have already seen, I assure you, it is only wine. Drink, please, let the spirits unburden your mind." He patted the girls on the head. The one on his right rose. He whispered in her ear. She stepped over to Devin, pressed her breasts to his chest, and kissed him. She pulled away, taking him by the hand, and led him past Alex, and through a group of fornicating figures beyond that I hadn't noticed. He never looked back. I held the wine glass, not yet convinced.

"Your friend will be fine. Come, Mr. Lachance, I wish to share something with you," Alex said, pulling up the other naked imp by her chin as she sucked on his thumb. I felt movement in the front of my pants. As if she noticed, the girl with the black lips smiled at me.

Alex led me past more sexual trysts; thankfully, there were no more cannibal sightings. I already doubted what I had seen, or what I *thought* I'd seen. Could it have been some sort of illusion by my host? I thought of the rumors at school, mind reading, levitating (like the wine glasses that floated to our hands), and in those few seconds, worked hard to convince myself that's what it was–magic.

Ahead of me, Alex whispered to his mistress. She smiled back at me, and wandered off to the right, vanishing into the shadows.

A trick. Another trick. She couldn't have–

"I suppose you're wondering why I invited you here tonight?" he said.

I continued following him, looking back to where the girl had disappeared. "Uh, yeah, I mean, I didn't know you–"

"Knew who you were?" he answered. "I know every beating heart that resides in Bentleyville." He stopped at a curtain. "Please, my friend, after you."

"I- where's Devin?"

"Nolan, I hate to repeat myself," he said. I saw something that might be anger flare up in his twinkling eyes. "Your friend is fine." He placed a hand on my shoulder, and nodded toward the black curtain.

A dreadful feeling crawled over my heart. I didn't believe him that Dev was all right, and I couldn't shake the darkness swallowing me like an alcoholic's drink, as I was led onward, presumably, to my own private execution. As his hand gripped my shoulder, those thoughts became murky. I felt *off*, but better. His smile made me smile.

"Go on. This is where the real show is," he said.

I noticed the glass of wine in my hand, I thought I had sat it down, but here it was. I put the glass of wine to my lips, downed its warm, bitter contents, and parted the curtains.

The basement stretched out on and on. The room Alex ushered me into was a village. There were youthful-looking men and women all sitting single file, ten rows wide, at least a dozen to a line. They were all directed toward the stage on the far side of the room. At the back of the stage, surrounded by red and black candles were two thrones, and sitting in them, two skeletal forms.

Mr. and Mrs. Cucumber.

"Who are all of these people?" I said.

"They are the missing, the lost," he said, placing his hand upon my shoulder again, and looking me in the eyes; "The found."

I felt his power– intoxicating, seducing me.

"They were like you, Nolan, now, they serve a much higher purpose. They are no longer chained to the world outside of these walls," he said, urging me forward. "Walk with me."

I had never felt so good in my life. My mind, my body, my blood tingled–it was euphoric. And my host, Mr. Mojo Rising, the Amazing Alex Cucumber, continued his speech as he walked me to the stage. His voice spoke not of peace frogs or riders on a storm, but of belonging, and family.

"*They* offer money, they live by it, for it, they are only their possessions. Here...we have none. We reward your efforts with love, with companionship, with truth. What they have is fleeting. What they have are lies," Alex directed me up the stairs to the left of the stage. I climbed the steps. "Look," he continued once we stood before the congregation of youth. "Look at their faces. Do you see it?"

I did. Their eyes were upon me, each and every one smiling. I couldn't recall what I was outside. I couldn't remember my family, my friends, my life. I searched the crowd of beautiful faces, and spotted someone familiar.

"Yes, you know that one," Alex said over my shoulder.

It was Gina. Gina Colby.

"She is one of many, much like you, she wandered through *their* regimented series of make-believe freedoms, thinking she was an individual. We open eyes here. We welcome those who have no idea they have been deceived by the world around them; pulled in by the technology, distracted from the real world...the old world. Here, our eyes are wide open," Alex turned me away from the crowd; I managed a smile at Gina before turning to something unexpected. Devin, being held under his arms by unseen hands, was naked, and shivering. He looked at me, but he was no longer there. His lights were on, but someone had snuck him out the back door. I should have been scared, angry, sad...

"We ask only one thing of our new members," Alex said, handing me a knife. "A sacrifice."

I wanted to do it, but part of me resisted.

"Children see this world free of confinement. They haven't been told that ghosts are not real, so they see them. They are not yet confident that monsters cannot exist, so they fear them. They are handed lie upon lie by those they trust most. They are fed fantasies of a man who brings presents, a fairy who comes for lost teeth, and a bunny who carries eggs of candy. We only want to give back to you that which they have ripped away–your innocence, your truth."

There was a tin pail in front of Devin.

"One act of brutal truth and you can have it all back. Free yourself."

The knife was now in my right hand, the pail in my left. Neither had been there seconds before.

"Do it," Alex whispered in my ear. I turned to ask him why Devin couldn't come, too, but he was gone. His advice was repeated, chanted by the throng behind me.

Do it, do it, do it...

I tried to weigh my options, but my thoughts were drowned by the chanting voices.

Do it, do it, do it...

The next few seconds flashed past my eyes as if in a dream. I looked up at the Godparents of this cellar dwelling movement—hollow sockets looked back, their skulls appearing to where smiles; Alex—or Jim as I saw him—and Gina Colby standing at the edge of the stage nodding, prodding me onward; my hand with the blade out before me like that scene at the beginning of the first Halloween movie; Devin's neck spilling blood into the bucket.

My head spun like a top, my eyes fluttering as I fell into darkness.

I awoke to the sound of rain thrashing against my bedroom window, the same window where I had found the invitation from Bev—the lady in black. My head hammered away in unison with the wind whipping around in the grey world outside. I sat up, noticing the odd scent secreting from my slick, pale skin; mildew, like the cellar of the Amazing Alex Cucumber. A dream, it had to be a dream. Loud music burst to life from my right—♫ *faces come out of the rain, when you're strange, no one remembers your name, when you're strange, when you're strange* ♫—startled, I slammed my fist down on my alarm clock radio. I knew the song; it was from one of my favorite movies, one about lost boys that had nothing to do with Peter Pan. I noticed something on my wrist, and followed its faint red trail down my forearm—it was blood, dried and staining my pale skin.

Knock-knock-knock

"Nolan, there's a girl here to see you," my mom's voice said from the other side of the door.

"Yeah, who is it?" I said, sounding like I'd downed a whiskey and broken glass concoction as I slipped out from beneath my covers, scratching at the red stain on my wrist.

"It's Gina, Gina Colby...from your school," my mom said. In my mind, I could see her holding the laundry basket with an ear cocked at my door. "She wanted me to let you know that *Beverly sent her?*"

I froze with my jeans halfway up my thighs, my mind flashing back to the events in the basement of the Amazing Alex Cucumber, to the words of the great one himself: *"We ask for one thing...a sacrifice."*

"Nolan?" My mother said. I watched the door knob begin to turn.

Glancing down I saw the knife was once again in my hand.

"Nolan?" Gina's voice.

"Oh, hello dear, he should be right out," my mom said to her.
I knew what I had to do. Why Gina was here.
I pulled up my jeans, and slid the knife behind my back.
"Mother, come in, I have something I want to show you."

My mother's blood was still warm, slicking my wrist and hand. Gina was wearing the same beautiful smile she had shared at Sunday school, all those years ago, when we were just victims of our parent's ignorance. She took my crimson hand in hers as we stepped over the bloody mess in my room, and moved with swiftness and eased down the hall and out the door like a whisper on the wind–unheard by most, but cherished by the chosen. We were *his* chosen. The Amazing Alex Cucumber. Our liberation of a town undone by its own want for modern distractions, and naive concepts of truth, had begun.

Paul Greystoke
Dreamer

"Sorry for your loss, Sam."

John Templeton smiled sympathetically as he sat by my side, wiping his sweaty hands on the crumpled Armani suit trousers which were caked to his legs. His natural body stench was enough to make my dog wretch but I was glad of the company. The room was crowded, yet for the past two hours no one had given me so much as a second glance; perhaps they knew something John was unaware of. Personally I think he was there for the free buffet.

It took five minutes of uncomfortable silence, with John slowly shaking his head whilst desperately trying to find the right words, before he finally offered his own comforting sermon "First your best friend, now your dad, and in as many days. Are you ok?"

I thought this would be a good opportunity to take one of the metal skewers from the lamb kebabs on the table and drive it into his forehead whilst shouting, "Of course I'm not ok you drooling moron!"

I simply stared at him. My internal message must have been clear because he rose from his seat, picked up a plastic plate and began stocking up on quiche and tuna sandwiches before retreating out the front door. If nothing else at least I had lightened the load on my greedy neighbour's food bill.

Mother was in the opposite corner, my daughter Margaret sleeping on her knee. I wanted so much to comfort her, to let her know everything was going to be alright. She looked broken, lost almost as she sat running her hands through Margaret's hair, observing the crowd of casual onlookers as if they were not real.

I closed my eyes to shut out the images that surrounded me, the only escape my claustrophobic mind could conjure. Through my inner darkness I took a couple of deep breaths. The sound of my heart beat seemed to drown out the pointless chatter from my guests.

It took a moment to register but the room seemed too quiet for comfort. I held my breath and listened.

The chatter had completely stopped. The rustling and clinking of glasses, too, even the Andersons' annoying daughter from down the road, who had been talking to her would-be boyfriend on the phone about what she should wear when she meets him tonight, completely silenced. The sound of my heartbeat completely filled the room.

Slowly I opened my eyes.

It was as if someone had taken a Polaroid and replaced my living guests with it. Everyone and everything was completely frozen. One lady's coffee cup had slipped from her hand and was making its way to the floor, the contents escaping and coating the tail end of my sleeping dog; except it wasn't, it just stayed there, in mid-air, motionless.

Through the silence I heard a sound; Mother in her chair still stroking my sleeping daughters' hair. She looked at me, trying to hold back the tears. Suddenly my little girl sat up and opened her eyes wide. Her head tilted to one side as she looked at me brushing the sleep from her left eye.

They didn't seem to find it at all strange that they were the only moving parts in an otherwise motionless environment. Both their gazes were fixed firmly on me.

A bright light stole my attention as the front door swung open. In walked a silver haired lady. Her dress, a blinding white, made me want to cover my eyes. As she turned to face me, any anxiety that was inside my body began to slowly diminish. She slowly approached, moving through my still guests as though they were mere phantoms. Mother started to cry. The lady stopped, distracted for a moment. I saw in her eyes purity entangled somehow with my mother's pain. She feigned a smile whilst uttering the words "no change."

I blinked and the lady disappeared. Mother was once again stroking the hair of my sleeping daughter. The guests were milling round as before. The dog was up and yelping un-amused by the order of coffee his rear end had not requested and Marie Anderson had decided on the pink turtle neck sweater her aunt had bought her the Christmas before.

Save the occasional glance in my direction the guests continued to pay me no mind at all, instead offered their condolences to Margaret and my mother before leaving.

"I'm going to take Margaret for the night," Mother said as she buttoned my daughter's red duffle coat. "You need to rest." Margaret kissed me on the cheek before leaving.

I was alone. I had been alone for two days, the only difference being now the house was empty.

I couldn't be bothered to tidy the place. I sat there for what seemed like hours, trying to make sense of what, up until now, I had dismissed as mere coincidence.

Two nights ago I dreamt my best friend was killed crossing a stretch of highway. I didn't bother to warn him. It was just a nightmare, surely? A nightmare, when, hours later, the evening news reported the accident as fact.

Then there was my father.

Dad always told me, "Never give up on your dreams, Sam." You gotta love the irony here.

Sleeping last night I had a vision, my father's clapped out old banger complete with flat tyre being jacked up by the side of the road. Honks from opinionated drivers as they sped past only served to piss him off. "I'm not here by choice" he shouted as he fought to free the flat from the wheel arch.

Less than a minute away on the same stretch of road, unaware there was any hazard ahead, I was fiddling with the volume on the car radio, trying to drown out the repetitive sound from my daughters Buzz Light Year action figure.

Dad had resorted to kicking the stubborn tire, anything to loosen it. He knelt again, taking each side of the wheel, and pulled with all his might. The tire came loose and dad fell back with it across his chest.

He never got up. The oncoming vehicle's impact killed him instantly.

As if that wasn't bad enough, I was driving the car. I'd got up in the early hours to clear my mind, unable to sleep for fear the nightmare vision would return.

I sat on the roadside cradling my father's lifeless body in my arms wishing with every fibre in my soul that I could trade places with him, that he would at least wake long enough for me to say how much I loved him. That he would just wake.

The tears that fell from my face and rolled down his cheeks were not enough to bring him back, but did send a clear message. I may be a psychic but I'm no healer; in fact, I think I'm cursed.

In Eastern philosophy it is said that the five people closest to you directly represent your own personality and state of mind. The philosopher in question failed to mention that as each one is taken, it would leave a gaping hole where they once belonged or that as they left, your heart would be ripped to shreds and you would do anything to escape the pain you were going through.

en route to hang an out of order sign.

The emotional hurt from the previous two nights had already started to have a physical impact, spreading through my body like a ravenous cancer. I just wanted to sleep.

I rose and slowly walked the desolate wasteland that was my living room, a place that in the past had played host to some of the finest moments of my life. Without my family here it was more like a shell, empty and meaningless.

I glanced over to my bedroom door. There was a strange glow escaping from the gaps in the frame, a glow that seemed to grow in intensity the more I looked at it. Suddenly the silver haired lady in white appeared, walking through the closed door as though it were not there. She simply stopped and stared into my eyes before returning to the bedroom.

Who was she? A ghost? An angel? I had to find out. The light that protruded through the cracks in the door frame dimmed with every step as I moved closer to the bedroom. When I eventually opened the door the room was in darkness, the lady was gone. Yet the bed had never looked so inviting. Yearning for rest I lay down and rested my eyes.

Barely moments later a vision of my daughter crying, shouting my name shocked me from my sleep. I couldn't lose her. I didn't want to dream of her demise. I wouldn't. Tired and exhausted but with my heart pounding so hard my ears hurt, I rose from the bed and made myself a black coffee, spending the remainder of the night sitting at the kitchen table, trembling.

The sun beaming through the blinds the next morning was enough to give me a migraine, to make me want to close my eyes at least. One of the curtains was jammed; typical. When you've had no rest sunlight can be a killer. I considered moving into a darkened room and wait there for the solar flex to go annoy someone else but the thought of accidentally falling asleep was too much to bear.

I needed my daughter with me, and to know that both her and my mother was safe, so decided after a quick phone call to let her know I was coming to pick her up. Mom was asleep when I got there. Margaret answered the door, duffle coat in hand.

"Grandma was worried about you." Margaret paused before continuing. "I missed you last night." Smiling I picked her up and held her close. My baby girl's arms wrapped around me, tight. "I'm always with you," I said as we walked to the car. Once the door was opened she jumped into her child seat and I strapped her in.

The journey back home was longer than expected. A traffic jam on I465 brought us to a complete standstill. Margaret picked up her Buzz Light-year action figure from the seat and flicked the switch at the back of his head repeatedly on and off. I closed my eyes and pinched my fingers between them, a futile effort to ward off an oncoming headache.

Suddenly a bright light through my closed lids stunned me into opening them. I couldn't risk falling asleep, especially not on a busy road. Looking ahead I expected to see a long line of cars sitting patiently waiting so they could continue on their way. Instead the road was completely clear, not a car in sight. Cautiously I put the car in gear and began driving.

I was travelling at a constant sixty miles per hour, Margaret, in her child seat behind me. She was playing with her Buzz Light-year which with the switch on repeatedly announced "To Infinity and Beyond" every time it was placed at a horizontal angle.

Ten minutes into the journey, I'd heard all I cared to from Mr Light-year. "Sweetheart, do you think you could turn Buzz off so we can listen to the music on the radio?" No response apart from the continued galactic announcement from Buzz. "Baby Girl, Buzz is giving me a bit of a headache; just flick the switch on the back of his head ok?"

Out of the corner of my eye I saw Buzz drop to the floor and on he went, "To Infinity And Beyond." I swear the cocky little toy actually winked at me. Now out of reach of my daughter and even closer to my ear I had to pick it up before the announcement transformed to an internal one: "Lack of Sanity and Beyond."

It was a fleeting thought. One quick glance at the road before I turned around to retrieve it, two seconds max.

As I turned to pick up the toy the radio volume increased. "We now change the scheduled programming to cater for all you grieving parents out there." Buzz sat up on the seat and started to shake his head whilst Billie Joel started singing say goodbye to my baby over the airwaves.

Buzz turned his head once more then stopped moving, his lifeless gaze now directed at my daughter. Her eyes met his and paused momentarily. The silence seemed to blanket a moment of pure understanding and clarity between them both, a moment I desperately wanted to share but could not.

Margaret lifted her head and smiled. A single red teardrop made its way slowly down her cheek and fell to her lap. As she lifted her hands in my direction, scarlet tears began to free flow. I felt a shudder and a cold spot on the back of my neck. Shards of glass were floating past my head in slow motion effortlessly cutting my face as they attempted to pass me and find their way to my baby girl.

My eyes began to throb as if hot needles were being pushed outward from the inside. I clamped them shut, too afraid to reopen them and unable to move, very aware that I was the human shield protecting my daughter from whatever danger that had sought her out.

The radio volume increased. "Say Goodbye To My Baby" repeated over and over, accompanied by an orchestra of smashing glass, crumpled metal and a piercing soprano that was my daughter as she cried out in pain. My eyes were still closed. I pushed my hands to my ears and prayed for this nightmare to end, and it did.

When I reopened my eyes I was facing front, all in the car was as it should be, but outside everything was happening at super speed. Traffic, people and trees became nothing but momentary blurs. I looked at the speedometer which moved rapidly from sixty miles per hour to one hundred and five then back again to sixty fixed in a constant time loop.

There was a voice, a warm comforting sound that eased my pounding heart. "I realise you're concerned." The voice continued. "I'm here to help as much as I can." In the distance, but moving ever closer the silver haired lady approached. Her high definition image contrasted with the surrounding environment.

I wasn't even alarmed when she glided through the roof of my car like a heavenly apparition to look me in the eyes from above, her stare now both hypnotic and frightening. The pain in my head and body returned and amplified.

I turned to check my daughter was ok, but when I looked she wasn't there. Her red duffle coat was laid out on the empty child seat as a blanket for the Buzz Light-year action figure. Slowly the car seat began to fade from focus, and my entire environment was becoming a hazy image like a repressed memory till it disappeared altogether.

I heard my father speaking behind me. "You can do it Sam, stay with us." Dad? But that's impossible, I thought. My daughter's pleading voice joined his: "I love you. Please don't die; I'll be good always, I promise." She cried like I'd never heard before. Facing front again I looked at the lady in white who returned my smile. The name on her badge read Nurse Rebecca Walker.

The mist that had been shrouding my perception was finally lifted and my memories once again clear. There had only ever been one accident with myself as the only victim. A wave of relief passed through me as I saw my family and best friend standing in the hospital room with me. I felt gratitude for the nurse who had been there through my fleeting moments of consciousness and sorrow for the loved ones I would leave behind.

"There's nothing more we can do," Rebecca said as she stepped back to allow my family to approach. Behind me the bedroom door I'd seen earlier opened once more. The light from the room was inviting and warm.

The bleep from my heart monitor was slowing gradually. "Take care of my daughter" I managed to say. "I love you all so much" My family's tears made me want to stay but I knew I couldn't. I approached the light and lay down on the bed. The heart monitor's unrelenting beep turned to a constant drone as I slowly closed my eyes.

Charie D. La Marr
A Touch of Indigo

Dedicated to Flannery O'Connor

Debbie Wayne walked through the kitchen and noticed the cellar door was open. Downstairs she could hear records playing and boys laughing. It was her brother Mark and his friends.

Their mom had always warned them about keeping the cellar door locked. But now that Mark was thirteen, he and his friends had started hanging out there. They dragged an old sofa that someone was throwing out down there through the bulkhead door and he took his record player and his 45 record collection down. She knew that sometimes when Mom was asleep, they opened the bulkhead to get light and air. They also smoked cigarettes sometimes.

It had been over a year since Debbie and Mark's father died. He was a policeman and had a heart attack on the job. Since then, their mom had taken a job working nights as a nurse and her sister Judy had moved in with them. Judy was also a nurse, so she worked days and watched the kids at night. Mom had a hard time sleeping during the day, so she started taking sleeping pills. That left Debbie in charge of the three-year-old twins a lot during the afternoons. Mrs. Kramer was right next-door and she stopped by sometimes.

It also left her older brother Mark to do pretty much whatever he wanted. What was she going to do? Tell Mom? That would have made her a total rat in school. Mark would make sure everyone laughed at her. So what if they hung out in the basement and listened to music? There was nothing down there but Dad's workbench, a washer and dryer and a few spiders. He didn't care. It was better than crowding into his little shared bedroom.

But that wasn't the point. Mom had lectured them a million times. Dad had put many people in jail and when they got out, some of them wanted revenge. She didn't go into any graphic stories, but she'd heard of cops and their families who were killed by ex-cons who had vengeance in their hearts. Mark was the man of the house, and yet he was only a kid. He couldn't protect them. She hated that bulkhead door. Someone could easily break into it. That's why it was important to keep the cellar door locked. After Dad died, she put a second lock on it.

Debbie sighed and went in to watch cartoons with the twins. The picture was terrible. The twins didn't seem to care. She adjusted the antenna anyway. She wanted to watch the soaps like all her girlfriends did, but it was impossible with the twins. If they didn't get their own way, they'd scream and cry and wake Mom up. And she needed her sleep before work.

A lot of the times, when the girls at school talked about the soap operas, Debbie would smile and nod her head and act like she watched them. She didn't want the girls to know she spent her days watching stupid cartoons. She couldn't even watch the news. Anything could happen and she wouldn't know about it. Sighing, she got a book and settled down on the couch to read. Aunt Judy would be home from work soon, and they'd make dinner together and wake Mom up for work. Once the twins were in bed, Aunt Judy would let her stay up for a while and watch some real TV. They loved the crime shows. Mark did, too. Dragnet and The Fugitive were their favorites.

After a while, she heard the boys coming up the stairs. It was their daily raid of the refrigerator. They would make peanut butter and jelly sandwiches and grab as many sodas as they could carry. Probably even a bag of chips. They were such pigs. The cellar was beginning to look like a garbage dump.

But there were other footsteps. Heavy ones. Debbie listened carefully. She could swear she heard the sound of chain rattling. She grabbed the twins and pulled them behind the couch.

"Hey!" Michelle said. "We were watching Bozo!"

Teddy seemed a little more interested. He walked over to his sister in his favorite coonskin hat. "Are we playing a game, Debbie? Are we hiding from the monsters?"

"Yes, something like that," Debbie whispered. "Only we have to be really quiet because the monsters have really huge ears and they hear every sound we make. So the first person who makes a sound gets eaten, because they have big, huge teeth, too. And great big tentacles to reach out and grab you and throw you in their giant mouths."

"Cool!" Teddy said. "I hope it's Michelle. She's a pest and she always hogs the television. And she makes me play house."

Debbie heard the footsteps coming closer. "Shh, 'cos the monster's almost in hearing distance." She slumped down and held the twins close.

"Debbie? Where are you? You'd better wake Mom. We need her in here." Mark was in the kitchen. He sounded really scared.

"We should do what he says," Michelle said. "It sounds like he's in trouble."

"Part of the game," Debbie said. "Mark's playing, too."

"Mark never plays with us," she said.

"Well, he is this time, so hush."

Then she heard the rattle of chains and the voice that went with them. "How many more are in the house? Tell me!"

"My two sisters, my little brother and my mother. She works at night, so she takes a sleeping pill in the daytime. She's hard to wake up."

"Well, let's go find them."

Debbie could feel her whole body shaking. "Come on, time to move," she said to the twins. They slipped up the stairs and into their mother's bedroom. She was sleeping soundly. Her starched white uniform was hanging on the back of the door. The nurse's hat she was so proud of was on her dressing table. Debbie loved seeing her mother in her white uniform. She looked like an angel. An angel of mercy. She worked in the wing of the hospital for children. Debbie felt good to know that when they woke up during the night crying or in pain, her mother was there to help them and comfort them.

"We're gonna hide under her bed," she said, pushing the twins under and then sliding under herself.

There were more footsteps. It seemed as though the owner of the heavy footsteps was following the boys. It sounded like they were in the living room.

"The television is on, kid. Where are they?"

Debbie could hear the voice more clearly. It was a man. He sounded very big and scary. Mark and his friends must have been terrified.

"I . . . I don't know," Mark said. "The twins are little. Debbie watches them in the afternoon. They watch cartoons."

"And who takes care of you at night?"

Debbie closed her eyes and prayed. "Please don't say it, Mark. Please don't say it." Aunt Judy would be home soon. Maybe she would see something was wrong and run for help. She might be able to see the open bulkhead door from the driveway.

"I'm thirteen and my sister's almost twelve. Mom puts the twins to bed after dinner, before she goes to work. Debbie and I take care of ourselves."

"Where's your father?"

"He died last year."

"Sorry to hear that kid. What happened to him?"

"He had a heart attack on the job," Mark said, almost in tears.

"Yea? And what was his job."

Debbie started praying again. "Remember the stories Mom told us," she whispered. "Don't say Dad was a cop."

"I'm not really sure. He worked in an office. Like a businessman, I guess."

Debbie breathed a sigh of relief.

"So where are these two sisters and one brother?" the man asked.

"I don't know," Mark said. "Maybe Debbie took them to the playground for a while. Sometimes they get so noisy she's afraid they'll wake Mom. They're probably in the park."

"And left the television set on?"

"Looks that way," Mark said. "They do that sometimes."

Debbie had a new respect for her brother. He was doing everything he could to protect them. He really was trying to be the man of the house.

"So let's go wake up Mom," the man said. "Where's her bedroom?"

There was no response from Mark.

"That's okay, kiddo. You're trying to protect her from the big, bad man. But it's a small house. I'm sure if I take a look around, I'll find her. You and your friends lead the way."

Debbie heard his footsteps moving again, this time up the stairs. And the sound of chain. He was getting closer. There were only three bedrooms in the house. Debbie and Michelle shared one and Mark and Teddy had the other. Mom and Dad's room was the biggest one—at the far end of the hall. There would be no way to get past him. Besides, he had Mark and his friends. She couldn't leave them behind. Did he have a gun? The prison was only three miles up the road. The men worked along the highway in chain gangs. That had to be where the chain came from. But how did he escape? Were they looking for him?

She heard someone approaching the bed. It was Mark.

"Mom?" he said. He was crying. "Mom, you have to wake up now. Please? I'm so sorry, Mom. We opened the cellar door and we were down there. The bulkhead door was open, too. And a man came in. Mom, I'm so scared. Please wake up. I need you now. God, I wish Daddy was here, he would know what to do, but you have to help me, Mom, please?"

Ruth Wayne sat up and took off her sleep mask. She took one look at the man and gasped. "Boys, get behind me, now!"

"What are you going to do, lady? Protect them from this?" He held up a gun. "Admirable of you, but you must realize I can kill you all. And what have we here? A little foot sticking out from under your bed? The rest of the family, I presume. Well, tell them to come out too, or I'll start killing you one by one."

"Michelle," she said softly. "Are you under my bed? Are the others with you? Come out now, baby."

"Debbie said we were playing a game, Mommy," the little girl said.

"Well, the game's over now, sweetie. Come out from under there and get behind Mommy with Mark."

As Debbie slid out, she noticed the dark stain on the front of Mark's pants. He'd wet himself. Ordinarily, that would be material to use to tease him for a year. But she was trying very hard not to do it herself.

"You got money in the house?" the man asked. He was tall and balding and wearing the familiar black and white striped uniform that told the world he was an escaped convict.

"Forty, maybe fifty dollars in the cookie jar. Another twelve in my wallet. That's about it. I'll go get it."

Ruth started to get up but he pushed her back on the bed. "You ain't goin' nowhere, lady."

"Then you go get it. The cookie jar is in the kitchen. My pocketbook is on the table in the foyer, next to the front door."

"Do I look that stupid to you, lady? I go lookin' for money that don't exist while you push the brats out the window and call the cops?"

"Out a second floor window? Then how are you going to get the money?" she asked. "It ain't gonna bring itself to you."

"Maybe I kill everybody first then I go get it, if it even exists."

"It does," Ruth said with a choke in her voice. "Mister, my husband died over a year ago and I've been working day and night to support these kids and keep them together. You never know when you're gonna have an emergency—a flat tire or a broken window or one of them gets sick. Every mother in my position has a cookie jar she tosses a couple dollars in every week. Where else would I get the money from? I made myself a promise when we laid Ted to rest. I wasn't ever gonna ask his parents or mine for a dime. And give them a reason to take my kids away from me because I couldn't support them? I don't know who you are, but I'd clean toilets or stables before I'd let anybody lay a hand on my children."

He chuckled. "And a fat lot of good it did you, huh? Because fifty bucks in a cookie jar ain't gonna save them now."

Michelle tugged at her. "Mama, is this man playing the game with Debbie? He says he's gonna hurt us. I'm scared, Mama."

Ruth hugged the little girl, never taking her eyes off the man. "Nobody's gonna hurt you, Michelle."

She glared at the man. "Look Mister, if you lay one hand on any one of these children, sooner or later you'll get caught. And then whatever your sentence is now, it'll get commuted to life. You'll never see the light of day again."

He laughed. "Lady, I'm already in prison for the rest of my life. I killed two men. A couple more murders ain't gonna make a bit of difference one way or the other. Once ya get a life sentence, that's that. The rest of you would just be icing on the cake."

"Oh, really?" Ruth said. "That's what these children are to you? Icing on the cake? Do you ever think about your afterlife? Do you realize that in hell, you can be punished for each and every murder you commit? And that you would have virtually no chance to confess your sins in the hour of your death and be accepted into the Kingdom of Heaven?"

"Who told you all that hooey, lady? Because here's a clue for you. It ain't true. When you die, it's over. The end. Finished. There's nothing after this life. Absolutely nothing. When it ends, it ends. You think if there was a God, he would have let me rob and murder two priests? You really believe that? God didn't even protect two of his own?"

"I don't have an answer for that," Ruth said. "Sometimes bad things happen to good people or for good reasons. Sometimes bad things just happen. I don't know why. But I know one thing, bad people get what they have coming to them. I'm sure of that. You start out as a baby, you struggle to be born. You grow up; you suffer through problems, illnesses, deaths, hardships. And I don't care what you say but you don't do it for nothing! There is something more after this life—there has to be! I won't believe my husband is just gone to nowhere." She was crying.

"Lady, let me tell you this. I ain't had nothing but suffering and hardships in my life. Not since the minute I pushed myself out into this world and took my mother out of it. You talk about having to give up your kids? Well, I was given away. Only I didn't have any grandparents who wanted me. Just the County Home. And when I was old enough, they bought me a new pair of pants and a cheap pair of shoes and turned me out on the streets. And every night when I went to sleep, I didn't know where the next meal was comin' from or where I'd be sleepin' the next night."

"So you lost your faith," Ruth said, wiping her eyes. "That's understandable."

"No!" he screamed at her. "I didn't lose no faith. I never had none. And you can stop tryin' to preach to me because I ain't gonna get none. All I got to look forward to is life on the run and then it's over. And there ain't gonna be no angels or devils waitin' for me neither. Just nothing."

Ruth closed her eyes and shook her head. "The children and I will pray for you."

"You better start prayin' for yourselves. Because it's time. You sure you ain't got money hiding anyplace else? The kids got no piggy banks? No saved up allowance money?"

"No," she said quietly. "Nothing more. And if you want, you can take it all and go. We'll stay right here and we won't tell anyone. You can be gone. The keys to my car are next to my purse. It isn't much, but it'll get you where you want to go. And you can even have some of my husband's clothes. He was about your size. You'll even find a bolt cutter on his workbench in the cellar for that chain."

He shook his head. "Too late for that now, Missus. It won't be long before they come around here asking questions. Once they learn I have your car, they'll be on me like white on rice. Nobody's gonna believe no colored man drivin' a car like that. The roads is probably blocked off by now anyways."

"There are back roads. You can find a way. There's maps in the glove compartment. More in my husband's nightstand."

He thought for a moment and walked over to the nightstand. He snapped up a photo and stared at it. It was Ted's favorite photo of the family on the day he became a detective. They looked so happy and proud of him. But she'd made a mistake—a mistake that could cost them all their lives.

"A cop?" he asked incredulously. "Your husband was a cop? That's it, Missus. Time's up. I'll take the boys first. In the next bedroom. Put a pillow over that little girl's ears so she don't hear."

A tear rolled down her cheek. It was his first display of compassion. She held Michelle tighter. "Go with him, boys. Be brave. And pray. Mark, Teddy, your father will be waiting for you in Heaven. Someone will be waiting for all of you in Heaven."

"No, Mom!" Mark cried. "Don't let him take us!"

"Mister, you win. The kids can't get away. But could you just give us a minute alone? To say good-bye? Could you just wait for a moment in the hall, I'll send them out when I've said good-bye and told them I love them."

"Sure. If you think it'll make any difference to them when they're gone. One minute." The man nodded and left, closing the door behind him.

Ruth grabbed Mark. "Your father's uniform. The one he wore every day. It's hanging on the back of the closet door right where he always kept it. His gun. It's in the pants pocket. I didn't want to keep it in the lock box. I thought the time might come when I had to protect you. Get it. Throw it to me."

Mark ran to the closet and tugged the weapon from the pocket of the dark blue pants. Just as he was about to toss it to his mother, the front door opened and Judy walked in. "Good evening, little Wayne's," she called out. "Mark, go wake your mom up. Debbie, meet me in the kitchen. You can make the salad for dinner. I brought home TV dinners. The turkey ones you like."

The man panicked. He pushed open the door and saw Mark standing there with the gun in his hand. The boy glanced quickly at his mother, held the gun tightly and fired. Ruth hid the twins' eyes as Mark fired again and again. The man went down but as he did he fired a shot. It missed Mark and passed through the sleeve of his father's uniform. And then there was silence.

She threw a blanket over the dead man and pushed the children past the body. "Go downstairs and tell Aunt Judy to call the police. Tell them there's been a shooting."

Then she went to Mark who was standing very still, the gun pointed at the ground, his eyes on the body. She wrapped an arm around his head and took the gun away from him. He didn't resist. Ruth reached out and touched the torn arm of Ted's uniform.

"I kept it there, Mark. I couldn't bring myself to move it. I don't know, I guess it just seemed to me like he was still here, looking after his family and protecting us. But as of today, that's your job."

She put another blanket over her son's shoulders and sat him on the far side of the bed, where he couldn't see the body.

"I killed somebody, Mom," he said.

"No, you protected your family. You did exactly what your father would have done. Nothing is more important than protecting your family. Nothing."

The following day, some of Ted's friends from the police department came over. When they were done cleaning up Ruth's room, they dragged the sofa out of the basement. Then they nailed the bulkhead door shut and built a little laundry room behind the kitchen. They put a stronger lock on the cellar door and new locks on the front and back doors, too. Locking up the basement spelled the end to Mark's gatherings in the basement.

He would just have to use the bedroom he shared with Teddy when he had his friends over.

When they were done, Ruth stood in the kitchen, her body pressed against the door that led to the basement. "Whatever you do, kids, don't ever unlock that cellar door again."

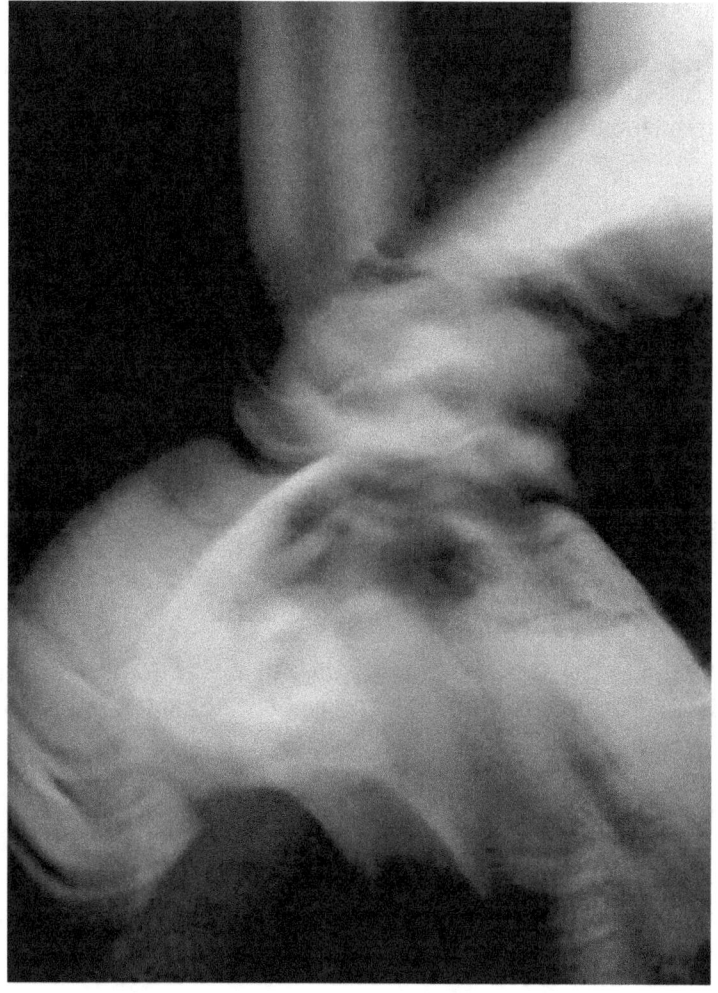

Scathe meic Beorh
Comic

Sanders, Indiana, June 1972

I found my little brother naked and hanging from a dogwood tree in a burlap bag. He was dazed, and had a pretty high fever, and when he tried to talk, his voice was so hoarse he sounded like a toad frog. I cut him down, wrapped him up in the sack, and cradled him in my arms. Next day, when he was feeling better, I asked him what happened.

"I borrowed the Haggard horse. Without asking nobody," he said.

"Again?" I asked him. "That makes you a horse thief sure enough, Mitchell."

Mitchell smiled big. "I know. But I needed Ol' Rags to get down to the post office."

"Where's your bicycle, partner?" I asked my brother.

"It's got a flat tire. Hey Randy?"

"Yeah Shorty?"

"I think the Haggard kids hate me more than they hate their drunk old man."

"I wouldn't doubt it, Mitch. I mean, look at all the things you've done to them just this year alone. First off, you killed their prized rooster. Now, I know that was accidental, but you still killed him. The main problem with that was you did it with the shotgun you so-called 'borrowed' from Seth Haggard. Then you stole Ol' Rags and was gone with her for two whole days. Then a week after that, you knocked their baby sister Rhiannon down with your bicycle and broke her finger. Accident again, I know, but it's still no excuse. You know how to ride a bike."

"And I'm good at it too, Randy."

"You remember who taught you, don't you?"

"You did."

"That's right. And don't you forget it. Anyways, now you've done gone and took the Haggard horse again without asking. It's a wonder they didn't string you up *outside* the bag, if you know what I'm sayin'."

"You mean gone and hanged me?"

"That's what they would have done in Grandpa's day. C'mon, partner. Let's get a big bowl o' that homemade vanilla ice cream I just made. What you say?"

"Well, all we can gather so far, Jerry," said Sheriff Jones, "is that your son Mitchell got Ansel, the youngest Haggard boy, interested in goin' in on a series of comic books with him. Mail order. Then when the books got here, for some reason Mitch didn't let Ansel have his share. So..."

"I tried to raise that boy right... if only his mother was still alive..."

"I'm sorry, Jerry. We'll find Mitchell's... *ah...* we'll find the rest of his... his body... *god...* I promise you that."

"I want justice, Tim. And I won't rest until I get it, now. You know me! *You know me...*"

"Well... that's the other part of why I'm here, Jerry. When we went to question the Haggard family..." Sheriff Jones closed his tired eyes and shivered. "*Damn it was awful...*"

"What, Tim? You *did* put the bastards in jail, didn't you?"

"Well... it seems..." Jones took his cap off, ran his fingers through his greasy blond hair, and then plucked at the gold star pinned to his shirt until it came unclasped and fell to the floor. "It seems, Jerry, that the oldest boy, Seth Haggard, has been trampled to death by a horse. We checked Ol' Rag's hooves, but they were clean."

"*My lord...*"

"That's not all. Ansel Haggard... has been killed with a sawed-off shotgun, Jerry. The gun was... apparently held up to his face. And . . . We found Elaine, the oldest Haggard girl, dead in the barn loft."

"My lord... how... what...?"

"It's the damnedest thing, Jerry. She was... *nude*, her mouth gagged and her feet tied together... and them nailed to a post. And then if that wasn't enough, a bicycle tire has been taken apart, and the spokes pushed into... all the... *lord...* all the soft parts of her body. *My god....* as deep as they would go. We found flesh and hair under her fingernails. She tried to fight off her killer. But why she was in such a vulnerable position to begin with... well, we can only speculate. I mean... I *hate* to have to ask you this, old friend, but Jerry, where's your daughter Randy?"

Gary Murphy
Donkey Jacket Man (Return of the Prince)

Andrew 'Prince' Paisley woke up that evening on his lounge sofa wondering where the hell the frigging day had disappeared to, since the last remaining thing he remembered was coming in from the Hornets Social Club last night around 11 O'clock (essential booze palace for every prince and princess living in the town of Cleator Moor, a place that can be found next door to Whitehaven in West Cumbria), watching a bit of late-night TV and getting bored, and eating a micro-curry, and a frankfurter sausage, and then crashing. Had he slept all night and all day?

Donkey Jacket Man to his friends, Andrew was off work yesterday. But tonight he had to go to work at the Morgue and he had little time to sort himself out and get ready. He was due at the Dead House in less than an hour. Donkey Jacket Man had to get his groove on.

They called him that stupid name due to a fault of his own, in that he wasn't seen without his black donkey jacket. He wore it everywhere he went, whether it was to church, going shopping, to work, or even when he bar-crawled looking to pick up women in the wee small hours after a night hitting the sauce! He wasn't picky, and like he, usually neither were they.

He had worn the donkey jacket for years, the coat becoming part of his personality, from his time in Secondary School at the Whitehaven School when he walked out aged fourteen and never went back, due to a misjudged caning. Something he was blamed for and had to suffer the punishment accordingly, for something he didn't do. Nobody could blame him for walking out. He had been a ministerial scapegoat for the pansies running that so-called institution of education. Did they single him out because his family couldn't afford to pay the fees for the Grammar School across the road, the natural progression from Secondary? Donkey Jacket Man wouldn't have put it past the wankers!

But was he bitter?

Absolutely . . . So bitter, it stained his soul. He sought solace in thoughts of burning the fucking place to the ground and taking that bamboo cane and ramming it up Headmaster Pearson's arse! Or flail his skinny scrawny arse as many times as he had whipped his that one fateful summer afternoon!

Now, Donkey Jacket Man was twenty-five and he took shit off nobody.

But he still thought of school.

It was on the bus on the way to the Workington Town Morgue when his nightmare visualized in the shape and form of a long but not forgotten figure from his schooldays: Board Duster Man.

Percy Dart, aka Board Duster Man, was a little chubby man, short with wire-rimmed spectacles which sat uncomfortably on a thin crooked nose, a nose that was hooked like a buzzard's beak. The eyes, too . . . sharp, narrow and squinted, forever alert, and burrowed into psyches of innocents, once he fixated on the chosen, dislikeable character.

On the bus, Donkey Jacket Man was looking out the window when he spotted Dart, the Board Duster Man from school. He was called that due to his employment in History Class. Boris Clondyke would scribble on the blackboard with his blue chalk and afterward, as was his paid job, when the board was full and Boris needed more room to scrawl, Dart would shift forward off his chair nearby and wipe the board clean in order for Neo-Nazi Boris to continue, and progress through the Ages. Board Duster Man . . .

There had been grisly slayings across this part of West Cumbria recently, and the killer was still at large in the community, committing obscene acts to male and female, murdering indiscriminately. It had been going on for months, and every time the police thought they had a lead or a suspect, their revelatory discoveries were scuppered and their investigations were knocked back. Across the country the standard of police work was definitely improving, and the men and women of the law did their best to succeed in their jobs, but foiling stuff like this was becoming quite a pisser for people considering leaving their homes at night. People, and good people, wanted to booze and once drunk, not get butchered. The sooner they found this maniac the better.

One thing that made Donkey Jacket Man think of Percy Dart was that on every one of the killer's victims' backs was a chalk imprint, made into an X.

Maybe by thinking of him, he had conjured him up somehow. It might even have been his spirit or ghost, since it was a while since he was at school and observed Dart, and by now he must have been well into his sixties. Was he physically capable of stalking those people, cornering them and cutting their throats?

Who could tell these things?

There was solace in believing he was long dead.

But as the bus passed the Workington Swimming Baths on his route to the Morgue, where he saw Percy Dart standing outside the Baths, the tiny fat fellow looked more than a double. Donkey Jacket Man would never forget that face, those eyes and that nose so hooked and horrid, and he could have sworn it was him for sure.

And Donkey Jacket Man had serious reservations concerning this old bastard.

On the bus going by, he watched as Dart looked directly at him, making eye-contact. It was cold as ice and the shiver it powered along the back of his neck spread to the rest of his body; within that moment of realization it was *him*. When he looked at him, sitting up in his seat, Donkey Jacket Man's eyes widened and he breathed a sharp inhalation, for not only did this man look overtly sinister and evil, but he smiled, and this made the incoming feeling of dread intensify further.

"Percy Dart . . ." he muttered, "It can't be, surely . . . "

But it was, without shadow of a doubt . . .

The situation was only clinched when another bus going past on the other side of the road obscured his view, and once past, Dart had disappeared.

It was 10 O'clock when the Prince started his Night Shift at the Morgue. Thirty minutes later, the place, with its marble floors furbished in clinical white and the cold white rooms were deserted and he had free reign to do as he wished. This was Donkey Jacket Man's job. He worked at the Workington Dead House. And he was trusted wholly.

He loved his job.

But perhaps for reasons unacceptable and inappropriate to others.

He "enjoyed" his job.

There were two dead males on the slabs tonight and for the Prince this factor was a truth he knew he could exploit in glorious fashion. The females he never bothered with. Only the men . . .

He removed the plastic transparent sheet from the first and scrutinized the dead man's face, like a child eyeing up chocolate. He was young, maybe forty-something, broad-shouldered and handsome, bluish-skinned in death. Now the fun would begin . . .

"You bastard," he said, grimacing, "You think you can screw with me and get away with it? I'll teach you a lesson you'll never forget!"

He brought his right fist into the side of the dead man's face. And his left, again into the upper face and head. He punched the ribs and chest, moving down to the stomach, abdomen and groin, and pummelled his way up and down fevered and frenetically. He cursed all the time, gurgled with perverse joy as he drooled and laughed like a maniac, all the time punching and punching the lifeless corpse.

No blood.

This was good.

Once tired out, he headed toward the viewing room. He picked up his bait-box containing his supper, cheese-and-ham sarnies caked in ketchup, and without so much as washing his hands, took the first sandwich and crammed it into his mouth. All that strenuous and punishing work had given him quite an appetite.

Donkey Jacket Man was hungry now, but as he devoured his bait he was already excited about the next corpse on the other marble slab, which he had examined and discovered was a bit older. He didn't like battering pensioners. But it had to be done. They had to be taught a lesson. Just like when he was at school and they taught him a lesson. All that pain he felt had to be shared, experienced by other innocents. Like he was innocent . . . oh yes, everyone was innocent, and had to be taught a lesson . . . those coming into the Morgue was a good place to start.

He chewed on the cheese-and-ham sandwich greedily, drooling as he envisaged in his mind the cold flesh against his knuckles. He could feel the "punishment" as he clenched his fists into tight balls.

He grinned as he looked through the window into the Death Room from the viewing room. But Donkey Jacket Man was barely aware of the reflection of the figure standing there directly behind him. He first became aware of the presence when he heard the singular, short rasping breaths which issued from the short gentleman's mouth, and when he turned it was with grave horror he confronted Board Duster Man.

" . . . Percy Dart?" He stumbled to speak, ". . . Board Duster Man?"

The serial-killer still very much active in the community claimed his latest victim as the razor-sharp blade lashed out, slicing a nick in the Prince's jugular. A squirting scarlet stream spurted forth and Donkey Jacket Man was dead before he hit the floor. The little tubby man reached into his bag and extracted a board-duster, which he applied chalk to and left his signature X on the dead man's back. All those times those pesky kids pissed him off and made his life miserable, while he just tried to do his job as teacher's assistant. Now they weren't so clever. In fact, not clever at all;. just stupid. And he would punish every single one, in the same way he had been punished. He hated his schooldays just as much as any of those snivelling snot-nosed brats.

Mike Jansen

Alex Stephens and Vada Katherine
Mary Me

1.

David Stone noticed the woman. He didn't know her name yet, but he would come to know it. He counted the mice around her feet. The woman's hips moved to the pounding bass from the speakers like a snake moving across a hot desert highway. She wore a blue dress, like Mother. Normally David ignored women like her, their desperation darkening the sweat on their brows. These women thrived on the blood of genius, as if they could suck intelligence from the tip of a penis. But the mice: their number was growing; now swirling around her ankles like debris around a tornado, their mouths open in terror.

When David was a child of nine, his mother, wearing one of her countless blue dresses, found a mouse and her litter in a seldom used closet. David watched her as she picked up each of the pups and squeezed the middle until its pink and red guts burst out. His mother told him this was how to treat vermin. No mercy, no hesitation—just extermination.

David roused from memory. A woman in a red dress passed him. She was covered head to toe with scuttling cockroaches, even her open eyes, except for where expensive crimson cloth covered the woman's body. *It's too late for her*. David closed his eyes, the time-released chemical prescribed by Dr. Payne flooding his brain: *none of this is real.*

David did not see the bodies of the men in the dance club. Their heads were the body of ticks buried deep and sucking blood. Any exposed flesh on them was transparent, like a child's lie. He was alone with the damaged women. They smelled of lavender and dirt.

David opened his eyes. *She can be saved, the woman with the mice.* He looked at his gold Rolex. *There's still time; her infestation is manageable, and she may be of use.*

His approach was classic; brief eye contact from across the dance floor followed by the saunter. The hunter and the willing prey played the timeless game. Chemicals flooded David's brain and body. His focus narrowed to the woman and her luscious curves. He wanted desperately to squeeze her. He stared at her, took her in, swallowed her whole like a sumptuous chocolate petite four. He felt the endorphin-rich blood flow through his veins, bringing strength to his heart and vigor to his limbs. Mary filled the cracks in his brain.

2.

She felt the chemical reactions of attraction. Her mind filled with hazy visions and vague hallucinations of mystical wholeness, as her body became soft and pliant, and her senses heightened to their utmost. She felt every heartbeat, every brush of fabric, every soft breath that passed her moist lips, and his warm palm upon her cheek. She moistened, and wondered if the man scented her.

"My name is Mary." She sighed. "I noticed you noticing me. I knew it was just a matter of time. It always is." She lit a cigarette, inhaled and exhaled through her nostrils.

People nearby stirred. How dare she smoke in here? David grunted, and those with objection looked away, a palpable sense of insanity souring their breath.

"My name is David." He breathed through his mouth, preferring to taste the woman than grieve her aroma. "Mary, there's still time for you."

"Are you my savior?"

"Perhaps." He smiled at Mary. His teeth glowed white in the club light.

"And how will you save me?" She drank from her glass of red wine, then flavored the sensory input with a final draw from her cigarette. Smoke embellished her hair, adding silver to black.

"I am a thanatologist."

Mary blushed, lit another cigarette.

"I study death, Mary. Think about it. What happens when we die? The human body is best represented by the number two. The brain has two hemispheres. We have two lungs, two kidneys. The liver has two halves. The human heart has four chambers, devisable by two. Humans hold within themselves both good and evil. What happens to that coupling of good and evil upon death? I propose that at death good and evil separate. But what happens then?"

David lit his own cigarette. "I'm not speaking the language of seduction. I'm sorry."

"Death. Seduction. They're two basic drives. We seek them in equal measure. They serve similar purposes and function in similar ways. Where death is a parting of pairs, seduction is a pairing of parts." Mary laughed. "You think you can save me? You can see death upon me? Smell its stench? Well I believe you can. But what is the price you charge? You didn't get that expensive watch doing charity work." Mary smirked. "I bet there are a lot of freaks that would love a girl like me. And I bet you're the guy they go to."

David looked about the crowded room. The Vermin were multiplying. "I have a place in the countryside, a forty-five minute drive. I can show you . . . secrets".

Mary stood. "Let's go."

3.

"You may not believe this, Mary. But I have invented a machine . . ." David hesitated, rubbed his cheek. *Dare I say? Yes. She is mine to squeeze.*

"Go on. A machine?" Mary prompted.

"Yes. It . . . Well, it captures the good and the evil as they separate, captures the energy at the moment of death." David looked at Mary. "I believe I can cycle the energy back around to . . ." David laughed at the absurdity of what he is about to say. "Well, the machine, if it is set up properly, will cycle the good and evil energies around in such a manner as to harmonize their frequencies and reanimate the body. One becomes healthier than ever, and in symphony with life."

"And if it is not set up properly?"

"I guess it wouldn't bring you back."

"Could it bring me back imbalanced?"

"You mean pure evil?" David laughed. "According to my theory of twos, that should not be possible."

"But that is just a theory."

"True."

4.

The two-story house stood in an open field. The crescent moon illuminated a few details: spires at the corners, several crumbling chimneys, floor to ceiling windows. A crack in the foundation was apparent, running from the cellar to just below one of the chimneys.

David helped Mary out of the car. Mice scurried alongside, as they approached the door.

"Are you sure you want to do this?" David opened the door, and pretended not to notice the cock roaches as they scattered.

"There's something you need to know. I have a secret."

David, his mind beset by a torrent of contradictory thoughts, led Mary by the hand across the creaking, warped floor of the foyer to the left. They entered the library, which was lit only by moonlight through the large windows.

He seated her in an over-stuffed leather chair the color of coffee. "Mary, may I offer you a drink?"

"No. But perhaps you should."

David poured a brandy, discreetly swallowing two of Dr. Payne's pills. The swirling in his brain stopped like a bird slamming into a window. But the window cracked, and David experienced the cosmos peering at him from behind the glass.

This took the form of a blurry figure as it often did. The dark apparition occupied the corner of the library and mumbled with many voices. David glanced at the dark, shifting form. He felt its heavy presence in the room. Rats scurried from the corner and set about chewing the walls and floorboards.

David pressed his eyes together tightly for a long moment. He returned to Mary, taking a chair across from her. He crossed his legs, sipped again from his brandy, and asked, "Please tell me your secret."

5.

"The 'good' you speak of that resides in every human being, does not reside within me." She paused for affect. "I am a killer. My first murder was my fraternal twin named Oscar. We were five years old, and it was Christmas Eve. I entered his bedroom and smothered him with his pillow. Oscar was weak, pathetically puny. I think in a way I murdered him in the womb, stole his will to live somehow.

"I wanted his Christmas presents. Nothing more and I got them. 'Poor little Mary' my parents said.

"I did not grieve the loss of Oscar.

"Over the years I have murdered countless people; mostly vagrants and worthless types, but some decent people, like Oscar, who's only flaw was his weakness."

David nodded his head thoughtfully. Inwardly, he was elated; the extreme lack of polarity in her soul made her perfect for his true purpose. Yes, he had the machine. Yes, if it were properly calibrated, it could reanimate the dead. But it certainly wasn't calibrated to harmonize energies, as he had long ago lost interest in reanimation.

"Mary." David finished his brandy. His face flushed. "I am not worried about your misdeeds." David watched the mice scurry into Mary's hair and noticed her struggling to breathe. "You have what I need; the strength to finally be one or the other." David reached for an ornate black onyx box. He gingerly removed a scarlet cloth and passed it to Mary. "Breathe deeply. This is the first modest step."

Mary did as requested without hesitation, and her heartbeat grew erratic and weak and her head began to nod.

"My family has lived in this house for generations. Well, actually this is the second house on this spot. When my great, great, great grandfather, Roderick, lived in the original house, the whole thing split in two and sank into the swampy land beneath." David's eye twitched and he licked his lips. "My father says I take after Roderick. He was a sensitive man. He was convinced that the original house was alive." David rubbed his forehead. "I believe it was, and this house, the second house, it is alive as well. But it is quickly being destroyed by the vermin and--."

David twitched. He jerked his head to the side, as a large chunk of plaster fell from the ceiling.

Mary's head fell to the side and the mice ate into her skull.

"It's time, Mary." David took Mary by the arm.

"Yes, David." Mary whispered.

David lifted Mary from her chair. Mary tried to resist but faintness had overcome her. David carried her limp body down the stone stairs. Her feet skidded across each step and thumped onto the next. When he had reached the bottom, David dragged Mary into his workshop. He stripped off her clothes, his erection ostensible, strapped her onto a large wooden table, and attached electrodes about her chest and head.

Mary breathed heavily. Leather restraints pressed into her flesh. Sparks flew, as David hurried to adjust some setting on a control panel and disconnect a few wires from the spiral filaments above the table. He jammed the bare wires into the back of his neck at the end of his spine and waited.

The dark form shrieked with several voices from the corner. The house shuddered and groaned.

Mary drew a few sharp breathes.

Her heart stopped.

Gradually the spiral filaments began to glow. Sparks jumped from point to point on the apparatus and Mary's pure dark energy flowed into David's nervous system.

David's body shook.

The shadowy figure produced a multiplicity of screams, which, as David's body and mind were overwhelmed by Mary's energy, condensed into the mad snarl of a single voice.

David fell to the rough stone floor. He was dead for a moment. When his heart resumed beating, it did so with greater gusto than ever before.

David removed the electrodes and stood before his unwitting benefactor. Mary's flesh was ashen. Her face expressed an ease and comfort that was lacking during her tormented life.

David, with rough, powerful movements, disconnected the electrodes and removed the leather straps that held Mary tight upon the table. He moved onto the table and began stomping Mary's middle and did not stop until her eyes burst outward and her guts smashed beneath his feet, as if making wine.

Exhausted and complete, he dragged her depleted body to a large fireplace, doused it with gasoline, and set it alight.

David watched her flesh burn with single-minded attention. He smiled.

On the open field, the house loomed; large and foreboding. Dark smoke wafted from the chimney.

Mike Jansen & Michael Blommaert
Hoosier infestation

Jeff runs. Because running is all that is left

The old warehouses along the White River were one of the few spots that haven't been rejuvenated by Indiana municipal development projects. Many of the small panes in the high windows are broken and those that are still intact are nearly opaque from dust and silt. The residual paint on the window-frames is World War Two brown. The entrance is boarded up, just like most ground floor windows, except for one, at the back, hidden by low brush.

William climbs inside and hears the cracking sound of old, discarded syringes beneath his worn out boots, a familiar sound, almost soothing, because it associates, somehow, with home. In addition there's a wisp of fear, a scent perhaps, something animal, old newspapers, moist, moldy, the soft drip-drip of a far off, leaking tap. Memories of nights filled with dark thoughts, drowned in vodka and heroin, topped off with weed and loud punk rock, anything to silence the mess of warped images in his head. This is not his personal hell, but it is his torture room, filled with the tools of his trade. He calls it 'home,' and he is all too happy to share his misery with the street scum even more down on their luck than he, and they gladly ingest his specific poison.

From his bedroom windows on the first floor, Jeff sees the middle-aged man amble along. He wore a long rain coat, wrinkled, with large sweat spots below his arm pits, tattered and torn. In each of his coat pockets is a bottle without a cap, the contents invisible. Every second lamppost the man leans his head against the cold iron, as if he is trying to cool his face on the metal. A swig from the left bottle is followed by one from the right bottle. Jeff wonders how this man has gotten this far down on his luck to be getting drunk on the street. He has seen his parents drink too much, but only on nights out with friends or family. Never just like that, with so much aggression, as if the need for the next swig controls the man. Jeff wonders if that brought the man to his current state, but at that moment he spots, just for a second, two dark creatures clinging to the man's pants, with unearthly red eyes that seem to glow in the light of the afternoon sun and with claws and teeth visible and stained red.

Jeff blinks and looks again, but there's nothing. He rubs his eyes and wonders if his mother was right when she said he might need glasses. He looks again and it seems a small horde of dark creatures surrounds the man. The scene reminds him of a pack of wolves surrounding a wounded caribou, waiting for it to succumb, at which point they will attack the defenseless beast like a living tidal wave of flesh, bone and teeth. Blink, the street is empty. Jeff shakes his head, considers, and decides. He takes his coat and a key and leaves. When he closes the door he sees the man a few hundred yards away at the bus stop, taking a bus to the Amtrak station.

It's happening again, Neil thinks. He leans against the next lamppost to rest his head and the support helps him in taking sips from his left and right bottle. The combination muffled the world around him and was enough to keep the rats off. Oh, he knows they're around, they always are, waiting for a chance to take a bite, but the booze keeps them away. It was one of the first lessons he learned, years ago, when he saw them first. And he calls them rats, but they're not. He really never managed to get a good look, as if they somehow avoided his direct gaze and he only sees them from the corners of his eyes. But that is enough; he has witnessed their work often, especially with the other homeless. During winter they showed up in large numbers, as if their intention was to suck the warmth from him and the other homeless people. And perhaps it was. Like with Uncle Buck, who they found behind the Amtrak Station frozen to death inside his cardboard box. At least, that's what the officer said he called to the alley, but Neil had seen the bite marks and the red eyes that stared at him from underneath dumpsters, as if saying: "Your turn will come."

He takes another swig from the left bottle. Whisky, cheap stuff, but together with the Vodka from his right pocket it keeps him just drunk enough that the rats don't want him. But he feels his head spin, his thoughts churn and run through his head and he sees the world around him twist and change, like looking at two or maybe three strange worlds simultaneously, worlds that are not Earth, but strange and Bosch-like, filled with devils and demons and he has this uncomfortable feeling they can see him too, although there seems to be no real reason for it.

He increases his pace slightly, his thoughts clear momentarily: *It's happening again*. As usual only very little will actually help, except for a visit to Mr. Ink. He knows his dealer's name really is

Will or William, no last name as far as he knows, but the bright colored tattoos on his arms and shoulders, pictures of fantastic monsters surrounded by intriguing Celtic patterns, have earned him the nickname "Mr. Ink."

The bus for the Amtrak Station drives just around the corner and as soon as the doors open, he pushes inside. One look from his bloodshot eyes at the driver is enough to earn him a free ride. Some people you don't mess with.

The sun is merciless and nearly burns his eyes out, but his eyelids refuse to close. William has been here before. He knows this is his personal Hell, the big rock with the sharp points that press up into his back in exactly the wrong places, the too-blue sky with the too-large sun that singes his pale skin. Around him only desert, no vegetation, and no sign of life, to the horizon that seems to shimmer in the scalding air. Occasionally he thinks he sees pale eyes, observing him, the vague outlines of the head of the Jackal god, but when he tries to focus it is no more than air.

His arms are tied to the rock, the ropes cutting into his flesh. His feet too so that he is stretched out, his naked body a helpless prey to the glowing hot sun. In the white light the pictures of monsters that he has had tattooed on his body in the past years, stand out clearly. There's still enough white space left to last a long time, but the thought of what will happen when that's no longer the case, frightens him on a deep, primordial level. *Jesus,* he thinks, *help me!* But he knows his cry for help falls on deaf ears, which he himself may just be the redeemer, no matter how bizarre that thought really is.

He never remembers arriving here. Perhaps it's a dream, perhaps a hallucination, but he cannot be certain, too much alcohol and drugs. A cause for his appearing here he also never found, all he knows are the consequences of his short, sometimes longer, painful stay on this rock.

His first tattoo he did himself, not with ink, but with a razor sharp knife that he used to cut the outlines in his skin of the creature he had seen crawling from his body there on that rock, or that had tried to leave his body. But his skin stretched, painful as that was, with too many small sharp clawed legs pushing against his muscle and bone. His skin appeared more tough than usual in the bright light, allowing it to stretch and turn nearly translucent, displaying the nightmare that was trying to crawl from it in all its horrific glory.

The scars the knife left behind were enough to give him relief and the horror that haunted him days and nights, departed him through its likeness in angry red healing skin, during one of his deliriums. At least, that's what he thought, he could never be certain.

One of the free places on his shoulder started to burn, a feeling he knows well. As he watches, something moves under his skin, a sickening squirming that seems to create room for itself and pushes against the outer layer, like it wants to get out and be born.

However, William knows it will not survive this world, let alone come out and he prepares for the agonizing pain that is about to follow. He is not disappointed and the head of a dark creature, a horror, presses against his outer skin layer, pushes it outward until it is stretched across teeth and too big eyes. William screams until his throat is sore and his screaming becomes something remote that seems to emanate from a different mouth.

His final thought is that he needs to visit a tattoo shop soon, now the image is still fresh in his memory. Darkness ends the pain.

Jeff takes the next bus, only a few minutes after the last one that the middle aged man entered. With luck he might still find him at the Amtrak Station. He did not walk very fast and his young legs will allow him to catch up.

Except the driver there are three other people in the bus. A young couple, he dark haired, she white blonde, who only have eyes for each other and busy exploring each other's mouths, and an old man with a skeletal face and a yellow, wrinkled skin. He leans on his cane and looks out the windows often. His face betrays wonder and surprise. Jeff can well imagine that this man hasn't seen Indianapolis in years and that all the changes he sees cause him to wonder. Whether that is positive or negative wonder is not important. Change is not always good, but most certainly not always bad.

He plays Rammstein, but focuses mostly on his own thoughts and the images he just saw. He still isn't sure if they are a reflection of reality or that he created a reality in his mind. However, he tells himself, that is what he wants to ask the middle-aged man. In fact he wants to ask more, because he cannot imagine how someone can let himself slide down so far and so deep, how all dignity and even humanity can be stripped from a person so thoroughly.

He really hopes a conversation with this man will provide him with answers. What did he think he saw, but also answers to the questions he has been wrestling with for some time, questions about the meaning of life, and existing, and the purpose of the things he must do. A different perspective to the protected environment he has grown up in.

The bus enters the Amtrak Station and halts at one of the many stops. Jeff gets out and just sees the man he was following cross the road in the direction of E South Street. Cars honk because he does not seem to care about traffic lights and just wanders ahead. Jeff hurries after him, but when he rounds the corner he no longer sees the middle-aged man. With a feeling of desperation Jeff looks around, but the man he follows is nowhere to be seen. He blinks a couple of times until finally his eyes notice a small, shadowy silhouette that appears to have two red, glowing eyes. He follows those eyes to a dark alley between buildings and he feels, he knows, that is where he must go. He puts his hands in his pockets, increases the volume of Rammstein and makes haste.

Neil is in a hurry. Usually booze or pills will sedate him, or maybe a large joint, and life is something he experiences at the speed that agrees with him, but the feeling that's coming up inside him forces him to act. It wasn't always like this, but in recent months he has had this nagging feeling more often and only one cure exists, that Mister Ink provides. For a price.

Neil's mind does not correlate the fact that the feelings never existed until he first met Mister Ink. Or that maybe there's a connection with his regular visits and the pictures of horrific creatures that appear everywhere on his body. He has a tattoo that he had placed on one of his shoulders, but he cannot recall any visits to the tattoo shop after that. And the horrific expressions staring at him in the mirror are definitely not his specific taste.

However, Mr. Ink has a special something, a potion that brings oblivion that scares the rats with their hungry stares away. Kwamor, Mr. Ink calls it and it is prohibitively expensive, but Neil obtained sufficient cash with which to buy the drink and enough pills and weed to stay intoxicated for more than a week. The first and also last time he tried to live without it, in fact the one time his money was late, shadows set upon him in the alley he was sleeping in. When he closes his eyes he again hears his own screaming and wailing of that night and he remembers the deep wounds tooth and claw inflicted on him, some of them physical, but most spiritual. From that moment on he makes sure. If his money is not there in time, he will get it from somewhere, regardless of the cost to him or to his victims.

He wanders from alley to alley and he keeps clear of places that are illuminated by the low sun. The bright light burns his eyes and rekindles bad memories related to the sun and a blue sky, memories that also include pale eyes and the vague outlines of a jackal's head. Fortunately buildings here are high enough that in this time of year the rays of the sun are often obstructed and the world behind them is cloaked in deep shadow.

He leans against a dented, steel door and takes a couple of swigs from left and right. It's not really helping, but the motion of putting the bottles to his mouth sooths him and already provides him with a slight buzz that is mostly just in his mind. His logical brain understands this, but the fear lurking in the background, fed by the red-eyed shadows that are always near, flood his body with adrenalin, making him more alert, and the awareness of impending doom drives him on and on.

He walks through a low tunnel and arrives at a set of low warehouses, dilapidated, messy, with a view of high rises and renovated office buildings. Four warehouses in a row, each more deteriorated than the next, with rotten window-frames and broken glass, either from old age or thrown stones. For a moment he imagines he is in the presence of old giants or trolls with dangerously sharp teeth from which pieces are missing, but he blinks and shakes his head. No time to hallucinate right now, oblivion waits.

The tattoo is fresh. Terrance looks it over in the broken mirror in his room. Three simple sixty watt bulbs light up the space. He does not remember going out, but the image on his shoulder must have been drawn by something or someone and he can almost feel the needles injecting ink at high speed underneath his skin.

The picture's detail is nearly bizarre. Every ridge, every spot, every sharp pointed fang of the small creature is visible. *Life like*, he thinks. His eyes in the mirror are blood shot and his head hurts something vicious. He knows what is coming what his preparations must be to mitigate the pain.

His hands shaking he opens a drawer of an old, decrepit IKEA cupboard that he found on the street. It contains plastic bags, some filled with yellow green, dried flowers, some filled with black or dark brown slices and a few that contain a readymade joint. He picks one of the latter and lights it near the window with his lighter. The sweet smoke fills his longs, calms him and almost immediately his headache recedes.

As always he remembers his time on the rock, he can almost feel the sharp points in his back. He inhales fresh air and alternates it with drags from the joint. Postponing the inevitable nausea as long as possible will result in his time above the bucket to barf his guts out being shorter. There's also a glass vase on the table to catch what comes after he has emptied his stomach.

He feels the wave of half-digested pizza rise and in two steps he is at the white bucket next to the table. The brown, acidic waves flood upwards through his throat and splash down again. He nearly chokes on small particles that enter his nose, causing more retching. When his stomach is empty, his bowels start to bubble and he grabs the glass vase above him on the table. He waits patiently until his midriff convulses and a stream of clear liquid leaves his throat, which he deposits inside the vase. Exhausted he leans against the dirty, fabric covered couch that was already old fashioned and filthy in the seventies.

Terrance breathes in great heaves then bursts out in laughter for several minutes. Suddenly he is silent and tears drop from his eyes. *This is no way to live*, he thinks. *But it's what I know, what I have.* He gets up with the vase and searches for and finds a few small glass bottles in the kitchen sink. The labels contain the word "morphine", only barely legible. He carefully fills them from the glass vase, puts a cap on them and places them in the nearly empty fridge. He shakes his head. *Stupid sheep even pay for it.*

He lies on the couch, exhausted, and not much later he begins to snore.

The bulbs start to flicker and their light output is drastically reduced, as if they were waiting for this moment. The shadows move and from below and behind anything that harbors shadows, red eyes stare at Terrance.

On his shoulder the fresh tattoo bulges and slowly the shape of the nightmare creature extrudes from his flesh until it is nearly loose from the sleeping man. It shakes its bony tail and pulls free from the shoulder. The tattoo is covered in bloody slime and the horror staggers along the back of the couch and disappears in the shadows, hungry for fresh meat.

Jeff follows the middle-aged man. Near a dark alley he waits a while so the man won't see him. This is a quiet part of Indianapolis and he rather no one sees or notices him.

When he leaves the alley, the sun sets in the west and in the dusk the shadows seem to jump forward and nearly touch his feet in the light circle of a street lamp that has just switched on.

The man he is following is nowhere to be seen, but the dilapidated warehouses were obviously his destination, there is no other option. On the first floor of the first warehouse a few lights are on, so Jeff surmises it to be the place he has to go to.

The lights on the first floor flicker and dim. It seems likely someone is inside. He hides behind an old, rusty Chevy, once sky blue, parked to the side of one of the warehouses, observers the other side of the road and waits.

Neil knocks on the window frame at the back, but no answer is forthcoming. It does not matter, he has been inside before, although usually he would be invited. Carefully he climbs through the open window. His sneaker he places on the floor cautiously. He remembers the needle sticking from the sole of his shoe, nearly in his foot, that last time.

He walks through the narrow hallway to the front, where the stairs going up are located. Newspapers were used as a kind of wallpaper here, the yellowed paper a living testament of the occupants of the mid-seventies that put it there. The smell here is musty, rancid almost, scent of old paper, urine, shit, vomit and something different, animal like, like a horde of rats built a nest here. The thought reminds him he saw them more often today than usual and it makes him shiver. He quickly drinks more, but the desired effect remains absent. *Need kwamor*, he thinks.

Each stair tells a story as he ascends, from miserable creaking to enthusiastic squeaking, and every sound in between. At the top of the stairs is a landing with a single door that is slightly ajar. Soft, yellow light shines through and he carefully pushes it open. The animal scent he smelled earlier is more intense here, although the sweet scent of freshly smoked weed masks it to an extent. Neil sniffs deeply and his body reacts with hunger.

He hears the soft snoring coming from the couch and he walks into the room. Next to the table is a white bucket with fresh vomit, from which a sour smell emanates. He avoids coming close and walks up to Mr. Ink. The fresh tattoo on his shoulder is clearly defined in the soft light and he blinks when he recognizes one of the horrors that he sometimes notices staring at him from the shadows.

He carefully taps Mr. Ink on his arm and even grabs hold of it and gently shakes the sleeping man.

Mr. Ink suddenly snaps awake, a wild look in his eyes. "Wha... Whasgoin' on?"

Neil steps back and holds up his hands. "Easy, it's just me, Neil." He points at the door. "It was open."

Mr. Ink shakes his head. He gets up, walks up to the fridge and takes a small bottle of fake coke, which he quickly drinks half empty. "What do you want? The usual?"

Neil shakes his head. He shows a small stack of dollar bills. "No, today I need the heavy stuff."

Mr. Ink grins. "It so happens a fresh supply just arrived." He waves at the couch. "Have a seat, you almost passed out last time, remember?"

"It's powerful stuff. I need it," Neil says. "I think you know what it feels like."

Mr. Ink nods. "Do I ever."

Neil sits on the couch and Mr. Ink takes one of the small bottles he just filled from the fridge. He holds it up against one of the bulbs and notices the fluid is now crystal clear, not a trace of impurity.

"Here you go," Mr. Ink says and hands Neil the bottle.

Neil reciprocates with dollar bills, then downs the contents of the bottle in one go. It tastes like water, but the feeling that immediately spreads through his body is divine. He sits back in the musty pillows that smell no better or worse than he himself and before his mind's eye worlds drift apart, the worlds with the demons in them become distant memories and all he sees is a blistering desert under a clear blue sky with the silhouette of a jackal god at the horizon, laughing at him. His eyes turn back and he begins to snore.

Mr. Ink closes the door, switches the lights off and throws himself on the filthy bed in the bedroom. Neil will be in a stupor for the next few days, no need to worry about him. And he has performed his duty, as always, which means that as a reward his sleep will have no dreams in the coming weeks, just the way he likes it.

Jeff gets up when the lights on the first floor are switched off. He crawls along the building until he reaches the back. Nearby a large truck thunders past and in the resulting noise he pushes through the brush.

The broken window in the rotten window frame is like a dark eye staring at him. He shivers but mans up and puts one leg over the frame. As he tries to stand up, he feels a sharp pain in his foot and he quickly pulls it up. In the weak light of a nearby street lamp he sees a used needle sticking from the sole of his shoe and he mumbles a string of curses. He takes it out and pushes it into the wood of the window frame. With his foot he first wipes the floor clean, before putting his weight on it.

His eyes need to adjust to the darkness, but when that happens, he sees a narrow hallway leading to the front. He follows it to stairs leading up. There is a scent of old, musty papers. The floor is mostly covered in yellowed paper, newspapers, magazines and unopened mail.

The bottom step creaks abominably and Jeff cowers. He carefully leans forward and takes the next step, which also creaks fearsomely. He looks up and in the darkness he sees darker shadows. A set of red eyes observes him. Quickly more pairs of red eyes appear, all around him, in shadowy corners.

He steps back and of a sudden feels something soft and hairy fall on his head and neck, small paws with sharp claws grab hold of his hair and neck and then a sharp, stinging sensation in the back of his neck. He grumbles and grabs it, a bony creature, skin over bones with a mottled, felt-like hide. He throws it from him in disgust.

Fuck, Jeff thinks, *rats, lots of them.* It seems like they are waiting, as if they have seen the strength he used to throw off their brethren and now they are careful. He turns and walks back to the rear of the building. Behind him he hears the patter of many small paws and nails scratching the wood of the stairs.

He dives through the open window, landing in the brush. He feels thorns cut his skin, through his clothes and he feels tears well up in his eyes. He wrestles loose, then takes off in the direction of the alley. He feels his neck with his hand, which comes back covered in brown in the artificial light of the street lamps. *Bastard got me good*, he thinks, *pfff, it's hot.*

He stops at a street lamp and presses his forehead against the cool metal. As soon as he lifts his head again, the world around him seems to change and he looks straight into the eyes of a dozen gruesome demons that appear to be looking him over. He blinks, then rubs his eyes and when he opens them again, the world is back to normal, although he feels the presence of 'something' and it frightens him.

Jeff looks around and in the shadows at the entrance of the alley he sees a few dozen silhouettes and corresponding pairs of red eyes that seem to glow in the darkness. He feels fear in his heart and a chill runs down his spine. Quickly he crosses the street and faster than he usually does, he hastens towards the Amtrak Station, or at the very least a place where many people come together.

He passes several people and they are different than he is used to. Two men with extremely long faces look at him from a quiet bar and he feels a deep coldness in the pit of his stomach. An old woman, covered in sores, crosses his path, pushing a baby wagon. He notices tentacles rising up from the wagon, accompanied by a penetrating baby wail that sets his teeth on edge and that seems to cling to him, no matter how hard he runs away from her. Drops of fear induced sweat prick his scalp.

There is no relaxing, as soon as he stops or slows down, he hears the patter of dozens of small paws with sharp nails and he knows he must continue.

From his window William observes the lonely figure running off through the alley, followed by dozens of dark shadows. He suspects it to have been the cause of the creaking of the stairs just now, someone trying to climb up, but for obvious reasons waylaid and now on the run.

Doesn't matter. He yawns and stretches, before returning to bed. *They always come back. Always.*

Jeff runs, because running is all that is left. Fear drives him, relentless, continuously. He runs around the corner, seeking the relative safety of the Amtrak Station that holds enough people at all hours of the day, enough to keep the monsters away. He nearly bumps into a woman. She turns. Her face is blank, no eyes, just a mouth that opens impossibly wide with teeth dripping black bile and a tongue that darts around, sniffing the air.

Curved razor claws swoosh through the air in the spot Jeff just occupied.

Because Jeff runs . . .

Sonia Fogal
Daddy's Girl

Five-year-old Lisa Caldwell beamed as she ran to her father, her yellow-beaded necklace bouncing on her chest.

"Come on, Daddy! It's time!"

As a child Michael had failed to save his mother from his father's brutal beatings. His pleas to his brother to seize the chance at a happy family life given to them by their mother's second marriage failed. Instead he chose life with a father he couldn't stand to be apart from, even if it meant a life of pain. Lisa was his salvation. The cycle of abuse that was his family's legacy would stop with her. He would not mess it up. He stretched his arms out toward her.

"Hop up here, big girl!"

She jumped onto his lap with a grin, her eyes wide.

"Ready?" he asked.

"Ready!" She screamed and laughed as they raced down the hall.

"Hop down," he whispered as they reached her bedroom. She slid off his lap and watched as he eased into the room and placed his right index finger in front of his lips. "Shhh." She poked her head around the doorway to watch him slide the door open and peer inside.

He looked at her and smiled. "No monsters!" he declared.

Lisa bounced on her tiptoes. "Mommy!" she called.

Mary worked the night shift at the truck stop by I-65 so she could tend to the needs of both Michael and Lisa. Henryville, IN wasn't exactly a bustling metropolis but it had a steady stream of truckers 24/7. She sometimes felt like a mother to them both. An exploding grenade in Vietnam left Michael paralyzed from the waist down so he needed help with some very basic things. Chronically sleep-deprived, she kept going on pure will.

"Here I come," she said as she pulled her hair up for work.

Lisa pointed to her bed and Mary got on her hands and knees to look underneath. "Nope, no monsters," she said and swatted her bottom. "Now into bed."

She hopped onto Michael's lap.

"Aww. Can I sit in Daddy's lap for story tonight? Please?"

They both stuck out their bottom lips and gave her the most pitiful look they could manage.

She tapped her foot and rolled her eyes. "Just tonight." She smiled and leaned over to kiss her cheek. "Goodnight, baby. I'll be here when you wake up."

"Nighty night, Mommy."

Mary leaned over and placed her hand on Michael's cheek. "I've gotta go. See ya in the morning." She kissed him. "I love you."

In love with her since they were fifteen years old, her natural and simple beauty still mesmerized him. He hated the burden his disability put on her. She deserved so much more. The moments she kissed him brought him peace like nothing else could. "I love you, too. Don't work too hard."

Mary turned and waved to them both. "Bye-bye". She blew them kisses as she walked out the door.

After reading "Are You My Mother?" for the fourth night in a row, Michael turned her lamp off. Her arms flew to his neck.

"I hate the dark," she told him. "What if the monsters come and get me?"

"There's no such thing as monsters," he lied. Monsters do exist. He knew two personally--his father and the evil creature known as war. "I'm right here. You'll be fine."

He pried her arms from his neck. A cool breeze drifted through the window by her bed and moonlight allowed them to see each other in the dark room. Michael rested his palm on the necklace she wore.

Vietnam was a real-life horror story full of haunting scenes. A man's ankle bones in his hands, his flesh falling from his napalm-burned feet; wartime bonds stronger than voluntary lifetime associations, terminated in a mere moment as mortar fire decimated bodies just feet away--these and countless other tragedies haunted Michael. This world of mindless violence didn't allow time-out for a human moment of mourning, or anything but a constant push toward the enemy soldiers they were expected to kill without hesitation.

Guilt tortured his conscience--guilt for not saving the lives of men he watched die during his service, and guilt for coming home to a life of safety while they stayed to fight for their lives. It was a Vietnamese girl that seared his soul with guilt the most.

Vietcong engaged them in gunfire and led them to a village where women and children scattered in an effort to escape the barrage of bullets. His conscience begged him to stop. These weren't soldiers. They were just people trying to live their lives in a war zone. He knew though that to stop shooting would be to die and leave one less person to protect the men he fought with, men like him that had families to go home to, so he kept going, firing only at the armed and hoping for the best, whatever that was in this nightmare.

The girl appeared to be about Lisa's age. He watched her clutch her yellow-beaded necklace as she fled. He ran to her when a bullet to her neck knocked her to the ground. Firing with one hand, he used his other hand to drag her away from the deadly chaos and trampling feet.

He thought of Lisa as he looked at her blood-spattered neck and face and wondered if she clutched that necklace to her death because for some reason she believed it would protect her.

Out of the sight of other soldiers, he collapsed on the Vietnamese girl's body in grief. No child should have to witness such violence. His commitment to stop the cycle of violence with Lisa and to create a world of love and security, free from such madness and danger was reaffirmed in that moment. He took the simple string of beads from the girl and when he returned home gave them to Lisa, a sign of his commitment to keeping her safe.

He placed his palm on her necklace after the story. "Don't be afraid. I'll sit here while you fall asleep. If you wake up and I'm not here, just put your hand on your necklace and think of me. OK?"

"OK, Daddy. Can I rub your back in the morning?"

The doctors called the lower back pain Michael suffered daily "phantom pain." They said the nerves in the area were dead, that the pain he felt was not real. It was very real to Michael. He and Lisa started every day with her rubbing his lower back. Even if massage would work, her little hands weren't strong enough to make a difference, but she felt like she was helping and he treasured the time together.

"Of course. I'd be sad if you didn't!"

"I love you, Daddy."

"I love you too, sweetheart. Now get in bed."

She kissed his cheek and did as she was told. He held her hand until she fell asleep.

Willie Jones slipped through her window that night, a shadowy bug in black attire and night-vision goggles. Her instinctive jerk upon waking was stilled by his knees on her legs. His clammy hand on her mouth muffled her yell. "If you want to see your crip daddy and pretty mommy alive again, you shut up and do as you're told. Got it?"

She nodded her compliance, her heart a jackhammer in her chest.

He used a rag from one back pocket to stuff her mouth and a rag from the other to blindfold her. He tossed her out the window with all the care of someone tossing a bag of garbage into a dumpster, then ran to his black van with her in his arms.

Once inside the van he cuffed her ankles and wrists, sniffing as his nose dripped on her. The pounding of his boots faded as he walked to the front of the van to start the engine and she let the tears flow.

Ten minutes into their drive he groaned and grabbed his stomach. He pulled to the side of the road and vomited, then got behind the wheel and continued driving. He pulled behind an abandoned house and backed up to some cellar doors. He opened both the van doors and the cellar doors, then drug her by her feet and threw her over his shoulder like a sack of potatoes, constantly checking his surroundings for witnesses.

Small animals scratched across the dirt floor, fleeing this intruder into their world of the unknown and unseen. He carried her to the farthest corner without a sound, then groaned as he leaned over and let her free-fall from his shoulder. Before she hit the ground he had a gun pulled and was firing at rats in a corner. "Oh yeah!" he screamed after his last shot, then turned and vomited. "God damn it."

He picked up his kills and dropped them on her tear-soaked face, then groaned and sniffed as he pulled her trembling body to his face by her cuffs. "Gonna score me some smack to cure my ills and get my share of a deal. Then we're out of here, princess." She collapsed into a pile on the ground when he released her.

"Your mamma and daddy underestimated me! Ain't nobody gonna take what's mine!" He slammed the cellar doors shut. They didn't open again for three days.

She slept by the bloody masses of fur and Jones' vomit after the slamming doors trapped her in that hell hole. She woke to the gnawing of cannibalistic rats instead of her mom saying "Good morning, Sunshine." She wanted to smell her daddy's cologne, but instead smelled her urine-soaked nightgown that now clung to her cold skin.

Was this punishment for something she did to this man she didn't remember ever seeing before? Her daddy--who would take care of his back? He would be sad if she wasn't there to make it stop hurting. She felt her necklace against her chest and it gave her temporary comfort and assurance that he would save her. She fell into an exhausted sleep.

A tickle on her nose woke her the next day. The glowing eyes of a possum stared back. Her heart pounded in her ears as she screamed. It hissed, baring its small pointy teeth, and crept closer. She watched it back away and begin feasting on the carcasses inches from her face.

She faded in and out of consciousness the next few days, wakened once by the splash of water on her face as Jones shoved a bowl in her face. "Got medicated but the money's gone. We'll be here a little longer. You don't do me any good dead though, so drink up." He lifted her head by her hair and dropped it next to the bowl. She whimpered when her head hit the ground. "You're like a little puppy, crying and drinking from a bowl."

Mary sat on the couch sobbing into her hands when the police arrived.

"It's all my fault. I was stupid. Young and stupid."

Officer Klein introduced himself and sat in the chair to Michael's right. Mary sat on the couch to Michael's left.

"Her father did this," Mary said.

Officer Klein leaned forward, resting his forearms on top of his thighs, and looked at Michael.

"You?" he asked.

"No." He shook his head. "My brother."

"Her and your brother?"

"She didn't know. Our dad abused us. Willie lived with him. I lived with my mom and her second husband, Henry Caldwell. I didn't tell Mary about my real dad or Willie until we were engaged. She was already pregnant with his baby."

Tears flooded his face as he remembered his brother's screams as his father's belt buckle smacked his bare bottom. He remembered his face, tortured by the violence as a young boy, defiant and determined not to show his pain as he got older. His father had stolen their childhood just as war had stolen this girl's childhood.

"I never told him Lisa was his. It wouldn't take much for him to figure it out though," Mary said.

"Your name's the same as the second husband. He adopted you?" he asked Michael.

"Yeah, but not Willie. His last name's Jones."

Officer Klein shook his head and laughed. "Willie Jones is your brother?"

Michael looked at Mary and then at the officer. "Yeah. Why?"

"Oh, I know Willie Jones. Home from Vietnam for a year and I've picked him maybe a dozen times. Drugs mostly. Picking fights a couple of times. A real piece of work."

"You have to find him before he hurts her," Mary pleaded.

"It won't take long. I'm familiar with the dregs of society he hangs with. I'll get them to cough it up."

He followed a trail to Willie Jones within a week then watched the house three days to figure out his routine. Then came the night he parked in an unmarked car, waiting for him to leave the house, backup waiting for his call. Right on schedule, Willie backed his black van out of the driveway shortly after 3 AM. Klein called for backup then pulled behind the house and shut off his engine. He saw the cellar doors and the padlock on them right away. He pounded the wooden doors with the soles and heels of his boots. His backup had just appeared when he called Lisa's name through the hole. She didn't respond. He called twice more and she responded.

"Daddy?"

Klein perked up.

"It's not Daddy, Lisa. I'm Officer Klein. I'm going to take you to your daddy." He told another officer to call for an ambulance.

She fell to the floor in tears while Klein and his men tore at the doors with their bare hands until the hole was big enough for him to enter the cellar. Rats scattered when he shined his flashlight.

"Lisa?"

"I'm over here." She wept.

He yelled to his men that he had found her and lifted her tiny skin-and-bones body and handed her up through the hole in the doors.

"Got her."

"I want my daddy," she cried.

"You'll see him soon, little one," he told her, then told another man to go in the house and get a glass of water for her to sip on until the ambulance arrived.

Officer Klein rang the Caldwell's' doorbell about 5 AM. Mary answered.

"We found Lisa. She's on her way to the hospital."

"Oh my God," Mary said, her hands covering her mouth and tears filling her eyes. "Hospital? Is she OK? What's wrong with her?"

"She looked dehydrated and she was weak. Just having her checked out to make sure nothing else is wrong and get some fluids in her."

"My poor baby." She turned from the door and headed for the bedroom. "Michael! Michael! They found her! They found Lisa!"

He broke into tears. "Where is she?"

"She's in the hospital getting checked out by doctors," she said as she helped him into his wheelchair. She rolled him into the living room, where Officer Klein waited.

"Can we go see her?" Michael asked him.

"Of course. I'll give you a ride. It'll be faster."

Willie Jones went to jail and Lisa's few physical wounds healed quickly. Her mental and emotional wounds were deeper and longer-lasting. Michael could relate to some of the things she struggled with. They both jumped at the backfire of a car, Michael because it reminded him of gunfire in Vietnam and Lisa because it reminded her of gunfire in the cellar. Michael feared crowds, not trusting who was a friend and who was the enemy. Lisa feared the dark and basements or cellars, not trusting what she couldn't see. She lay in his arms the first few weeks, refusing to leave his side, enter a dark room, or sleep with the light off.

One afternoon she fell asleep in his lap on the front porch. When she woke it was dark. She screamed and threw her arms around his neck. "No, Daddy! Please! Go inside! Go inside!"

"Lisa!" he yelled through her screams. "Stop! Stop! It's OK!" She cried on his shoulder. "Shh, shh," he said.

"Please, Daddy. Please. Go inside!"

"OK, OK." He rolled to the front door and Lisa opened the door for them to go in. Once inside, she laid her head on his shoulder and wept. She quieted in a few minutes.

"Lisa," he said. He set her hands on her lap and placed his hands on top of them.

"You remember the bully at the playground last summer?"

She nodded. "He wouldn't let me swing."

He nodded.

"It made you really mad for a while, didn't it?"

She nodded again.

"But what did you finally do?"

"I told him he wasn't gonna keep me from swinging!" her tone stronger.

Michael smiled.

"That's right! And then what happened?"

She smiled. "I got on the swing and he pushed me off. And I got back on." She was talking more quickly now. "And he pushed me again. And I got back on again! And he pushed me again." She smiled. "And then . . . I pushed him!"

"That's right!"

"And his mom got mad at me for pushing him! That wasn't fair!"

"I know. A lot of things in life aren't fair. But he didn't mess with you any more, did he?"

She sat up straight and smiled. "Nope!"

"Being afraid of the dark is keeping you from sleeping in the dark and going outside at night, just like the bully kept you from swinging. You have to stand up to it and tell it to get out of your way, just like you did with the bully."

She stared at their hands in her lap.

"Does that make sense?" he asked her.

"Kinda."

"Well, that's good enough for now. We'll beat that fear, just like you beat the bully. Don't ever let anyone or anything make you feel like you can't do something. They're not the boss of you, you are."

"OK, Daddy."

"So," he said. "What's the book going to be tonight?'

She searched her bookshelf and found the one she wanted. "This one!" she exclaimed and handed him "Chicken Little".

He smiled. "Good choice. Up on the bed now. And close your eyes."

She did as she was told and Michael did as he promised, sitting by her bed as long as he could, then going to his own bed.

Lisa fought her fear of the dark for years. She went to a couple of slumber parties, but ended up calling her parents to pick her up each time, afraid to go to sleep away from them. Trick or treating terrified her not only because of the dark, but also because of the masks and the unknown faces behind them. She had only a handful of dates and those were for daytime activities. There were no dances, or football games. Her fear cut her off from a social life and dictated her schedule. She never ventured out to the grocery at night or took the night shift on a job.

She also carried her fear of cellars and basements with her for years. She never owned a home with a basement and boarded up the window in her bedroom and slept with the lights on in every home she had.

One night as she sat in her boarded-up bedroom watching TV, her mom called.

"Hello?"

"Lisa, this is Mom."

Lisa sensed the tension in her mother's voice. "What's wrong, Mom?"

"I need you." She struggled to breathe between sobs.

"Mom, what's wrong? It's dark outside."

"Please, Lisa. Please come." Her voice faded, followed by screams. Lisa hung up the phone and grabbed her keys.

The yellow necklace from her childhood was part of her keychain. It was her security and a daily reminder of her father. Her heart pounded and beads of sweat formed on her forehead as she stared out at the dark, moonless night, gripping her keychain and contemplating the walk to the car.

She knew it was crazy but she imagined Willie Jones or someone else lurking in the darkness, watching her. She opened her door and stared at her car then closed her eyes and remembered her mom's cries on the phone.

Come on, Lisa. Let's do this. You'll hate yourself forever if something happens to her because you couldn't get over your stupid fear.

She opened her eyes and focused on the car and thoughts of her mom as she stepped into the night.

As she neared her mother's home she noted the solid line of glowing streetlights on both sides of the street, with the exception of the one by her mother's driveway. As she pulled into her driveway she noticed the porch light her mother had turned on at sundown every day in memory was also out. She stepped out of her car and gripped her keychain once more before putting it in her pocket and heading for the porch.

Pieces of the shattered porch light crunched under her feet as she walked to the open door. She reached for the light switch just inside the door and called for her mother. Both the light switch and her calls yielded no results. She decided to feel her way to the single lamp in the room, a floor lamp in the far corner.

She carefully maneuvered around the coffee table and reached her destination only to find the lamp gone. As she turned to feel her way along the wall and into the kitchen on the other side she tripped over the lamp as it lay on the floor. She caught herself with her hands, pushing shards of the light bulb into her hands and hitting her head on the coffee table on her way down. She stood to go to the kitchen, where she could clean her wound.

The neighbors to the right had their lights around the edge of their patio, illuminating the kitchen a bit. Blood covered her palm. It stung like hell when she ran hot water over it. Her blood splattered the sink in black shadows as she shook the excess water from her hand.

A scream travelled up the stairs to the basement and through the open door behind her and to the left.

"Mom?" she yelled from the sink.

"I'm down here, Lisa!"

She wrapped her hand loosely in a towel and walked to the open door. There were shuffling feet, then a man's voice. "There's a flashlight on the table to your left. Pick it up and turn it on." She knew the voice. She heard it every night in her dreams. It was Willie Jones.

His voice ran through her mind along with the smell of her own urine, Jones' vomit and the rotting rats. She jumped when his shout brought her back to the present. "Now!"

She turned on the flashlight and aimed it down the stairs where she saw her mom and Bug Man, night-vision goggles and all. His left arm was wrapped around Mary's neck. His right held a gun he pointed at her head.

The gun--she remembered her mom kept one in the cabinet over the kitchen sink.

"Hey kiddo!" Willie said. "We got us a little reunion here-- a family reunion! Nice, huh?"

A rush of warmth spread through her body and her head spun.

Family? Like hell we're family.

She grabbed the door jamb to keep from falling as all the strength in her legs disappeared.

"Hey, I want you to come down here and join us in this little party. Put that flashlight back first though."

She turned and walked toward the kitchen table to her left but headed for the gun in the cabinet as soon as she knew she was out of Jones's sight. She grabbed the gun with her good hand and put it in the back of her pants, and then put the flashlight on the kitchen table along with the towel around her hand. She walked to the head of the stairs and gazed at the darkness.

"Come on. Mamma and Daddy are here. We'll take care of ya, won't we Mom?"

Don't you dare call yourself my Daddy.

She still didn't budge.

"You get your ass down here or Mamma goes bye-bye."

She took the first step.

"Good girl. Now shut the door behind you." She did as she was told. "Good girl. Come on."

He waved her toward him with his gun even though she was blind in the thick darkness.

She stopped halfway down the stairs, unable to go further.

Willie screamed "Get down here now or I shoot!"

She walked the rest of the way to the bottom.

"Keep coming. Keep coming," he said as he moved backward, holding the gun to her mom's head. "Stop."

You're like a little puppy.

She stopped.

"Good girl," he chuckled. "Sit."

She sat on the floor in the dark while Willie and Mary remained standing.

"Seems like old times, huh kiddo? You like a good story? I do. And this one's a good one. You ready?"

Silence.

"Okay, here we go. Once upon a time there was a pretty girl who was dating this bad guy in high school." His voice had taken on a condescending tone. "This guy was not only bad, he was stupid too, and broke up with her.

"Now this guy's brother had wanted a piece of that for a long time. This was his shot and he took it. He swept her off her feet, treated her like a queen. Then the bitch dumped the good brother and got back together with the bad one, without mentioning to the good brother that she was pregnant with his child."

She clutched the necklace in her pocket and tried to think clearly, ignoring what he was saying.

This is impossible. He can see me but I can't see him. Mom and I are both going to end up dead.

He fired a shot in the air. "I said, are you with me so far?"

"Yes." She curled up in a ball on the floor and listened

"Good. So the bitch and the bad brother get married."

If I get a chance I'll take a shot. Worst that will happen is I end up dead anyway. At least then I go out fighting.

She focused on the direction of his voice as Willie continued. "In the meantime both brothers turn eighteen and Uncle Sam sends them to Vietnam. Bitch has the baby. Good brother hears about it in Nam, does the addition and subtraction and figures out the baby is his.

"Bad brother comes home first. When good brother comes home he tries to take what's his and lands in jail. Messed up, huh?" Willie asked.

She was silent.

"Sit up!" he barked at her. "I asked you a question! Isn't that messed up?"

"Yes." She winced as she used her hands to push her upper body off the floor and then slipped a hand behind her back.

"Do you understand what I'm telling you, baby doll? I don't think you do! I'm your daddy, sweet britches."

Her chest burned with anger. She pulled the gun out of her pants with her good hand and fired it behind her back toward the outside wall. Willie instinctively snapped around to look for an intruder and lost his grip on Mary.

"Who's there?" he said.

Mary fell away from him and to the floor.

As Lisa brought the gun up and shot in the direction of his voice, Mary stumbled up the stairs and threw the flashlight down to the basement. Lisa scrambled to pick it up while Willie's attention was diverted.

The bullet grazed his skin on his right thigh. Panicked, he dropped the gun and reached down to check his leg. As he focused on his leg Lisa grabbed the flashlight and stood.

She pointed the flashlight at him and fired again. This time she hit his shoulder. "You are not my daddy, you scumbag" she yelled, and shot at his other hand when he reached down for his gun. She missed his hand but got him in his ribs.

He held his ribs in pain and shock as he looked pitifully at her and struggled to breathe. His life was in her hands and she found it intoxicating.

"That's right you S.O.B.. You're on the other end of the gun now. How's it feel?" she said and shot his knee. He fell to the floor, writhing in pain.

"Let's get something straight you sorry excuse for a human. I don't care if your blood is in my veins. Michael Caldwell was my dad and you're not good enough to lick his shoes."

"Mom, call the police," she said, as she pointed her gun at him. Sweat covered her forehead and her breathing was heavy. She kicked his gun out of his reach. Jones looked up at her from the floor, helpless.

"You may have donated your sperm but my dad gave me his life."

She shot at the ground next to him then walked to him and slipped his goggles off his head as he gasped for air, for life. "The Bug Man isn't so strong after all, is he?"

He struggled to keep his eyes open.

"Hey, Bug Man. Do me a favor. Play dead."

He looked at her and took his last breath. His eyes closed and his body went limp. Lisa smiled. "That's a good boy."

John D. Stanton

Gary Murphy
Horrorwerk

Professor Roberto Klaus was coming to the sorry point in his long illustrious career when he simply couldn't continue due to age and increasingly bad health. He had been informed that he would die by the end of the month of heart and breathing complications, and did he wish to spend his remaining two weeks in hospital the offer was always there did he decided to choose that option. He had shrugged and casually said no, that he would spend it at home in the bosom of his family, where he was loved and, most of all, respected, rather than spend his few remaining days shuffling around on a ward looking at clinically-clean white walls and floors, counting down the hours. There was no respect in that. Although, he had said rather candidly to the doctors that when the time came he wished for it to be mercifully quick and painless and that he would much prefer to simply "black out" and fall flat on his face rather than seize-up in a contorted rictus, agonized and wretched or twisted out of all recognition. Professor Klaus longed for a graceful demise.

Smoking didn't help, and he smoked a pipe to boot where the nicotine level was much higher than that of a cigarette and he always chose to indulge in the finest and strongest, a lung-dissolving Bulgarian brand he could only buy via a special Internet website. Never without the pipe, it acted as a constant reminder of perpetual ill-health and his stubbornness not to quit. Not that it would make much if any difference now. The hangman's noose was already and had long since been around his neck and tightening with every minute and every hour that passed...

Professor Roberto Klaus had a special gift, however. More importantly, one that he urgently wished to pass down to a family member before it had the chance to evaporate when he died. He did not want this remarkable gift to simply disappear into the pale ether or merely rise and dissolve into the air as his useless and burnt corpse would do in the flames of the crematorium.

Professor Klaus believed his mental powers could somehow be passed on to his 12-year-old grandson by means of a simple blood-transfusion. Or perhaps something that was easier, like the digestion of his blood orally. Either way, young Harley Klaus was the key.

At his home near Leicester Square in an affluent London location, Klaus held a dinner party one evening for family members and a few close friends, just to explain his health situation, his impending demise and say his heartfelt goodbyes. Young Harley he stated would be the main beneficiary to his wealth, his home and his every last asset. But the Professor included he would also leave quite a sizeable chunk of his estate to his only son, George, and his wife, Andrea. He wasn't a heartless, soulless bastard.

George and Andrea never really ever knew of Roberto Klaus' sensory abilities or to what effect they could be administered by mere thought or profound concentration. They had never had reason to be told and the old miser was a private man who spent most his days lecturing at colleges and universities around the world, from New York to Paris, from Switzerland to Moscow. He was a Professor of Science, the Paranormal, and the Holocaust. In his time he had travelled millions of miles, either by ship or by plane, and he was proud to admit that.

However, due to terminally ill-health and his smoking habit, he was forced to mainly keep to Europe, and for the better part stuck to his teachings in London. It was his hometown, after all, and where his heart belonged.

The dark-haired and cherub-faced young boy approached him at the party. Harley said, "Granddad, are you really going to die?"

Roberto Klaus smiled warmly at his grandson. But he felt wounded when he replied, "Nobody lives forever, my boy. But I'll be with you in spirit always. Never forget that."

"I thought professors could work miracles."

Strange that, and Klaus replied, "No man should ever try to eclipse the work of the Lord, Harley. Not as a professor and neither as a human being. Miracles are there to be solely performed by God." He took the boy by the hand. "Come with me into my study, I need to speak to you concerning a matter of great importance."

The study was a large but cosy room adjacent to the main lounge. Entering it for the first time with his grandfather, young Harley was astonished, because for the boy it must have been not dissimilar to being the man who first set foot on the Moon. It was like walking into a world totally alien. Leather and rosewood and mahogany, an air of richness and affluence and seniority, the huge wooden desk and bookshelves that towered to the high ceiling, and the smoky aroma of pipe-tobacco and malt whiskey. It was dark and creepy but also heralded a fascinating adventure for a 12-year-old boy.

"I want you to drink this, Harley. Don't worry. It's only red wine..." He laughed, almost mockingly, and added, "...I started young, and so should my sole begotten grandson."

Harley accepted the goblet without argument and gulped it down like a sailor.

"Good boy," the Professor said and grinned, "Today I'm very proud."

Harley hiccupped and handed the goblet back. "Taste's nice," he said, smiling back, "Can I have another?"

Klaus laughed and held his hands aloft.

"Listen," he said in a low whisper, even if they were in a secluded spot, "We must keep this our little secret. "Mustn't tell mummy and daddy..." He put on a stern face, adding, "...If you do, I'll be very cross. And mummy and daddy won't like the idea of their young boy drinking alcohol, right?" He turned the boy around and playfully slapped his behind. "Now run along!"

As Harley scampered off Professor Roberto Klaus knew his work was done. He leaned back on his paper-laden mahogany desk and chuckled, knowing his legacy was strong and fervent and that his search for a successor was over and completed. Harley would discover his abilities without hindrance and accidently, just as he had as a youngster during the Second World War. Oh Mister Hitler, what you would have offered to possess such a magical ability...

It would have spread throughout the Reich like a disease.

Shortly afterwards, the boy and his parents observed the night was a cool one and said their farewells, saying it was such a nice night they would walk and return in the morning to pick the car up before work. A frail Roberto Klaus seen them off and wished them all the best. He watched the boy in particular as they departed along the street towards the main epicentre of Leicester Square. Harley Klaus looked back over his shoulder and scrutinized the ageing Professor suspiciously.

And it was not long before the trouble, and Klaus" legacy, went into immediate effect in the most corruptive sense.

"My God, Harley," George Klaus implored his son, as the boy stiffened on the sidewalk, "Are you all right, son?" He put his hands on the entranced youth's shoulders and shook him. "Harley! What's the matter? Are you okay? Speak to me!"

Suddenly the worried dad was forced to retract his hands, almost "unsticking" them, for the boy seemed more than just icy cold but at a point of freezing. Removing his hands, he turned to his wife Andrea and despaired. "He's freezing cold," he said. "My God, he's literally like a block of ice!" Harley had begun turning blue with this strange abrupt coldness. George shouted, "Harley! Answer me!"

The boy was in a trance. Until his eyes turned and fixed on George when they seemed to open a secret lock inside the man and switch fear for his son's disposition into a fear for his own mental stability. George and Andrea retreated backwards, for Harley suddenly took on a cold grinning persona and appeared grotesque, almost evil-looking. He took off running across the busy road. And stopped in the middle as a huge red London Transport double-decker bus threatened to run directly into him and mow him down, killing him for sure.

Harley raised his hand and "stared down" the huge scarlet shape approaching.

When he raised his hand, however, so did the bus, giving the appearance it was levitating. And when he cast his hand to the right, the huge bus traversed through the air to the right, flying and crashing into a series of parked cars. And because the bus was occupied, it would later be confirmed there was serious injury caused amongst its many passengers travelling through the Leicester Square vicinity during this time of night.

The Professor heard the racket outside and ran out onto the street, suddenly brutally aware of this night's shameful misjudgement, solely on his part. He was an idiot and a damned fool!

However, the incident occurring did not go undetected by the law in the area and because the vicinity was on high-alert due to a terrorism scare where the miscreants had threatened to bomb the place, and the deadline was tonight, officers were carrying loaded weapons and were decidedly edgy. When the bus transported through the air, they immediately drew their own conclusions, and were deployed to the area en masse, cars and vans and army vehicles flocking from all directions, sirens blaring amid a sea of blue flashing lights. Some of the officers and soldiers saw what happened and pointed at the boy who was currently scurrying down a deserted alleyway – a dead end. They followed, for they only could, because the world knew just as the armed forces knew, terrorists were getting younger by the day.

When Harley reached the dead end he looked around angrily and faced the incoming authorities closing in on him in the alleyway, as they blocked off the only route of escape.

They had him cornered like a rat in a drain.

Soldiers and police officers had drawn to a standstill and were there poised to open fire on the young terrorist if he displayed any sign of confrontation. Harley stood and stared at the people pointing guns at him. But no more was the evil or corruptive instinct. Just a frightened young boy trapped. Yet the boy was ready to kill and he knew just how...

"...Harley, my boy!" Roberto Klaus shouted, and pushed and shoved his way through the crowd of authority. They tried to hold him back but his persistence paid off and he got through without any serious fuss. It was as if they knew the old man would prevent them firing their bullets into a young 12-year-old kid. "He's my grandson! I know this boy...he's completely harmless...I can help you...trust me, I can help...!"

A passageway formed in the crowd and the Professor used it. He entered the alleyway and approached the nervous youth.

Harley's eyes welled with stinging tears. He yelled, "You did this to me..."

Professor Klaus implored, "I know I did, Harley, and I was a fool. An obsessive fool and arrogant and selfish, but together we can both be delivered unto greatness..."

Harley gritted his teeth to form a snarl and reached out a doomed hand.

He said, "I'm going to kill you, Grandad. And everyone else in your family."

The authorities appeared dumbfounded. But they were ready and more than willing to open fire at a moment's notice as the strangest occurrence took centre stage in the darkened alley. The two great psychic abilities had gone to war and the authorities hadn't a clue what any of it was about. To them it just looked like a young kid and an elderly geezer were pointing at each other. Even though secretly they guessed something much deeper going on. After all, that huge bus that flew through the air and the possessed screaming populace of Leicester Square scurrying around looking for shelter or a safe-haven from terrorists.

The Professor was far outweighed by youth and fresh perspective as Harley channelled his ability to disrupt the body"s internal nervous-system. The older man folded almost immediately, his heart and lungs shuddering inside their delicate ribcage as a burning fury seemed to fill his stomach and chest. It was like a claw within scratching and ripping its way out, as the same claw clutched vital organs and threatened to remove them and take them with it.

Veins sprouted across the boy's forehead and cheeks, opening and spraying minor sprinkles of blood across his face until it was awash with redness. His eyes bulged like they were about to explode. His lips had turned a cold icy hue of dark indigo.

It was payback time and Harley revelled in his newfound power of concentration.

Roberto Klaus attempted to open his mouth to perhaps plead for his grandson to stop but all that emerged with a thick regurgitated flow of yellowy puss.

The boy's extended hand suddenly clenched into a tight fist so it gripped his Grandfather's very soul, squeezing it relentlessly so that it couldn't escape his hold. But he felt his own pain now, for while he tried to finish the job, there was no room for any lack or drop in concentration. The older man was strong but not stronger and the battle of wits was closing. It now approached an end where there could be but one victor, one survivor, and one remaining dishevelled soul to continue this instrument of destruction's legacy. Whoever this proved to be, they would be afflicted so badly by tonight's confrontation that it would leave one tragically dead and the other grotesquely disfigured.

The soldiers opened fire on the boy as the elderly Professor Roberto Klaus fell dying to his knees clutching his expanding and shattered skull in agonized pain. When the old man hit the deck, his body was a mashed lump and his face unrecognizable. Harley Klaus" powers were not adept in magically assisting him to dodge bullets, and his young body slumped to his death in a hail of blazing firepower.

Nobody would ever really know what took place that night in Leicester Square. Professor Klaus" little experiment worked, that's for sure, but with an unforeseen circumstance that even he as a man of science and a man of the world would never have anticipated. It was like the old saying in America that he had picked up on his travels whilst lecturing there, "Everybody loves a hotdog. But they don't want to see how a hotdog is made..."

Justin Hunter
Echoes

Jeff lay down on his son's twin-sized bed and stared at the foot long, oval shaped water stain in the ceiling. He shifted his weight and the wooden bedframe gave a short but urgent creak. Jeff made a mental note to lay off the late night binging at the fridge. His son's cheaply padded mattress was rough on Jeff's back, but he wasn't going to get the kid a new one until he stopped wetting the bed. Their boy, Kyle, had been potty trained shortly after turning two years old, except for staying dry through the night. The kid slept so deeply that he couldn't listen to his body telling him to get up and use the bathroom. Kyle was beginning second grade and his need to wear pull-up diapers at night was embarrassing to him, but there wasn't any other option. Jeff wasn't about to do a whole bed's worth of laundry every day.

Jeff snapped out of his reverie when he saw a heavy drop of water fall from the middle of the stain and splash into the bucket he had placed below. He sighed. There was no reason to put it off any longer. He had been watching the water stain grow over the last several months.

He hadn't done anything to fix it. His time was eaten up by the needs of work and family. The project would involve taking down a portion of the ceiling, which was a messy job and not one easily done with a kid underfoot.

He didn't have that problem now. His boy was off visiting his grandparents up in Wisconsin. His wife was away leading a work conference in Texas. He had the house to himself. Jeff begged off tagging along with either his son or wife by telling them that he had to work.

As soon as they were gone, he took a week's worth of vacation. He felt a bit guilty about it at first, but that soon passed. He realized that he hadn't spent any real time on his own for the past fifteen years. Jeff wanted to experience a bit of what life used to be when he was single. He wanted to have a lot of time to do whatever whim came over him at the moment. It was a letdown experience. The first half of the day was excellent, he felt euphoric. Jeff watched three Die-Hard movies in a row and was drunk on beer before noon. After that, he didn't feel too much like doing anything.

He began to wonder what his wife and child were up to. Jeff didn't want to admit it, but he was a bit lonely. He spent the rest of the afternoon cleaning up the house and ended up lying in a sweaty heap on his son's bed upstairs. Then he saw the water stain and decided to do something about it. His wife would be pleased when she came home to see that he fixed it. He wished that she was with him now.

Jeff got out of his son's bed and moved a stepladder under the water stain, careful not to knock over the bucket underneath. He put on his tool belt and went to work. Jeff took a razor knife out of his belt and cut a long rectangle around the water stain. He used the knife to saw through the ceiling spackle and cut through the drywall. He lowered the cut piece of ceiling down carefully, but it was sodden and came apart in his grasp. He cursed and wiped his hands on his jeans. Jeff took a broom and pushed the insulation over with the handle.

He climbed the stepladder and shined a flashlight along the underside of the roof, trying to find the leak. The reason for the space above his son's room always mystified him. It was like a small attic with no entrance. Jeff wondered why the builders didn't just slant the ceiling with the roof and make the room larger. There was no ductwork coming from above, and the only electricity was a line extending to the ceiling light. Jeff thought he might expand the room himself one day, but that was probably another project that would only amount to an idea and nothing more.

Jeff cursed. He couldn't locate the root of the leak. He had worried that this would happen. Just because the water coming through the ceiling at one part of the room didn't mean that the hole in the roof would be right above it. Water could travel along the beams from anywhere and seep its way to the low spot of the ceiling.

He climbed further up the ladder until the upper half of his body was through the hole in the ceiling. He shined the light along the far, upper corners of the space and stopped the beam on a large black object that looked transfixed to the far wall. It was an oval shape, about six feet in length. It was a mottled black and red with leathery looking skin. Jeff thought he could see it pulsating like it was breathing. Jeff shined his light on the pod from one end to the other. He had no discerning notion as to what it was.

After a couple minutes, he walked back down the ladder and picked up a four-foot, metal T-square. He climbed back up the ladder and reached out with the t-square to touch the object. Whatever it was, he didn't feel like he wanted to touch it with his hands. The T-square was too short, and Jeff had to climb up another rung of the stepladder and lean his body forward onto the floor of the attic space. He was still about a foot too short to touch it. He was about to climb up into the attic completely when the pod dropped off the wall and onto the attic floor.

Jeff startled and kicked the stepladder over. He fell to the floor in a heavy thud. Bits of plaster rained down on his body. He groaned and swore weakly. His wind was knocked out of him. He looked up into the darkness of the rectangular hole he had cut in the ceiling and tried to regain his breath.

He began to panic when he heard a scraping sound coming from the attic. Whatever dropped from the attic wall was moving toward the hole. Jeff scrambled for the bedroom door, skinning the palms of his hands on some of his son's carelessly scattered Legos. He crawled outside the bedroom and into the hallway, slamming the door behind him. His breath came out in ragged gasps. A stench came to his nostrils. The smell was a mix of burning hair and rancid meat.

He turned to look through the door's keyhole. Something was blocking his view. A sharp crack made the door tremble as the creature stabbed a claw through the cheap wood, exploding splintered bits of particle board into Jeff's face.

He felt a sharp sting of pain and saw his shoulder impaled by the creature's appendage. Jeff tried to shove his way backward but was stuck. The claw had gone through his body and stuck out several inches though the back of his shoulder. Jeff could see the creature's ragged claw end in a thick finger-like appendage. Its skin was jet black with hair covered knuckles. The claw twisted sending another flash of pain through Jeff's body. He heard the creature make a low, gurgling sound from behind the door. It was like it was laughing.

Jeff fumbled with his tool belt and found his razor knife. He slashed hard at the creature's finger. The blade sank deep. The creature screeched and withdrew its claw. Jeff fell to his back. Darkness closed in at the edges of his vision.

The doorknob turned and the door was pushed outward. Jeff kicked it back closed and turned onto his stomach. He made a shambling, bent-over run down the hallway and fell into his own bedroom.

He heard his son's door explode off its hinges. Jeff slammed his door home and rose to his full height. He overturned his wife's huge curio cabinet and shoved it in front of the door. He fell backwards as the creature violently attacked the door, threatening to break in at any moment. The creature's claws began punching holes in the door, scrambling to rip it open. Jeff took a hammer out of his tool belt and smashed the devilish fingers as they came into view. Suddenly, the attack stopped. Jeff saw a large, yellow eye peer through a hole in the door and at him, then vanish.

Jeff piled his wife's hope chest on top of the curio cabinet. The wound in his shoulder tore with his effort, increasing the flow of blood from the wound. He ripped out baseboards and window framing and nailed them across the doorway. He remembered the ease with which the creature ruined his son's door and railed against the hopelessness of his efforts. When he had done all he thought he could, he stopped and stood stock-still, listening. He couldn't hear anything beyond his own haggard breathing. He looked out the window and saw the sun was setting. It would be dark soon.

Nothing more happened until nearly one o'clock in the morning. That was when the light turned on in the hallway. Shadows played in the dark bedroom from the cracks in the door. The creature was moving.

It made Jeff think back to the first night he had ever spent on his own.

He had flunked out of college after only one semester. He spent his first, and only, months of college in a drunken stupor. College was the first time in his life where he had total freedom. No parents telling him to get out of bed, no boss harassing him on the phone. His college loan covered his room, board and classes. He might as well have saved himself the money on classes and spent it on Vodka. He went to his classes the first week only and blew them off the rest of the time. He looked for a party every night of the week, and he invariably found one.

He never thought of the consequences until his father came to pick him up right before Christmas. He even partied the night before and took the three hundred mile ride home drunk and hung-over the whole way. His Dad didn't say much to him during the drive. Jeff was left to his self-loathing. He remembered getting out of the car and bringing his suitcase into his parents' house and up the stairs to his old bedroom. He fell onto his bed and stared at the cracks in the ceiling he knew so well. He had no plan, no dreams and no future that mattered. He fell into a restless sleep.

He woke up to see his father sitting at the foot of the bed. His father was more than six feet tall, but never stood up to his full height. His shoulders slumped forward, creating a small hump on his back. His face was calm and loving, but serious. He was looking at his hands.

"I don't think you can live here long," his father said. "It wasn't really working out for us when you were before."

"I know," Jeff said.

"Do you have a plan?"

"I guess I need to go and get a job."

"Is there anything you want to do? Are you interested in anything?"

"Not really. I can work hard at whatever job I have. I don't really have any real skills though."

"Probably should have let you work a bit more during high school," his father said.

"You always told me that school was my job."

"Didn't do you much good though, in the end."

"I guess not," Jeff said.

His father let the conversation drop for a moment and continued to study his hands. "I didn't mean that to sound as rude as it did," his father said.

"I know."

"Your mother can help you get a job at the bank by her office. She knows one of the managers there. You could be a bank teller."

"Okay."

"There are also some apartments near there above some of the local businesses. They are small studios. I've been looking into them," his father said.

"How long have you known I was flunking out?"

"I signed off on your loans when you went to college. When you weren't making good grades, I received notices that you weren't going to be funded for the next semester. I guess I just assumed that you would have spoken to me about this sooner."

"I don't know what to tell you. I wasn't really living in reality at school."

His father stood up and walked to Jeff's bedroom door. He turned off the light and turned toward his son. "Welcome to reality. We should have you at work and in your own place in about two weeks. Your mother and I will take care of the apartment deposit and the first month's rent. We expect you to figure it out on your own after that."

"Thanks, Dad."

"I love you son. Your mother said that you figuring things out on your own doesn't extend to you doing your own laundry. You can bring your things on Sunday to be cleaned when we have family dinner."

"You think I'm going to show up?" Jeff said. He was trying to be sarcastic but didn't know if he sounded as light as he intended. His voice came out too mean, nearly vengeful.

His father didn't seem to take offense. He even smiled. "At what you're going to make at the bank, it will be the best food you're going to eat all week. However, if you don't want to show up, don't. Just remember, you will be missed." His father closed the door to Jeff's room and left him to the darkness and his own churning thoughts.

Ten days later, Jeff was in his apartment. His father wasn't kidding when he said it was small. The whole apartment was one long and thin rectangle, a thirty by twenty foot room. The bathroom wasn't even walled off completely. The only privacy was a half wall that covered nothing. Jeff was sleeping on the top bunk of his futon bunk bed. The lower half was folded into the couch position. It was a present from his parents, and Jeff was thankful. Any way he could save space was a good thing.

Jeff remembered trying to sleep that first night alone. He could hear his neighbors, the walls were rather thin. One of his neighbors was a tiny, gothic girl. She had bad skin and scars running up and down her forearms, like crisscrossing strands of grass.

"I cut myself when I'm bored," she said.

"Why?" Jeff asked.

"I told you. I get bored."

Jeff heard the Nirvana song 'Rape Me' being played in her apartment when she opened the door to go inside. She must have had it on repeat since he could hear the melody over and over the rest of the day and still into the night. The neighbor on the other side was an awkward man who taught Biology at the local community college. His poofy, jet-black hair was cut into a mullet. He spoke endlessly when hailed, so Jeff tried to avoid him. The man gave Jeff an open ended invitation to come over and hear him play the violin. Jeff gave him the empty promise that he would stop by sometime.

The hallway outside his apartment was always lit. The lighting played under the crack of his apartment door. He watched the shadows of people walking along that hallway. He heard their voices, their laughter permeating into his solitary room. Some of the voices sounded normal, some drunk and some angry. He felt unsafe as he watched the shadows play through the crack of his door. He thought of his pitiful door chain, so cheaply made that anyone could break in.

He laid, an adult on a child's style bed, and spent his first night alone feeling small and unsure in a world where every decision was now his. His life spilled in front of him in a vastness he couldn't grapple with. He tried to clutch at his wandering mind, tried to simplify his situation and make things small and easy in his mind. Jeff found he just couldn't, so he stayed awake and watched the shadows. He felt afraid and unequipped. His fears were useless. No one ever came to his door. No one knocked.

The memory was more than a decade old, but it felt a fresh fierceness for Jeff at that moment. The beast was behind the door. The shadow had become real. He was alone. His family would be back in six days.

Jeff wondered if he could live that long without water.

David W. Landrum
The Science Teacher

People ask me what was the greatest moment in my life. I've said it was when I got my first recording contract, my first number one hit song, when I opened for Janis Joplin in Indianapolis and did a couple of songs with her at the end of the show, when I won a Grammy for my band's third album. I don't tell anyone about what was really the sweetest moment in my life. It was when I got even with my junior-year Science teacher, Mr. Davis—a memory that fills me with joy to this very day.

Davis was one of those people they used to hire who were not qualified but got a job in a school because the baby boomer generation was filling up classrooms and anyone with a college degree who knew the basics of a subject could get hired to fill the gaps.

I don't know where Davis went to school. He must have had a degree of some kind. But he was the most incompetent teacher I've ever been bored to tears by. He taught science. I don't know how he convinced the administration at Ethan Allen High that he was qualified to teach science, but somehow he made the cut.

He was really a construction boss who owned a small company that built driveways and contracted road repairs for the city and state. It was based in Kokomo, my hometown, and where I still live (I've never wanted to live in a celebrity enclave like Nashville or Hollywood). He might have been good at pouring concrete and laying down asphalt, but he was not good at teaching science.

He did two things in science class. He showed films and went on and on about taking notes.

I particularly remember the notes part of the classes. He never lectured. When not showing films, he gave us time to read in class, during which time we were expected to take notes out of our textbooks. Occasionally he would hold up examples of a good set of notes, almost always done in neat handwriting by studious girls who copied charts and graphs out of our textbook. Like most incompetent teachers, he gussied up to the women and hardly even spoke to any of the men in class. I assumed he felt safer around girls and assumed they were nice enough, and passive enough, not to censure him for his poor performance as a teacher.

Davis knew nothing of his area of teaching. The endless films and his monotone lectures on taking notes raised contempt in me. I guess he noticed this, because one day he lit into me in front of the whole class.

He had run out of films so he gave us "reading time." We were supposed to take notes during this reading time. I had not brought any paper to class that day. My mind was far from pointless classroom exercises and boring reading about the periodical chart of the elements.

My band had started to make a small splash in town. This was in 1968. Rock and roll had come in a new wave from Britain and from American groups like the Byrds and the Doors. Everyone was forming bands (garage bands, we call them now) and doing cover shows. We had played a few times at sock hops and done a couple of shows at local teen clubs; and we had not done badly last year at the annual competition they held at the Indiana State Fair. This had given me a certain notoriety in school. I was riding the wave of popularity and minor celebrity one can suddenly stumble on in high school. My success as a musician exacerbated my contempt for Davis. He nailed me that day.

He walked in halfway through the class period. I was whispering with the girl next to me. I had not opened by book and taken no notes. Davis walked up, leveled his gaze at me, and started to shout.

"Parker, you've been sitting in this class for thirty minutes and you haven't done a darn thing! Now you get busy and start taking some notes right now!"

I collected my thoughts enough to take action. I had to get some paper. I got up, walked over to Cindy Howlitch, a smart girl with glasses and bobbed hair, and asked if I could borrow some paper. She tore off two sheets and gave them to me. I sat down, opened my book, and began copying.

Now you may think this was not such a big deal. Teachers yell at students. It's a part of the game, however unfair—and this was especially true back then. That little episode with Davis, however, had some dire consequences.

I said playing in a rock and roll band had gained me some recognition in our school. It had also generated some hostility. I played music, my hair was longer than most students wore it, and I tried to dress a little hip. This earned me the contempt of the redneck faction there: football players, crew-cuts, and bullies from that stratum of school life. They didn't like me, but the complex social codes that governed the students at the high school stopped them from expressing their disapproval. I was, after all, popular. People admired me. I was not a geek or a loser. When Davis lit into me that day, it gave a group of them the excuse they were looking for.

I was walking across the common between two buildings on our campus (Ethan Allen was a large school) when three of those bozos blocked my path.

"Hey, Parker. I heard old man Davis got on your ass today."

They stood in a semi-circle in front of me. These guys were big, all on the team, and kahunas in their niche at our school. They were used to bullying and to students cowering before them. I did not like being bullied and did not like the swaggering way they stood there. If I had answered meekly, they would have been satisfied, laughed, and gone their way, but I decided I was not going to play their game.

"What's it to you?" I answered.

Williams, the leader of the trio, gave me a look.

"Don't talk to me like that, you faggot."

"Fuck you."

I did pretty well against them—at least at first. I gave Williams a black eye and scored some good hits on the others. But it was three against one, and they were big and tough. They worked me over pretty badly. Some teachers saw it and intervened, but not before the football boys had cracked a couple of ribs when they knocked me down and started kicking me. I ended up going to the emergency room.

Our school policy with fights is to expel everyone for three days, no matter who started it or how it came about. After that, the administration investigated and took further action based on who was at fault. The principal judged that Williams had started it. I was exonerated of wrongdoing. But they were easy on the guys who beat me up because they were on the football team—a fact they did not let me forget.

But the worst fallout hit on Lynda, my girlfriend.

She and I had dated for about a year. Lynda was cool, with dark skin and long black hair. I loved the Bohemian way she dressed: short skirts, boots, bright blouses, shawls. I think to this day I might have married her if the episode with Williams and the others had not split us up.

Lynda's parents always seemed uneasy about me. I mean, after all, those kids who played in rock and roll bands were all dope fiends and sexual predators, right? I did not seem that way to them. I made good grades, treated them respectfully—I even had a job stocking shelves at the local Kroger Store. But the fight gave them an excuse to act upon their suspicions that everything was not on the up-and-up with me. They ordered Lynda to break it off.

She pleaded, wept, argued, reasoned, but they refused to listen. They told her not to talk to me. They would not hear my side of the story. We split. She eventually began dating one of the guys who beat me up. Her senior year she disappeared from school. Lynda's parents were devout Mennonites, so I don't think she took off to get an abortion. I think it was to have the baby. I never saw her again after that. When I made it big and had some money, I hired an investigator to track her down. She lived in Santa Monica, California and was married. At the time, I assumed things had worked out for her, though they had worked out without me. Or at least I thought as much. Two years later I found out different.

Back in those days there was still a considerable stigma attached to have a child out of wedlock. Lynda had to take what she could get as far as men went, and her choices were limited. The guy she ended up with was a jerk. He beat her and made her life so nightmarish she left their kid with a friend, drove up to one of those California highways that are built on cliffs above the sea, parked her car, got out, and jumped.

In all my years, I've never met a girl as sweet and lovely, and as sharp and creative as Lynda. We lost our virginity to one another. I played her songs I had written. She was the first audience for at least four numbers that later became mega-hits millions of people sing yet today. She believed in me. She was (not to get sappy) my muse. I have no doubt I would have married her and stuck with her in spite of the successes of celebrity. I have never married—maybe never will, and I spent my time screwing groupie girls and have high-profile affairs with Hollywood glamor chicks. None of them even vaguely comes close to Lynda. She died due to a sequence of events caused by a loudmouth outburst from an incompetent teacher. My desire for revenge turned to obsession.

For the rest of my time in his class, I made sure I had paper and took those useless notes he was fond of going on and on about. I studied hard and aced all his tests—not difficult if you even bothered to do a quick reading of the textbook. He was magnanimous and familiar with me after that, as if to say, "Well, we had our spat, but now we can be friends." I played along. He never suspected my constant plotting to get even with him for all the sorrow he had caused me.

In Mrs. Marshall's literature class we read "The Cask of Amontillado" by Poe. The guy in that story understood what I felt strongly then but with infinitely more intensity when I learned about Lynda a couple of years later. In Poe's story, Montressor endured injuries, but when someone insulted him it was time for revenge. And, he said, he would be revenged in a way that would not have consequences or repercussions—exactly what I wanted. Only I didn't know how I could pull it off.

Then one day I knew what I would do. I got the idea after Frankie Waterman did a short stint as a guitarist in my band.

By that time we had got more gigs and were playing all across north Indiana. One of our guitarists quit. We auditioned some guys. Frankie seemed the best, but he was only in the band six months before I had to can him. He liked to smoke dope too much and often came on stage so stoned he couldn't play. When he could play, he was fabulous, but more often than not he missed cues, chorded when he was supposed to be doing a lead, and missed gigs. When we played at the Indiana State Fair the second time, he forgot to lock our van and someone stole half our equipment. We finally had to let him go. He agreed he had not been very reliable and we stayed friends. You could always count on him if you wanted some good stuff to smoke.

He also worked for Mr. Davis.

Davis hired guys who would work for low pay. He had three or four on his crew who were experienced, and he paid them well. He kept a rotating contingent of down-and-outers to do the grunt work, carry things, and perform the dirty jobs his regular crew didn't want to do. He hired Frankie to operate the dump trunk he used to spread asphalt.

I got together with Frankie one night. We smoked grass and talked. I asked him what it was like working for Davis.

"He's okay. He remembers you. He said you guys had your differences but you worked them out. He likes you."

As we smoked, talked, and, after a while, got out guitars and jammed, I asked him questions about work. He worked on the asphalt crew.

"It takes a lot of training to do concrete—laying curbs and building sidewalks. His regular crew does that. When he puts down asphalt, it's usually just him and me. I dump, he rakes it out, and then he uses the road-grater to level it."

"Just the two of you can do that?"

"Sure. It's not like we're paving a road. We do driveways. Davis can get a lot of work down by doubling up. He puts his concrete crew on a job, gets it going, and then goes off with me and maybe one more worker to do driveways. It only takes about an hour to do them. We can do four or five a day that way. It works.

Beginning of summer now, and we have more paving jobs than we can handle."

I told Frankie I had no hard feelings about the band. We hung out a lot. I kept him supplied with money to get dope. One night at a bar he told me they were swamped with jobs this month.

"Everybody in suburbia wants their driveway covered," he complained over a sweating bottle of Rolling Rock. "We've got a lot of construction and cement jobs too. It's just me and him on most of the paving jobs. When he gets under pressure, he can be a real bastard."

"Yeah, I know."

I asked him more questions. I asked him if he wanted to go out to MacDonald's for lunch tomorrow.

"Can't afford to leave. Davis goes to the Wagon Wheel every day, but if I'm not on site and ready to work when he gets back, he goes nuts and starts screaming at me. I pack lunch and eat it in the truck. I don't want to risk one of his shithead temper tantrums."

"I'll bring you a Big Mac tomorrow," I told him.

I went back to my apartment. I remembered something and got out my notes from Mrs. Marshall's class. The part I wanted to look at was easy to find because I highlighted it in class and underlined it in red pen later on. It's the part in *Hamlet* where King Claudius tells Laertes, whose sister commits suicide (like Lynda did), that he will arrange vengeance on Hamlet in such a way that "no wind of blame" will blow on Laertes. "Vengeance should know no bounds," he says and, at his sister's funeral, when Laertes is angry and wants to ring Hamlets' neck, tells him to be patient. "This grave," he says, "shall have a living monument"—meaning Laertes will get his revenge and live to enjoy it and know that justice was done. Nothing would happen to him. We had studied that part of Shakespeare's play long before I knew Lynda had killed herself, but it came to mind and I found my old notebook and text and did the red underlining the night I did find out. I learned about how she died. Her grave, I resolved, would have a living monument. I would arrange it so no wind of blame would blow on me.

And not on Frankie either.

The next day I went to MacDonald's, got stuff to go, and brought it to the site he had told me they would be working at. When I got there Davis was gone. Frankie sat in the cab of a Mac dump truck loaded with a smelly, smoking load of asphalt. The tarry scent of the stuff wafted through the air as it sent up waves of blue smoke. Davis had parked a steam roller beside the truck and gone to lunch.

We ate and I got out a hash pipe.

"I ran into a guy from Chicago. He sold me some really good stuff," I said. This was the truth. This particular dealer laced his hashish with opium. You could see the white flecks of it in the fifty-cent piece I had brought along. We went out to a small wood close to the house so we would not leave a scent in the truck, loaded the pipe, and smoked.

When we were finished, we stumbled back to the truck. Inside, Frankie thumped the back of his head against the back window.

"Jesus," he said, breathing out. "What did you put in that?"

"Like I said: it was good stuff."

"I feel like my arms are glued to my body. This isn't good, Gary. I'm too damned stoned to do my job."

I felt the effects of the dope as well, but not as much as he seemed to feel it. I think I was full of adrenalin or super-focused because of my plan.

"When you see him coming, pull the lever," I suggested. "That's all you have to do."

I left him there. I took the trash from our lunch, hopped out of the truck, and hurried off. I had parked my car a few blocks away.

I knew I was taking a big risk. But I also knew it could work for me. I went home, took a cold shower to wake up, and constructed an alibi. Yolanda, an on-again, off-again lover, would cover for me if I did get implicated. But I didn't think I would even be mentioned after Davis got what I had worked out for him. I didn't think Frankie would either.

Things didn't work out exactly as I had planned. They worked out better.

From what Frankie told me later, Davis came back in a hurry to get the job done. He yelled for Frankie to dump the load. Startled, stoned so much as to impair his response, he reached for the lever and pulled it all the way back.

My idea was that Davis would get scorched by the hot asphalt. He was probably too savvy about the hazards of his job to stand close to the truck bed after instructing one of his crew to dump a load of hot asphalt. Chances of the load burying and killing him were next to nothing. And I didn't want him to die because that would get Frankie in trouble. I thought my ex-guitarist would hit the lever too soon; the tar would splatter on Davis, burn him, hurt him, and maybe leave some scars on his face as a mark of what a nasty shit he was.

I did not know he had belted down five beers at the Wagon Wheel Restaurant. He had a drinking problem, as the investigation revealed. He was drunk that day and standing too close to the truck. As Frankie's reactions were disordered by the hash, Davis's were by the alcohol he had drunk. He said he saw the bed tip and the asphalt cascade toward him but could not react quickly enough to get out of the hot, tarry avalanche descending on him.

It buried him up to his thighs.

He screamed and shouted for help. Frankie heard him. The dire tone of Davis's voice, and the realization of what had just happened, catapulted Frankie out of his drug-induced torpor. He sprang out of the truck, pulled Davis from the heap of asphalt, took off his own shirt, wrapped Davis's burned, bleeding legs, and ran into the house of the people whose driveway they were doing. They called Emergency.

The EMTs rescued Davis—but not entirely. He lost both his legs in the accident.

Frankie did not get in trouble. Adrenalin did the same thing for him, I think, that it did for me. By the time he ran to the house to call for help, he was sober. No one even suspected he had been doing dope. The doctors who examined Davis detected his blood/alcohol level right away but noticed no signs of intoxication in Frankie. He was not even questioned about it.

Further, Davis had told Frankie to dump the load and Frankie had not heard him. Davis grew in incensed and shouted, "Dump it," and then used a racial epithet (Frankie is black). The people in the house and two kids passing on bicycles heard him. Davis admitted his drunkenness and admitted he did shout "dump it" loudly and intimidatingly and—yes—he did use a racial slur. The investigation exonerated him Frankie. He said Davis told him to dump the asphalt and he did. Davis, the report concluded, was drunk, standing too close to the truck, and was too intoxicated to react to the wave of hot tar coming down him. Frankie lost his job, but only because Davis's construction company went out of business after both his legs had to be amputated at the thighs.

This grave shall have a living monument.

Frank felt bad about it. Only he and I knew his smoking hash had contributed to the accident. "Davis had as much to do with it being drunk as you did being stoned," I told him. "If he hadn't been plastered he would have got out of the way the minute he saw the bed go up."

"It will be hard for me to get a job now," he said. "I'll probably end up leaving town."

He did leave town, but not the way he thought it would be.

I made it big the next year. Frankie was still around and I hired him as a back-up musician—not a regular band member but someone to fill in when needed. A couple of years later, when I started my production company, he worked as a session man, playing guitar for recordings, laying down sound tracks for TV, movies, commercials. Frankie was a damned good player, and he began to get his life stable enough to hold down a career.

He met some musicians from Barbados, cut a record on my label, and enjoyed moderate success touring. His group recorded two more songs that were only minor hits in the US but were all the rage in the Caribbean. He eventually settled in Barbados, where he is a star, married, and lives comfortably, performing locally, occasionally touring, and sometimes opening for my band when we do concerts.

Davis still lives in town. I've heard he has returned to teaching. I imagine he has had to develop a degree of competence now he did not have before the fact. I'm satisfied with that. I like to imagine Lynda is as well.

Timothy Frasier
Broken Consort

The black Cadillac idled slowly down the street. It seemed in its natural element under the dim quarter-moon. Hard Rock, Tennessee was smothered in a suffocating blackness with the only sign of habitation being an occasional house with lantern light bleeding from carelessly drawn curtains.

The car increased its speed as a faint, flickering glow appeared in the distance. At First and Cemetery Streets, the last intersection before leaving town, it came upon the source of that glow. On the corner to the right, next to the remains of a convenience store, a small bonfire battled the vast darkness like the Spartans at Thermopylae. A dozen men stood around the fire while several more shuffled about in the shadows.

The Cadillac's screeching tires broke the calm like a banshee at a funeral as the car stopped abruptly, out of instinct, at the dead traffic light which had not worked in over a year. The plastic-wrapped, human head on the floorboard behind the driver's seat rolled forward. To June, it sounded eerily similar to a mouse rummaging around in a garbage bag. She lit a stale cigarette and frowned at the taste.

A raggedy dressed man emerged from the shadows and trotted to the passenger side of the car. June stomped on the accelerator as he reached for the door handle. Her palms were sweating and her mouth felt as if it were stuffed with cotton. She looked in the rear view mirror and saw the man standing stationary in the road like some horrid scarecrow, watching her drive away. The head in the floorboard rolled as she went around a sharp curve in the road.

Tree saplings crowded against the edge of the deteriorating asphalt, creating the feel of a great tunnel as the headlights sliced through the blackness. The forest had been relentless in reclaiming its stolen territory. June's hand trembled as she reached for her pack of cigarettes before realizing she still had one between her fingers. She cursed and dropped the pack on the console.

June slammed on her brakes a couple of miles out of town as she glimpsed a break in the vegetation to her left. She turned onto the gravel road and traveled another three miles until she reached her driveway. Like most of the yards in the country, hers was an overgrown mess of knee-high grass, thorn bushes, and weeds. Two paths, one on each side of the driveway, led from her parked car. The path on her right curved around to the side door, which opened to the kitchen of the large, Victorian-style house. The straight path on her left led to her laboratory, which had been her grandfather's toolshed before the outbreak. The headlights shut off automatically a few moments after she killed the engine.

June sat with her eyes shut, giving them time to adjust to the darkness. She remembered her summers here as a child, visiting with her grandparents. They were the ones who encouraged her to follow her dream of becoming a neurosurgeon. Her parents were worthless pieces of shit, only interested in who they could screw in order to "one up" the other. By the time she was eight, she knew more about adult matters than a child should have known. She blamed her parents for her still being single at thirty-two years of age...and a virgin until this very night.

She opened her eyes and scanned the yard. A vague shape near the lab made her catch her breath momentarily, until she realized it was a cluster of tall weeds. The crucifix swinging from her rearview mirror caught her attention and gave her comfort. That was another thing she gave her grandparents credit for: introducing her to religion. Her parents were both atheists.

The Sig 9mm felt good in her hand as she retrieved it from the console. She stepped out of the car and scanned the darkness, wrinkling her nose as the light wind carried to her the scent of death and decay. A light mist was beginning to form, giving urgency to her mission as she opened the rear door and fished the head from the floorboard with her left hand. The pistol in her right hand was at the ready as she walked to the rear of the tool shed and started the generator. Light glowed from the single window of the shed and from the kitchen window of the house. For a moment, it looked as if her grandfather was peering out the kitchen window.

"You're dead, Grandpa." She shut her eyes and reopened them. The window was clear. Grandpa was dead, just as Grandma was also dead. June knew this, but for the life of her, she couldn't remember when they died. June turned to the lab and opened the door. Once filled with farming equipment, the room was now the equal to the most advanced labs from the old days. When things began to fall apart, her colleagues had persuaded her to let them set up the lab here so that their research could continue away from the chaos of Atlanta. She pondered on where her colleagues were for a few moments before giving up and returning to the task at hand.

June wasted no time as she prepared the head. She shaved off the blond hair that she'd ran her fingers through not more than an hour earlier. The man, Eric, had pouty lips that she had found extremely sensuous. His partially closed eyes seemed to open slightly as she tightened the clamp around his head. With a practiced hand, she cut the flesh and pulled back on the scalp while slicing the flesh beneath with a scalpel until the blood-stained skull was exposed.

The Barstow bone drill, a device created with major input from June three years earlier, made an unpleasant sound as the two inch diameter, cylindrical blade bore into the skull. As soon as the resistance decreased, the floor plate locked in place, preventing the blade from compromising the dura mater. She hit the release lever and dropped the disk of bone onto the table, and then shut off the water flow to the hydration line. The bright, Chiron lamp illuminated the exposed brain. The dura mater was intact. June took her scalpel and sliced through the thin leather-like membrane, following the path of the removed bone. She held her breath as she peeled it back. The color was normal, and more important, there was no sign of the dancing parasite. It was just as she suspected since he had shown no symptoms.

She removed the top of his skull with a bone saw, cut his spinal cord, and carefully removed the brain, placing it in a plastic container. She then picked up the container, wiped her hands off, and left the lab. The mist obscured her legs as she made her way to the house. Grandpa was nowhere to be seen as she entered the kitchen and placed Eric's brain on the countertop. Ever frugal with her propane, Jane turned on the stove and placed a cast-iron skillet over the flame. She then dumped the brains in the skillet along with a couple of eggs she'd swiped from her laying hens earlier in the day.

June swayed and spun slowly as Fleetwood Mac's song, "Dreams," filled her head.

Now here you go again--You say—you want your freedom. Stevie Nick's voice sent chills through June as she danced her way to the stove and stirred the brains and eggs with a spatula. She'd often been told her resemblance to Stevie was uncanny, though she didn't see it. The song replayed itself continually, fading only when she said grace. After finishing her meal, she entered the living room, lit a cigarette, and began dancing in front of the large mirror to the left of the front door. The cigarette felt strange in her hand. She'd never been a smoker. Her dance ended near dawn when she passed out from exhaustion.

June opened her eyes around noon and coughed. She nearly gagged as she rubbed her tongue around in her parched mouth. The music was gone for now. Every muscle in her legs screamed in agony as she stood.

"Fuck!" she cried when she realized she'd soiled her pants. She stripped her clothes and tossed them in the hamper. Her temper flared when she realized she'd let the generator run all night, and it was now empty of fuel, which meant no water.

June wrapped herself in a bath towel and walked out into the September sun. She filled a can with diesel from the above-ground tank, re-fueled the generator, and started it. The purr of the generator masked the sound of the approaching car until it was nearly to her house. From her vantage point on high ground, she'd caught the glint of sunlight off its silver hood, sending her scrambling to the house. It passed without stopping, just as she reached the door, but she went on in and retrieved her pistol.

A shower was now out of the question, so she took a quick whore's bath and then dressed in jeans; a red, sleeveless flannel shirt; and Nike sneakers. She went to the shed with the pistol shoved in the waistband of her jeans, just in case the driver of the silver car had seen her dashing to the house.

The details of the previous night were foggy in June's mind, but the soreness between her legs and the head resting in the clamp brought two things home to her. She had lost her virginity...and it was to this man. Tears flowed as she looked into his dead eyes.

Now here you go again – you say – you want your freedom.

"Shut the hell up!"

Well who am I to keep you down?

The song stopped at the sound of a car door being slammed shut. June was thankful and terrified at the same instant. She pulled the pistol from her jeans and stepped out of the lab.

"June Kemp?" The man called from beside the silver Challenger that had passed her house earlier. He was a tall, thin man of about forty wearing black pants and a white tee shirt. His long, brown hair was wild and unkempt. "I'm Dr. Anton Ross. I recognize you from the company profiles. You would not believe how long I've been searching for you."

June walked toward him cautiously with her pistol hidden behind her back. "What do you want?" The music was faint, just teasing, causing her to sway slightly from side to side. His face seemed familiar to her as well. "You were with the viral team helping the Russians at Lake Vostok."

"Yes. And as you obviously know, we failed. But we now have a retrovirus that is absolutely devastating to the parasites with minimal side effect to humans. It burns through cells like a wildfire and is highly contagious."

"Has it been implemented?"

"That's why I've been searching for you. We need to know what happens to the mature parasite while still attached to the host, as well as any possible residual damage to the host brain." He frowned. "You wouldn't believe how small our team is now."

"It's about to become even smaller." June brought the pistol around and fired at the man the same instant her teeth clicked shut and the world exploded in light and pain. Her body stiffened and she fell, face first into the weeds. The world was silent except for the pounding of her heart. She counted the beats as she pondered what had just happened. Was it another hallucination?

"You'll be okay," the man said before he broke into a coughing fit. "The Taser knocks them on their ass as well as you. You do you realize you have a parasite, don't you?"

June moaned and raised herself to her knees. Her nose was bleeding so she wiped it with the back of her trembling hand. "What the hell?" June started picking the tiny barbs from her clothing and skin. "Why did you say I have a ..." She dropped the last of the barbs, stood unsteadily, and looked at the man. He rested with his back against his car door and his feet sprawled in front of him. A growing circle of crimson stained his white tee shirt in the center of his chest.

"It appears we're both good shots." Ross fished in the back pocket of his jeans and pulled out a stun gun. "If things begin to get hazy or you hear music, zap yourself in the forehead with this. It brings you back for a little while."

June rushed to the man and examined his wound. "I'm so sorry!"

"There's no time for this. You must get the parasite out of you. Where is everyone?"

"They've..." She shut her eyes and frowned. Disconnected images raced through her mind. Images so horrifying, she stood and vomited, turning her head away so not to see the vile remains of her last meal.

With Ross forgotten, she walked back to the lab. A fly buzzed about Eric's head as she removed it from the clamp and carried it outside. Visions from the previous night threatened her sanity. June went behind the building and down a path which led to a ravine, which had been used by her family as a dump for several years. Her mouth salivated as she remembered the taste of Eric's brains.

The stench of decay and the buzzing of flies grew stronger as June neared the wash-out. She rounded a corner and stopped a couple of paces short of the ravine. Corpses in various stages of decay were intermingled with discarded couches and rusting appliances. Severed heads were scattered about, peeking from the mass of corruption like pumpkins sunning themselves amongst tangled vines. One of the most weathered corpses wore one of her grandmother's long dresses. Some of them wore lab coats. Every head that was visible had cranial trauma. A rat climbed out of the large opening in her old friend, Mimi Down's, severed head and scurried under an old refrigerator.

"No!" June cried as she dropped Eric's head, fell to her knees, and dry-heaved. She staggered to her feet and ran back to the lab.

"Dopamine!" June shouted as she reached the door to her lab. "Fuckers! I'll be the end of you!"

Now here you go again – you say – you want your freedom.

June fished the stun gun from her pocket and stuck it to her forehead as she felt her body begin to sway. She hit the button and released one hundred thousand volts, which sent her writhing to the ground. The music stopped.

She stood on trembling legs and entered the lab. Everything needed for removing the parasite was here. Without hesitation, she ran to the house and returned with one of the heavy, wooden kitchen chairs and two of her grandfather's leather belts. Her focus on the task at hand was so intense she failed to notice that Ross was gone. She placed the chair below the Chiron lamp and then positioned two adjustable mirrors in front of her. It took several tries to get everything adjusted to her liking. A table was rolled to each side of her chair, containing everything she thought she could possibly need. An extension cord was necessary for the bone drill.

June ran back to the house and entered the master bathroom. She retrieved the electric clippers from the vanity and buzzed her head. Her long, blond hair nearly filled the sink. The face in the mirror made her smile and she sang a line from the Eurhythmics' *Missionary Man* before snatching the stun gun and holding it to her head. Her smile faded as she lowered the gun. It was not the parasite this time. She placed the stun gun back in her pocket and left the house.

The sun was sinking in the west as June walked back into the lab. She rehearsed what was to come over and over in her mind, trying to anticipate every possibility. She sterilized and rearranged the tools several times until she was satisfied. Her last act before settling down in the chair was to scrub her hands and head with an anti-bacterial agent.

June strapped herself to the back of the chair with the leather belts, one around her stomach and the other thinner belt around her forehead with a rolled up towel to keep the blood out of her eyes. She said a prayer and then shocked herself with another charge from the stun gun, causing her to bite her tongue. The stun gun fell to the concrete floor.

"I'm coming for you, Motherfucker!" She reached up with a marker and outlined where she would make the cut. Every one of the dozens of parasites she had removed while at the CDC had always been positioned above the frontal lobe, which made it easier for June to reach.

What if something goes wrong? Her hand trembled as she lifted the scalpel to her head. *Then I'll no longer be a puppet!* There was no time to waste since the stun gun was out of her reach and possibly broken. She sliced through the flesh of her scalp until she felt bone and followed the outline of her marker until three sides were cut. The pain didn't come until she grasped the flesh of her scalp with forceps and peeled it to the side while slicing beneath with a scalpel. Blood flowed freely, soaking the towel and covering her face, thankfully leaving her eyes clear. June moaned loudly through gritted teeth as she clamped her scalp to the side.

She reached up, switched on the hydration system, and then fumbled the bone drill, almost dropping it twice before she held it securely in her trembling hand. The hum of its electric motor sent chills through her as she lowered the spinning blade to her head. Her stomach lurched from the aroma of burning bone and the cramping muscles in her right arm screamed as she cut the two inch circle of skull separating her from the parasite. After what seemed an eternity, she placed the drill on the table and hit the lever, releasing the round disk of bone.

"Okay, let's see what we have." June looked into the mirror and began to sob openly as she saw the small, starfish-like parasite fastened to the dura mater covering her brain. Knowing and seeing were two different things. "I have something for you a little stronger than dopamine," she whispered as she carefully grasped a syringe, stuck the needle into the creature, and injected a drop of sulfuric acid. It quivered and thrashed in place, lifting itself away from the dura mater far enough for June to grasp it with a pair of forceps and pull it slowly from her, the three inch spike appendage flailed wildly as it came free from her brain.

It felt as though the sun had burned away the clouds in her mind. June dropped the creature into an open jar and secured the lid. She cleaned the disk of bone and the inside of her skull, and then applied fast setting calcium replicating epoxy. The bone was placed into the opening and pressed into place, where it bonded in seconds.

"Would you like some help?" Ross smiled at June as he approached her from the doorway. He stood tall, exhibiting no ill effects from the gunshot wound.

"Stay back!" June shouted as she tried to reach the pistol resting on the table near her. Ross scooped up the pistol and placed it in her hand.

"You can shoot me if you'd like, but I hope you don't. I don't want another hole in this shirt, it's my favorite." He smiled a boyish, mischievous smile. "I'm sure you have questions. I'll do my best to answer them while I place your scalp back in place."

"You have a parasite." June's statement sounded more like an accusation.

"Yes, but a different species altogether. I still control my thoughts and actions, my parasite is along for the ride. It offers many benefits as you've witnessed first-hand." Ross raised his shirt and showed her his nearly healed chest wound. "They've been at war with the dancing parasite for countless generations. When the Russians drilled through the ice covering Lake Vostok, that war spilled into our world." Ross removed the clamp from her skull and began spreading it over her scalp. His work was fast and precise.

"Are you going to infect my body?" June asked after a long period of silence. She toyed with the Glock, resting her finger gently on the trigger. *I'll die first!* She swore silently to herself.

"They've entered no one without their permission. Well, not since the first accidental ones." He walked to the front of June and removed the two leather belts, oblivious to the pistol pointing toward his head. "I'm still the guy I've always been. Though a lot healthier."

June stood unsteadily as she began to wipe the blood off her face and neck with a towel. "I need something to drink."

"I'll get you some water." Ross was out the door instantly.

She gave him time to get to the house and then followed. The kitchen light was on as June reached the glass storm door. She watched as Ross poured the water and swayed back and forth with his eyes shut. He pulled a tiny bottle from his pocket and poured it into the glass of water.

"I'm not so thirsty, now." June fired the pistol from ten feet, sending the bullet between his raised eyebrows and blowing out the back of his head. The blood splattered across the white front of her refrigerator like a ragged rainbow.

"Now here you go again – you say – you want your freedom." June sang as she scooped Ross' brains from the floor and placed them in a pan. A smile spread across her face as she realized that this was her actions and her singing, not some fucking bug in her brain. She truly had her freedom.

T. S. Woolard
Ashes to Ashes

"Nelson," shouted Jake over the top of a curio cabinet Patrick assisted him in loading into their company's box-truck. "Hey, Nelson!"

"Yeah, boy," Nelson answered in his general fashion while he wiped sweat from his wrinkled brow, and sleeked his hair back with his one free, flat hand. In his other hand was a white, plastic, ordinary box.

"Don't worry about that box. The customer only wants to keep the furniture. Throw everything else away and sweep that last bedroom out," Jake instructed before whispering just loud enough for Patrick to hear, "You old, deaf bastard." Jake received a charitable chuckle.

"But I think someone's ashes are in it," said Nelson. He sat the box down on the rail of the front porch and began opening it.

"I don't give a damn!" Jake yelled. He lowered his end of the cabinet with caution. Knowing that he was the youngest member of the crew, and Nelson was new, Jake would have to be harder than he liked to make his role as the crew's supervisor clear.

Jake strutted over to Nelson who looked taken aback by the young man's aggressive nature. Patrick stared behind him, aware of what the new, old man was about to endure having been on Nelson's side a few times himself. Patrick felt sorry for him.

"If this is Aunt Nag or Uncle Bobo in this box," continued Jake as he jerked the box of ashes from Nelson's gnarled, vein marked hand. Jake pulled a plastic grocery bag from the crew's cleaning kit, and spiked the box into the bottom. The gray, powdery remains plumed up in a morbid wave. "It's going in the *damn* trash, like I said."

Jake tied the loop handles in a double knot, whirled around like a shot putter, and slung the bag in a high arc into the dumpster that sat in the driveway. Nelson watched in silent disagreement for the way Jake handled the dead.

"I think that was a little uncalled for," he said to Jake.

"That's too bad," Jake said. "That's where whoever in the hell that was will spend eternity. Now finish sweeping so we can go."

After a brief pause where it looked as though Nelson may object and things go from bad to ugly, but the old man bit his bottom lip and turned inside the house, shaking his head as he went.

Jake walked back to the truck with his chest bowed out and his shoulders swinging. Patrick waited, watching, holding his end of the cabinet still.

"Get 'em, Jake." Patrick laughed.

"I hate doing that to the old codger," Jake lied. He loved flexing his superiority muscles. "But he's got to learn to listen to me."

"I hear ya." Patrick gripped the cabinet when Jake got close. "I don't believe he liked what you did with them ashes though."

"It's just some ashes. It was nothing more than a pretty ashtray as far as I'm concerned." Jake lifted the cabinet. "I bet that room will be swept out before we're through though."

"**Y**es, my name is William Riley, Junior. I go by Bill." The tall, rounded man in the gray suit said into the phone at his ear. He had been waiting all morning for the cleaning company to open. "I was wondering if you could tell me what happened to an item one of your crews moved from a house."

"What is the item, Sir?" The lady asked on the other end of the line. Her voice was nasal, and her tone was flat.

"My father's ashes," Bill said.

"I'm sorry about that, Sir." The lady, still in the same bored way, said. "Can you give me the address for job?"

Bill did as he was asked while his sisters, Jan and Judy, sat around the kitchen table listening to the conversation on Bill's end. They stared as he paced up and down the long hallway and back out into the kitchen, giving numbers and information when prompted. His sisters whispered to one another behind cheap, pottery cups of coffee about how long it would be before Bill lost it with the lady on the phone. Judging by the shade of red of his face, Jan's guess was spot on.

"What the hell do you mean thrown away?" Bill ejected from a dead silence in the mouth of the hallway.

A pause went by while Bill got an answer. One in which he apparently was not happy with.

"It was a Goddamn human, not an item!"

"Calm down, Bill." Jan said.

He held up a hand to silence her, and nodded indignantly while waiting for the lady on the phone to finish what she was saying.

"You better hope it's still there," Bill shot at the phone. "Or you can count on going to court. I happen to be the most respected lawyer in this town." He slammed the phone down, and shuffled his narrow shoulders and round body into his suit jacket.

"What's going on?" Judy asked with a foreboding voice.

"They threw Dad's ashes in the trash."

"You don't say," Jan joked. Bill cut a look of warning at her.

"The trash runs today." Bill pushed on, not wanting a fight. "Maybe, if I hurry, I can beat them there."

"What if they've already come?" Judy asked.

"Well, then Mom will spend her afterlife on the mantle by herself." Bill gulped as he straightened his tie. "I swear, if Mom wasn't getting cremated right now, she'd die."

"Yeah, Dad's probably rolling over in his grave. No, wait..." Jan said with a smirk.

"Now is not a good time," Bill cautioned.

"I'll go with you," offered Judy. "You can't dig through a dumpster in a suit, and we've got to go get Mom's ashes when we leave anyway."

"Okay, let's go." Bill agreed.

"Call me when you know something." Jan said, this time being serious.

"Yep," was all Bill said.

Bill paced the lobby of the funeral home like he did the kitchen of his own house just two hours earlier. He and Judy had come to pick up their mother's ashes. Tonight would be the memorial service for her, and it was being held at Bill's house. This was the reason for the sisters coming into town and staying with Bill. They arrived just in time for their mother's passing, and were staying until after the arrangements were seen through.

Their mother died just a week and two days ago. Bill ended up with controlling interest in their parents' estate that consisted of a small, three bedroom, stick-built house all three siblings grew up in.

Years ago the family had a meeting and determined Bill would be the executor. Their father, who passed some five years prior to this meeting, told their mother that he was proud of Bill, and trusted him more in the job of handling their affairs after death. *He made more of himself than just a housewife*, was how his mother said it.

To Bill, this did not make up for years of cussing, berating, denied hugs, or missed I-love-yous, but it sure as hell helped. He struggled with the idea of his father ever putting down his precious girls to lift him up in a quiet moment in bed beside his wife. His mother would, absolutely, but he could not see his father doing it. Regardless, it had been his mother's wish to sell the house, and the three kids split the money, with Bill's portion larger to cover expenses.

Bill did as he was told, swiftly calling the cleaning crew to get the house ready to be shown. *Save only the furniture*, he told them. These words haunted him now while he waited on Mr. Smith, the funeral home director.

"Mr. Riley," a thinner, balding man said as he came through the double doors of the casket display area of the funeral home with his hand extended toward Bill.

"Mr. Smith," nodded Bill, taking the man's hand into his own.

"I'm sorry about your mother." Mr. Smith said looking at Bill, but shaking Judy's hand. "She was a good woman. Your father loved her dearly."

"Thank you, Mr. Smith." Bill acknowledged the nice comment he did not care about. "I've got a question for you."

"What's that, Son?" Mr. Smith implored with a kindly gleam in his eye.

"The cleaning threw Dad's ashes away." Bill cut right to the point. "Is there anything we could do to recover some of his to put with Mom's? They always wanted to have their ashes combined when they died. You know, be together forever."

"No, Son, I'm sorry. There's nothing left of him to make ashes from." Mr. Smith said in a sad way. "We give the family all the ashes after cremation."

The doors Mr. Smith entered through snapped open with a bang. A giant black man with sooty, bare arms, aside from the blue latex glove he wore, stood with his hands on the tops of each door. He had on a dingy, formerly white apron that reminded Bill of a butcher's, over his green, sleeveless shirt. He sported a matching round cap that covered his bald head. The man's chin was squared, and the whites of his eyes exploded, like the cut muscles on his chest and arms, against his dark skin. "You say you fadda's ashes gone?" The titanic sized man asked in a thick, African accent.

"Y, Yes Sir." Bill stuttered. He always prided himself on being steel, but this man intimidated him.

"You fadda want to rest with you madda after death?" The man asked.

"Yes Sir," Bill gained some of his composure.

"My name Lofie." The man said. "I cremate you fadda, and now, you madda."

"Yes Sir. I remember." Bill nodded. "Is there anything that can be done?"

"No," Lofie shook his massive head. "There no way."

"Okay then," said Bill, trying to stop talking to Lofie. He turned to his sister and said, "Worth a shot."

"There be great trouble." Lofie stopped Bill from shaking him off. The man was serious, almost looked to be in pain. "You fadda not rest."

"Okay," Mr. Smith interjected. "Go on back to work, Lofie. We're going to go settle the bill."

Mr. Smith waved his hand almost like he was shooing the overgrown man back through the doors. Lofie obliged, and Mr. Smith shut the doors behind him.

"You'll have to excuse him," smiled Mr. Smith. It was fake, and everybody in the room knew it. Nobody said anything, but this only concerned Bill worse. "Where Lofie's from, they take the afterlife very serious. If you'll come with me to my office, you can get your mother."

Bill and Judy followed, with Bill's mind on matters he did not understand.

He felt light, like he was losing himself in some vortex sucking him away. He was floating away, getting further from what he loved.

A lurch.

A feeling of flying through the air, nearly weightless.

Then the feeling of coming to a jolting crash and scattering pieces of him all over.

The bag that held Bill Riley Sr.'s ashes came free from the garbage truck and landed on the highway. His ashes floated away with the wind.

"How do you think it went?" Judy asked her siblings in Bill's living room.

"Fine," said Jan, helping herself to a handful of leftover cheese cubes. "Mom would've hated it, but I think it went good."

"Why do you think she would've hated it?" Bill asked incredulously as he plopped down in his favorite leather recliner and loosened his tie. He turned the TV on and let the news play low in the background.

"She hated everything. Everything us girls had a hand in, anyway." Jan covered her mouth as she spoke because of it being full of cheese.

"That's not true," said Bill. He undid the buttons on his wrists and slid his shoes off.

"Yes it is," piped up Judy. "You were her favorite."

"Really?" Bill questioned. He usually took Judy's word before Jan's in every case.

"Yeah," Jan informed him. "You know how us girls were perfect in Dad's eyes? Well, you were in Mom's. Mom was by us the way Dad was by you."

Bill noticed Jan still smiled as she said her peace, but he also found that some of her hard shell was chipping away beneath her grin. He began to understand Jan's poking, prodding, and inappropriate comments at horrible times were a defense.

"She's right," confirmed Judy. "She was hard on us, but I'm not sure she would've hated it. This was nice."

"Dad would have kicked my ass for what happened today." Bill finally verbalized what had plagued his mind all day, but he still could not bring himself to state the actual incident aloud. "He trusted me with all this, and I may have messed up the most important thing of all."

"You're gonna take them to court, aren't you?" Jan asked, pushing the last cheese cube into her mouth.

"I can't," admitted Bill. "I told them to only save the furniture. They did exactly what I told them. I don't have a leg to stand on."

"You're right," Jan never pulled her gaze from the TV as she talked to Bill. "Dad would've kicked your ass."

This time, Bill laughed along with her.

Paul O' Conner drove down Interstate 6 on his way home from work. It was late and he was extremely tired, sleepy even.

He never liked his hours much as a C.N.A. Three to eleven was not his first choice, but it was the only opening at the hospital when he was hired a year ago. Not wanting to pass on a job he chased for years, he took it without hesitation. Now at eleven forty-five at night, Paul drove his little compact car home, regretting his decision.

There were never any cars on the road during the week at this time of night. Tonight would be no exception. The smooth blacktop spread for miles, sparkling in Paul's headlights like there were a million shards of broken glass on its surface.

Paul turned the radio up so he could listen to his favorite political talk-radio host talk about the new bill going through the Senate now. When he looked up, he saw a floating grocery bag heading straight for his windshield. It hit right in front of Paul's line of sight, and sounded as though it was full of padded bricks.

Paul let off the gas slightly and cut the wipers on. The blades stopped as they hit the bag. Paul could hear the motor of the windshield wipers bog down as it pushed to no avail.

Then, Paul looked into the bottom of the bag. From far away, like in a tunnel, Paul saw a demonic face screaming at him. Scared, angry, and confused, the face called to Paul. Paul leaned in, trying to make sure his eyes were not playing tricks on him.

The face shot toward Paul's, like it was trying to bite him. Paul jerked away, and covered his own face in terror with his arms. His small car's wheels caught the shoulder of the highway and careened off the edge of the road.

The car cut back on the interstate and barrel-rolled down the highway. Paul ejected through the windshield to his death.

The bag floated aimlessly down the interstate.

"Thank you two for coming." Bill hugged Jan in front of terminal four at the airport. Both sisters were leaving to go back to their homes and families. Bill could not believe it himself, but he was really going to miss them. "I'm glad I've had some family for the last week or so."

"It has been nice. Bad circumstances, but nice nonetheless." Judy took her turn hugging Bill.

The sisters grabbed the trolley's that carried their luggage and headed toward the door of the airport.

"I love you guys," spewed Bill, thinking of how his father never said those words to him. After the words left his mouth, he realized how long it had been since he told anybody that. His ex-wife, his son or daughter (who both lived with their mother), his own mother, or his sisters.

Jan and Judy both spun around in surprise. They stared at Bill for the longest of moments, both wearing a dumb expression. Bill saw their similarities, and how much they both favored their mother.

"For God's sake," smiled Bill. "Will one of you say *something*?"

"Oh Lord," Jan laughed. "We love you too, Bill."

The two ran back to Bill and hugged him once more, tightly, with Judy wiping away a quick tear.

After all was done and the women were inside, Bill steered his car out of the airport. He headed on his way home, merging onto Interstate six.

Bill listened to the news report on the radio explain that there was a crash on Interstate 6 the night before. It was said to be before exit 68. Bill just passed mile marker 65. His curiosity peaked, wondering if he would be able to see anything. The report said the man died in the crash.

He glanced to the right and saw the sign for mile marker sixty-six, and turned back just in time to get on the brakes along with everyone else in front of him. They were all slowing dramatically. Bill thought for a brief moment everybody was trying to see any evidence of the previous evening's wreck, but then he saw the culprit bouncing and weaving around, and over the top, of traffic.

It was an empty, plastic grocery bag.

"**M**r. Smith," Bill shouted into his cell phone. "I need to speak to Lofie."

"Hold on just a sec, Son. I'll get him to the phone." Mr. Smith said, noting the panic in Bill's voice. Just a short while later, Lofie answered from the other end.

"Hello," came his thick, African accented voice.

""Lofie, this is Bill Riley Jr. Do you remember telling me bad things would come from losing my father's ashes?" Bill asked.

"Yes," recalled Lofie. He listened hard to the background noise coming from Bill's end of the line. A reverberating buzz filled the silence between words, an ominous hum mixed with a few bangs.

"Well, you were right." Bill said, sounding scared. "I was coming down I-six, heading back into town. There was an empty bag that landed on my windshield. I swear, Lofie, I saw my father's face in that bag. Then, everybody slammed on brakes, got out of their cars, and flipped mine over in the middle of the Interstate. I'm afraid, Lofie. What do I do?"

Lofie acted fast. He motioned for Mr. Smith to head out to the car while Bill was talking. Without a word, his boss followed his orders.

"Stay there, Mr. Riley." Lofie said. "I be there soon."

"**W**hat's going on, Lofie?" Mr. Smith asked as he sped down Interstate 6.

"Mr. Riley possess drivers on road." Lofie said, calmly. The easygoing nature of his tone helped settle Mr. Smith's nerves.

"Bill Junior?" Mr. Smith asked.

"No, Mr. Riley Sr."

"How is *that*?" Mr. Smith exclaimed.

"Mr. Riley want to be with Mrs. Riley. This his final wish. Now his ashes scatter interstate. He not resting. He not whole no more." Lofie explained.

"What's going on with Bill Junior?"

"He attacked by drivers." Lofie went on. "Mr. Riley Sr.'s soul between planes. He possesses drivers to attack his son."

"How could he do that?"

"Ashes come through windows, or these." Lofie fingered the air conditioning vent in the dashboard of Mr. Smith's car. "No matter how; we stop them."

"How in the blue hell are we going to pull that off?" Mr. Smith asked, perplexed.

Lofie pointed to the opposite side of the interstate. On its side,

Bill's car was being pushed--or rolled--into a ravine that ran from one side of the six-lane road to the other, through a large pipe. Some of the possessed drivers heaved and strained, while others clapped and cheered jovially behind them.

"We need rain," said Lofie as Mr. Smith slowed the car to a stop. He opened the door before it was in Park.

"Of course, Lofie. Look in my trunk, I think there is some in there." Mr. Smith said sardonically at the dark man's broad back. "We're in Southern California; it never rains!"

Lofie peered through the windshield, smiling from in front of the bumper. "It will soon," he said. "I make it."

Mr. Smith stood beside the hunched over African watching, with flickering eyes, between him and the scene across the street.

The large, black man was mixing things together in a vial about the size of Lofie's palm. He combined dirt from the shoulder, a single blade of grass with the root ball intact, and a splash of water from the ravine the possessed horde was pushing Bill into.

Lofie corked the vial and shook it in his hand, like he was trying to get answers from it. He looked at Mr. Smith when he unstopped the glass bottle.

"Here's nothing," he said, and poured the mixture out on his upturned hand.

Lofie said some words Mr. Smith did not understand, and surprisingly did not sound like any of the Swahili Mr. Smith ever heard him speak. Mr. Smith expected some kind of dance, like in the movies, but none ever came. Lofie just continued to chant in the unknown language.

A cool wind blew in, rustling leaves in the trees lining either side of the interstate, and the short fine hairs on Mr. Smith's neck. The skies darkened into a smoky gray blanket, blocking the warm sun that formerly beat down on them. Sprinkles begun to drip, and Lofie shot his hands into the air.

Sheets of cold rain came down to the pavement so hard it sounded like it sizzled on the musty smelling pavement. The possessed group suddenly ceased one by one, looking at each other with confusion. Lofie smiled through the downpour at Mr. Smith as Bill's car lie on its roof, now un-harassed.

"It's working," shouted the African over the pounding rain.

"I see that, but *how* is it working?" Mr. Smith asked.

"The ashes wash away," Lofie said, cleaning out the vial. "No more possession of drivers."

"Well that's all then, right?" Mr. Smith grinned.

"No," said Lofie. "We need the ashes."

Lofie crossed the interstate to Bill's side, splashing water up to his knees. He bent down to where the rain water cascaded from the pavement and filled the vial. After plugging the top, Lofie went to retrieve Bill.

They ran back, dodging the now moving cars that were swerving to avoid Bill's overturned vehicle. Mr. Smith saw blood trickling down Bill's forehead as they drew close.

"No time." Lofie waved off Mr. Smith when the pair reached his car. Mr. Smith was holding some paper towels he was meaning to clean Bill with. "Go to Mr. Riley's."

They rocketed down the road with a soft scream coming from the vial in Lofie's hand. It was an angry yell that sounded like someone screaming for help underwater. When Lofie held up the vial, a cloudy, demonic form of Bill Riley Sr.'s face pressed against the glass from the inside.

Bill sat, mute, bloody, and traumatized, in the front seat. Mr. Smith swung the car wildly into Bill's driveway, Lofie shoved the seat up, crunching Bill in the process, and went inside the house. Bill and Mr. Smith slowly followed.

When they got in, Lofie had the vial open and was pouring the water into the urn holding Bill's mother. Smoke issued from the mouth of the urn, and an odd hiss came from within. Lofie quickly put the lid on the urn and placed it back on the mantle. The urn vibrated violently to the point it nearly fell off before it stopped.

"Now you fadda rest in peace," Lofie said.

Bill smiled.

He felt happy, complete even. He could feel a love he waited years to feel again. His spirit faded from the body it animated, and he passed through to the other side.

The plastic grocery bag fell to the side of the road, damp and empty, forever.

Michael Faun
Jim Bolger's Secret Ingredient

Seamus stared at the battered silver guitar laying discarded by the overgrown railway tracks he was walking along. His functioning, non-glass eye scanned the instrument glinting in the blackish-blue Indiana summer's dawn. He inched closer toward it and picked it up; gazing at it with wonder.

Childhood memories flowed inside him. Lucid fragments of his old man playing Howlin' Wolf tunes for him out on the porch floated up in his mind.

Those magical summer nights before the devilish moonshine condemned Pappy's sweet soul and finally claimed his life and left Seamus out in the cold.

"Shit, you've been ramblin' foe many years now, Seamus..." he said to himself and pushed back the haunting memories into his internal coffin where they belonged. He wiped away the dirt from the guitar with his ragged sleeve. One rusty string was still left on the instrument, and Seamus, with a sad smile, began plucking it. Only a dull and dead strumming sounded. He grimaced.

Still, warmth spread inside his empty stomach because at least it was his crappy sounding guitar. He named his newfound traveling companion Geraldine.

"Still beats hearing one's thoughts at night." Seamus muttered and gripped the mud-slippery neck and slung Geraldine over his wool-coated shoulder.

Peering out over yonder, he began walking in the direction of his nose and minutes later, the new-born Sun was steadily climbing the sky, kindly defrosting his cold and weary bones. Goose-fleshed and content, he fished out a half-eaten tuna sandwich from the pocket of his patched coat and began stuffing his leathery face. Eating while pondering on where he might wind up next.

The small town didn't appear to have changed since the days of witch hunting. Early morning mist hovered just above the ground and ringlets of smoke arose from the chimneys atop of the old houses. Seamus was standing by the edge of town, surrounded by black bramble bushes and stinging nettle, looking for any sign of activity. Not a living soul or sound. Still, he knew better than to skulk around at this early hour, so he just waited patiently by the fringe. Waiting for the unnamed town to awake.

A sudden thrashing startled Seamus who whipped around and noticed a mangy crow sitting perched on a cracked gaslight next to him. It cocked its head and stared down at him with its black pearly eyes, cawing twice as if to either greet or warn Seamus.

Or alarm a third party?

"Hey, scared me good there, lil' fella'..." Seamus tore off a chunk from his sandwich and offered it to the bird. "You hungry my feathery friend?"

"Very kind of you, Mister. But Corbin here's just eaten."

The low creaky voice made Seamus jump a second time. He nearly dropped Geraldine. "Besides," the voice continued, "he only fancy those nasty li'l slithering worms anyway."

By a tree nearby, Seamus saw the person behind the voice. An odd looking man. Stately fellow by the looks of him, all dressed in black garments with a large straw hat on his head and a gnarled wooden cane in his knotty paw. His horse-like face was spotted with reddish vesicles.

"I-I'm terribly sorry, Mister, I don't want no trouble." Seamus stuffed the bread back into his pocket.

"Ain't seen you round here before. You here for the festival?"

Their eyes locked in a moment of awkward silence.

"Anything wrong?" the man with the crow said.

"Oh, no...I'm sorry. Just rumpled's all. I'm Seamus," he smiled broadly and reached out his free hand, "'tis your fine crow up there I reckon?"

"Pleased to make your acquaintance, Seamus. I'm Tin Cap Earl. Just call me Earl. And you're perfectly right, that's my crow right there." Earl returned the smile with closed lips, giving him a stern look. His big incisors made the skin around his mouth bulge slightly.

Seamus instantly knew something was wrong with Earl. He could discern a dark aura around the man. His mother had taught him that ability on his fifth birthday. Told him she'd passed over her 'gift' to him. That spring, Seamus knew he had received it: For he could clearly see the sickly crimson aura around his bedridden mother. She died from cancer two days later.

Her beauty and peacefulness after she passed away. Shit, she looked just like an angel, pale and brittle with silver hair...

He fought back the lost tears drawing close and focused hard on Earl and his crow instead. This wasn't a time to show weakness; he knew this man was a predator.

Seamus cleared his throat. "A festival you say?"

Tin Cap Earl let out a sharp whistle and Corbin leaped off the streetlamp and within two wing strokes landed on its master's strong shoulder. "Yes, why don't you come with me and I'll explain over some breakfast. I may have a little job you might be interested in. Please, right me if I'm wrong," Earl winked at Seamus, "but I suspect for a fella' of your kind, some gold in the pocket could come in handy, yes?"

Seamus eyes narrowed. "*My kind*?"

Tin Cap Earl grinned sheepishly. "Sorry, but are you not a traveling musician?"

"Suppose I could play me one or two Howlin' Wolf tunes if that's what you're looking for?" Seamus struck the broken string with his long thumbnail.

"Not quite, but let's be on our way to discuss the matter over some tea and pastrami sandwiches." Earl rubbed his hands in delight; even his crow looked pleased.

"That's awfully kind of you, Earl. Lead the way." Seamus courteously lifted his worn floppy hat and bowed his head. He had no damn idea what Earl had up his sleeve. Yet, beggars can't be choosers and with a stomach growling in response to the word *pastrami*, the choice was easy. The tea though, Earl could keep to himself.

They started walking down the cobblestone main street that ran through the sleepy ghostlike township and soon came to the outskirts. This part was somehow darker as it was encircled by a tall dense forest. There stood Earl's dilapidated house-a grayish-blue home with a small front yard. The looming trees in the foreground were so thick and hardly let any light through; thus cast a dull gloom over the ill kept yard with its overgrown weeds and wilted wormwood. Corbin the crow flew up and perched on the roof.

"Please, enter," said Earl and urged Seamus inside.

Soon enough, as promised, Seamus was wolfing down cold cut sandwiches from a plate on the kitchen table. Licking his sooty fingers between each bite, he felt like a king in rags.

"Man, these are some tasty nibbles." Seamus washed them down with generous slugs of apple cider from a copper jug.

"I'm glad you enjoy them. I'm convinced that one must help a fella' out to receive the same in return. Something I'm counting on you for. That job, remember?" Earl reminded of a statue sitting at the table across from Seamus; eyeing his guest like a hawk while fiddling about with a black feather between his knotty grayish fingers.

Seamus stopped chewing. A pang of both regret and guilt grew inside him as he realized he was in debt of gratitude to Tin Cap Earl, and that it was too late to back out now. Not after all the food Earl had shared.

Shit!

"Oh, yeah, about that job..." Shamefaced, Seamus gazed down at the clean-eaten plate. "I'm afraid I-I haven't been quite honest with you, Earl."

"No?" said Earl.

"I can't play the guitar. I-I lied because I was so damn hungry." Seamus' eye welled up with water. "I'm sorry..."

"Oh, don't fret, Seamus. In fact, have some more." Earl broke out in a comforting warm laughter and refilled the empty platter. "Just relax, my friend. I wasn't interested in your musical skills in the first place."

"I don't understand." Seamus dried his eye.

Earl grinned mysteriously, jabbing his index finger to mark each word in his following sentence. "That I did out of common curiosity. The real reason I need you, is because you're a man who, if necessary, can disappear from town without leaving any trails. Which leads me to the matter in fact." Earl jabbed his finger again, "I want you to ferret out what makes a man named Jim Bolger's stew so damn good. See, our town's traditional stew festival is just around the corner and I want to break the smug bastard's winning streak and for once shine myself. Find out what his secret ingredient is and I'll happily accommodate you for it. With gold."

"Huh?" Seamus arched his bushy gray brows in confusion while digging into the pile of meat slices. "Uh, so you want me to spy on this...Jim?"

"Oh, spy is an ugly word. I simply want you to—let's say—by chance happen to walk by Jim's place and peep through his window later this evening. Then, all you need to do is take notes on what he throws into his accursed pot. When you're done, get back to me and you'll get your reward."

Hours later, long after the mysterious town with no name had awoken, its residents had crawled out of their houses just to later clamber back for sleep, Seamus was skulking around in search for Jim Bolger's house supposedly located on the opposite edge of town.

Creeping along small unnatural alleyways, where the buildings ominously towered high above his head, he soon came to a house fitting the description of Jim Bolger's residence. Standing alone, it was more of a small detached white cottage with fiery orange light emanating from the tiny windows glowing in the bluish dusk. Seamus carefully drew closer, constantly checking his back. The thought of getting caught performing this degenerate act rankled in his head.

Shit, they'll surely lynch a Peeping Tom...

Seamus crouched up by a window on the back of the cottage. Peeping through, he spotted two people inside the wood panelled parlor; an elderly dark-haired gentleman and a much younger blonde woman. They were sitting by a large hearth, over which a large black kettle hung and simmered, discussing some matter based on a document the gentleman was holding while the woman now and then nodded in response.

Seamus sneaked to the next window to get a better view. Quietly, he fished up a monocular Earl had given him and brought it to his good eye. He zoomed in on the document and saw it was a map. An old looking map drawn on yellowed paper showing a brook by a clearing encircled by a forest. At the top of the map, baptized in black ink and written in fancy ornate letters it read...

"Blackbrook...." said Seamus quietly to himself.

Suddenly, the two people inside stood up. The gentleman reached for some chopped vegetables lying on a little side table by the hearth and threw them into the kettle and the woman grabbed a large white bucket and headed for the entrance door. Seamus got away from the window and began scribbling down the various kinds of veggies he had noted. The next moment, a door opened and slammed shut, followed by footsteps crunching on gravel.

Seamus froze. He saw the blonde woman walk away from the cottage in the direction of the main street, light-heartedly whistling and swinging the bucket to and fro with each step. When she was no longer in sight, swallowed by the darkness outside, Seamus set after her—guided only by the sound of her clogs; clip-clopping against the cobblestones.

He had followed the woman through the whole town, past Earl's house and into the gloomy forest growing there. And after having almost poked out his eye on twigs and sprigs and nearly sprained both his ankles from slipping on slimy stones; he finally came to the little brook by the clearing he'd seen on the map—Blackbrook—which looked more like a murky mud pit than a healthy brook. Also it oozed with smoke leaving a stark tangy odour that made his nose crinkle.

He sat himself down on a patch of moss, making himself as comfortable as possible, when his jaw suddenly dropped. The blonde woman, illuminated eerily by a thin streak of moonlight, began to fully undress and then wade out in the mud; holding the plastic bucket within her slim hand.

She halted when the mud covered her ass and stood perfectly still for some moments; looking around herself as if sensing something. Then, she swiftly dived, bucket first into the mud. After having been submerged for some time, she resurfaced; she looked like a brown sludge beast with seaweed clinging around her ample breasts.

Seamus sat watching the strange scene with his mouth and eyes wide open; trying to get a glimpse at what was thrashing about in the bucket she was carrying with some effort now.

You gone fishin' neckid using only a bucket? Crazy woman!

Before she could spot him, Seamus was already shuffling back the way he had came, through the gnarled, eye-poking trees and tricky roots; leaving the woods to head back to Jim Bolger's cottage. With a cold and shaking hand, he scribbled something down in the notebook provided for the mission.

Catfish?

Back at Jim's window, Seamus watched Jim the Cook stir his kettle with great precision and affection. So far no uncommon additives had been used in the stew. But Seamus suspected that would change as soon as...

She's back!

Seamus hid behind a shrub as he heard her come clogging back from the main street and entering the cottage. Whatever the thing in the bucket was, it sure didn't make a sound no more.

The following minute, Seamus was peeping through the window again, studying the weird duo's nocturnal cooking rite, when he made the strangest observance through the lens of his monocular. The woman's before fair, near anaemic skin, now had an oily, blackish-green touch to it; like chicken meat marinated in soy sauce.

"Oh, Lord, that devilish mire must've absorbed into her pores..." Seamus took notice as she now handed over the mysterious bucket to Jim who looked into it indifferently. He then uttered something in response and pointed right behind the hearth where there was a staircase leading downward. The next moment, they both descended it; Jim first.

"Goddammit! I need to know what's in that bucket!" Seamus looked around himself, biting his crusty lip while quietly deducting his alternatives with his dry husky voice. "Perhaps I could sneak into the cellar somehow...maybe there's a trap door...but what if I get caught? They'll surely lynch a thief in these parts...perhaps I could just tell Earl it's a catfish anyway...but what if he can sense me lying? He'll probably cook me alive and use me in his stew...even though my ole' flesh probably ain't that tasty...o-or I could just—"

Seamus suddenly stopped yapping. His eye locked on something he hadn't spotted before. A transparent screen, most likely one of those sun panels, was integrated into the roof and covered a rather large section diagonally from above the hearth. His heart sparked with adrenaline. God knew he needed the reward and he didn't want to lie to his employer, the strange Mister Earl. So without hesitation or difficulty, he began climbing up the downspout to the roof. Well up, he watched his step, crab-walking toward the four-by-four panel by the smoking chimney.

"Perfect view." Seamus peered down in the parlor, "Can't hide no ingredient from me now, Jim Bolger." He fished out his pen and notebook, awaiting the chef with a smile on his lips; a smile that soon waned as he spotted Jim Bolger ascending the staircase from the cellar. Wearing a butcher's apron spattered with blood and pieces of pink gut, Jim sluggishly carried the reddish-white bucket with both hands toward the slow cooking kettle.

Seamus gasped, grimacing from the raw sight of innards. Still, he couldn't be squeamish now. He needed to identify at least some part in that horrible bucket before they were going into the stew.

"After all, there's a hell of a difference between a catfish and a goddamn octopus..."

So, with a now deft hand, he produced the glass to his eye and adjusted the acuity before zooming into the bucket of gore. The fraction of a second he lay eye on its content, his head started spinning and he felt sick; then the first jet of vomit as he wobbly stood up and dropped the monocular; clattering as it rolled down the leaning roof and over the edge.

In the vertigo caused by the sight of the bucket's content as well as the sickening flesh, skin and burnt hair odour now wafting out from the chimney, Seamus fumbled down from the roof of Jim's hell-house and fled in the dark from that strange town and its even stranger stew festival, leaving his silvery Geraldine gold reward behind...

Bios

A. Henry Keene lives and works in Louisville, Kentucky. He has written and published under several names and is currently compiling a collection of his works to be published under his own name in the near future. He would love to hear from you at a.keene64@yahoo.com

Robin Wyatt Dunn lives in southern California and is the author of three novels. A member of the Horror Writers Association, he is proud to have been born in the Carter Administration. You can find him at www.robindunn.com.

Dale Hollin is a failed socialite and working writer from Indianapolis, Indiana. He has works published and scheduled to be published by Lovecraftzine, James Ward Kirk Publishing, Danielle Rose Publishing, Melange Books, and Anytime-Shorts.

Allen Griffin's work has appeared in the past two Indiana Horror Anthologies and several other cool places such as Innsmouth Magazine, Bizarro Central's Flash Fiction Friday, and The Mustache Factor. He has also appeared in several anthologies including Hell and Grave Robbers from JWK Publishing and is forthcoming in the Grey Matter Press anthologies Splatterlands and Ominous Realities. He plays bass in Profound Lore Recording artists Coffinworm.

Justin Hunter: I've sold several works to horror/thriller anthologies such as upcoming releases from JWK Fiction's Bones: The Anthology, The Ugly Babies Anthology and The Cellar Door Anthology, Robertson's Demonic Visions: 50 Tales of Horror and Emby Press Blood Trails: Monster Hunter. I have just sold a dark comedy/apocalyptic novel to Severed Press – Chet & Floyd vs. the Apocalypse: Volume 1. I also have another literary work being pitched by an agent.

Mathias Jansson is a Swedish art critic and poet. He has been published in magazines as The Horror Zine Magazine, Dark Eclipse, Schlock, The Sirens Call and The Poetry Box. He has also contributed to several anthologies from Horrified Press and James Ward Kirk Fiction as Suffer Eternal anthology Volume 1-3, Hell Whore Anthology Volume 1-3, Barnyard Horror and Serial Killers Tres Tria. Homepage, :

Dona Fox's short fiction and poetry has appeared in Eldritch Tales, Haunts, Thin Ice, Cemetery Dance (Issue #1), Beyond, and New Blood.

Bric Barker has been a dabbler of poetry since his university days where he was named Student Poet in Residence. He has published a few poems, and he won the Kay Megenheimer Poetry Prize. Bric has been a teacher of English around the world. His adventures abroad have informed much of his poetic musing.

Among other places, **Lee Forsythe**'s fiction has appeared in Blue Murder, Thou Shalt Not, and Cellar Door Volume Two. He has lived in Indiana, Armenia, Australia, Belgium, Russia, and the UK, but mostly inside his own head.

Kristin Roahrig's poetry and short stories have appeared in various publications. She is also the author of several plays and lives in Indiana.

Matthew Wilson, 30, is a UK resident who has been writing since small. Recently these stories have appeared in Horror Zine, Star*Line and Sorcerers Signal. He is currently editing his first novel and can be contacted on twitter @matthew94544267.

Glenn Rolfe writes his crazy tales of horror from his home in the Maine woods. His most recent publications include his essay, "The Rooster" in BLEED an anthology for children's cancer from Perpetual Motion Machine Publishing, and his short story, "Skull of Snakes", which appears in the COINS OF CHAOS anthology from EDGE Science Fiction and Fantasy Publishing. He is currently at work on his next novel.

Charie La Marr is primarily known as a ghostwriter in the field of sports - mostly baseball. She has had at least one book go to #1 on Amazon in 2 different categories. Currently working to establish herself as an author in her own name, she has created a genre called Circuspunk (listed at Urban Dictionary) and has sold a book of short stories in the genre to Chupa Cabra called Bumping Noses and Cherry Pie. She also has upcoming stories in Alex S. Johnson's heavy metal anthology Axes of Evil and Shwibly Magazine, James Ward Kirk's Bones, Sydney Leigh's Ugly Babies, In Vein for the benefit of St. Jude's Hospital, Chupa Cabra's We Walk Invisible, Dynatox Ministries' Witches!, Ripple

Effect for Hurricane Katrina relief, Surreal Grotesque and other anthologies. She was September's featured writer at Solarcide. She is known for writing in many different genres from crime to bizarro to erotica and even Seussian. She is currently editing a Circuspunk anthology called The New Wakazoid Circus—the Greatest Show on Paper.A redhead with a redheaded attitude, she lives in NY with her mother and son and fur children Bailey Corwin and Babe Ruth..

Paul Greystoke: I started life as a comedy writer, producing scripts for standup comics. I have also enjoyed success writing radio Situation Comedies in particular the 'Petal and Jonny' series which was aired on Metro radio 2010 – 2011. It was through this and the various books I have read by Stephen King, Dean Koontz and James Herbert that I discovered a passion for Horror slipstream work. I have written various short stories in this genre and am now working on my first novel. I consider myself forever a student in the art of creative writing and embrace the continued challenge that this work holds.

Gary Murphy: Originally born January 29th, 1969, in the North of England, Gary is the author of horror collections 'Scared Shitless', 'Lucifer's Rhapsody', 'Psychosocial – Dark Tales', and the blood-curdling novellas 'Bloodzone' and 'A Twisted Love Story', all available on Amazon Books. He is happy living in Egremont, West Cumbria, where he rides a black Vespa scooter and walks his dog, Chewy. He is a full-time writer, in between buying and selling his first love, antiques. He can be contacted on Facebook anytime and actively contributes horror shorts to many publications. Currently working on new stuff.

Roger Cowin currently lives in Centerville, IN. He is a lifelong resident of Indiana and his poems his lifelong connection and love for the Midwest. He has worked at Richmond State Hospital for 27 years and has been writing and publishing poetry for 3 decades. He has been influenced by writers as diverse as Eliot and Lovecraft, Joyce and Stephen King. He is the author of the poetry collections, *"Passing Through Darkness & Other Poems"* and *"Succulent Flesh,"* published by JWK Fiction. His new collection *"Pulp City"* will also be released by JWK Fiction.

Glenn Rolfe writes his crazy tales of horror from his home in the Maine woods. His most recent publications include his essay, "The Rooster" in BLEED an anthology for children's cancer from

Perpetual Motion Machine Publishing, and his short story, "Skull of Snakes", which appears in the COINS OF CHAOS anthology from EDGE Science Fiction and Fantasy Publishing. He is currently at work on his next novel.

Sonia Fogel: A graduate of the University of Louisville, I work for a health insurance company and am the mother of two teenagers. I spend every possible moment on several writing projects.

David S. Pointer has work included in the new "Indiana Crime Review" 2013, "The Bones Anthology," and other James Ward Kirk titles. David's latest poetry book is entitled "Oncoming Crime Facts" available at www.lulu.com

Justin Hunter has sold several works to horror/thriller anthologies such as upcoming releases from JWK Fiction's Bones: The Anthology, The Ugly Babies Anthology and The Cellar Door Anthology, Indiana Horror Review 2013, Robertson's Demonic Visions: 50 Tales of Horror volumes 1 and 2, Emby Press Blood Trails: Monster Hunter and Strangehouse books Strange Fucking Stories. Justin has published a dark comedy/apocalyptic novel with Severed Press – Chet & Floyd vs. the Apocalypse: Volume 1. He also has another literary work being pitched by an agent.

David W. Landrum: My speculative fiction has appeared widely, most recent in The Horror Zine, Sanitarium, Dark in the Limelight, Dark Edifice, and Sorceress Signals.

Timothy Frasier is a novelist, short story writer, and poet. His work appears in several anthologies. Frasier resides in Kentucky with his wife, Lisa, and German shepherd, Chief.

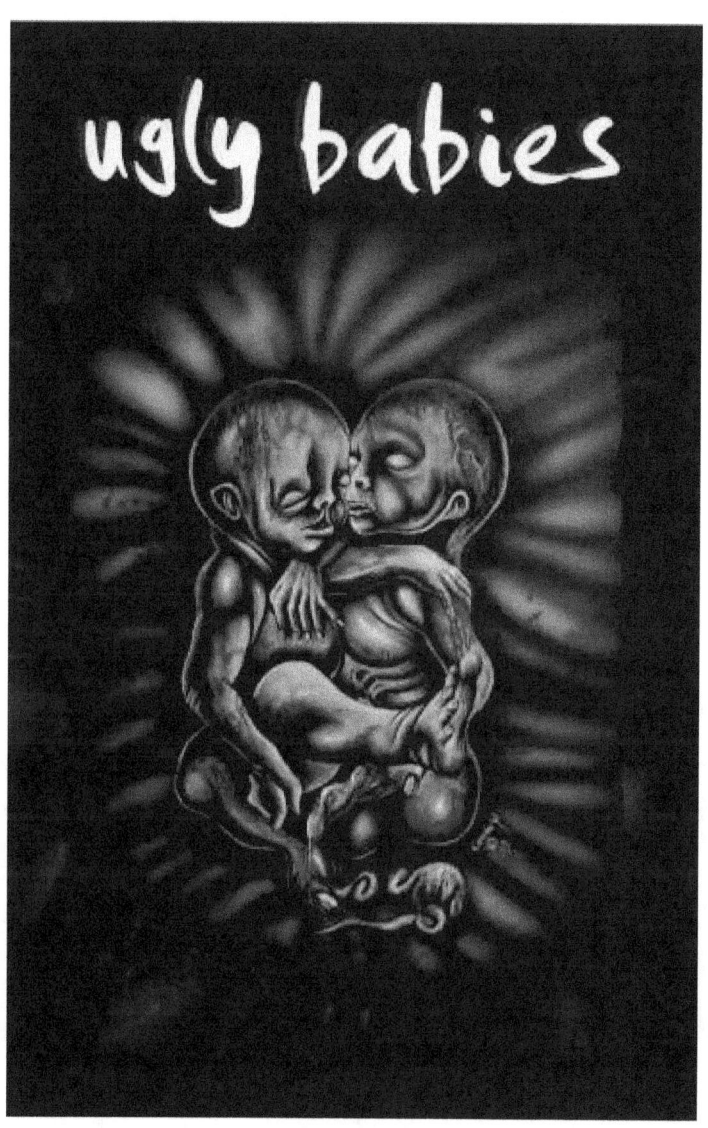

Also from James Ward Kirk Publishing